. . . and under the cover of night, there would be more than enough time for a warm sentient wave to glide through fleece to naked human skin.

The simple solution was executed flawlessly. Sequestered in the lee of a hillock, the flock of Hospah Ramirez settled for the night. Frequently Billichay trotted to investigate the deliberate straying of Dinay sheep. And once, long after midnight, the child leaped to his feet to scream under cold bright stars as he felt the deadly progress of a Thing within him, stealthy, satanic, horrifying and implacable. Hospah took three steps and fell, first blind, then deaf . . . no longer Hospah Ramirez. . . .

For Gina:
The Original
and Unretouched

ANASAZI

DEAN ING

SF
ace books

A Division of Charter Communications Inc.
A GROSSET & DUNLAP COMPANY
51 Madison Avenue
New York, New York 10010

ANASAZI

Copyright © 1980 by Dean Ing

An ACE Book

First Ace printing: December 1980
Printed Simultaneously in Canada

2 4 6 8 0 9 7 5 3 1
Manufactured in the United States of America

TABLE OF CONTENTS

Chronology:
"Devil You Don't Know": 1989
"Portions of this Program . . .": 1992
"Anasazi": 1996

ANASAZI

Part One

1124 A.D.: the planet throbbed with life, a promise of intelligent host organisms for the crew of the user starship. The users eased into orbit, their sensors scanning fruitlessly for radiomagnetic communication, subspace waves, or advanced energy sources. On some land masses, cautious probing revealed vast biped armies disputing by means of quadruped cavalry. Yet on two interconnected continental masses they found the bipeds without cavalry, or wheels, or iron. Though most of the primitives were nomadic, some had built permanent settlements where they grew cereals, legumes, and squash. Best of all, the bipeds were organically compatible with user protein and large enough to serve as hosts.

A user bulked scarcely larger than a human brain and could penetrate mammalian tissue with ease. There seemed nothing that might interfere with immediate colonization; certainly the users did not expect to meet disaster from a local weather anomaly.

The user tactic was to be straightforward: take control of a small sedentary group, breed more users within the hosts, expand their control to larger settlements, eventually to the other continents. Thus the landing site was near a small settlement and roughly equidistant from three larger ones. Eight hundred years later, ruins of the

larger settlements would be known as Canyon De
Chelly, Mesa Verde, and Chaco Canyon.

To the human inhabitants then, as now, the
land owned a terrible shining beauty. Buttes of
yellow, salmon, and umber were sandblasted first
to soft contours, then gradually to oblivion.
Cedar, piñon pine, sage, and tuft grass struggled
against dry winds that ransacked the unprotected
valleys. Moisture was so precious that the patient
Amerinds dug through powder snow to plant
corn that might, or might not, mature. Near most
settlements lay scores of tiny check dams, de-
signed to capture the occasional cloudburst or
snowmelt. During early summer days when rain-
fall was adequate, the land exhaled a musk of
cedar and wildflowers. In dry years the land lay
like a burnt offering, consumed by the sun. At
times even ocotillo cacti lost their scarlet blos-
soms, grew brittle enough to topple down
knife-sharp canyon slopes.

Forged between the bright-hued anvil of high
desert and the hammer of the sun, Amerinds
carved an ecological niche. There was no time left
to build a true leisure society. The users sought to
exploit this situation.

The shuttle craft detached itself from the starship and wafted down on repulsors, a crystalline
egg that tilted slightly as it settled on hardpacked
earth. A pitiless sun dominated the scene, though
of flock of clouds sulked on the horizon. Seven of
the eight male users sortied quietly in small crystal eggs on power broadcast from their shuttle,
floating above scrub and cacti in search of nearby
humans to be stunned and infiltrated. The eighth
male stayed with the shuttle to protect the eight
smaller females.

Though both sexes might best be described as amoeboid in shape, a user boasted nearly as many cells as a human. A female user needed several months to produce her offspring cysts, but a user's natural life span was a hundred times that of a human. They rarely hurried. All of the shuttle's life-support systems performed flawlessly, including the serenity beam, which was a male user's way of deluding its cells into behaving as if a female were physically present. Gender-anxiety had once been a survival characteristic; now it was merely an organic curb, easily overstepped by an omnidirectional subspace transmitter.

The transmitter, too bulky for the tiny sortie vehicles, lay within the shuttle beaming female emanations to which males were attuned. The beam was unaffected by intruding mass, but it did attenuate with distance. The male who sortied more than a hundred kilometers from the shuttle would quickly succumb to violent anxiety, exhaustion, and death. The serenity beam transmitter was even better protected within the shuttle than were the females themselves.

The shuttle owed its tilt to the gentle slope of an alluvial deposit from an arroyo nearby. There was almost no moisture in the soil, nor had there been for years. A user, forced to crawl over that parched surface, would quickly die of dehydration unless it had time to produce a thin temporary shell of gristle. This, too, was in the user bag of inherited tricks, but normally the user voided its gristle-producing chondroprotein as excrement. The sentry user felt relief when, in late afternoon, a few raindrops spattered on the shuttle. Perhaps, he thought, this sunbaked hell would get a little moisture.

Several kilometers up the arroyo, cloud formations were dumping furious curtains of rain on ground baked too hard to absorb it. Gradual mesa slopes became sheets of water that gathered in the arroyo's upper reaches, plummeted down declivities, became a hurtling fist of water that filled the arroyo and emerged from a bend toward the shuttle carrying boulders with it. Once or twice in a human generation, parts of this high arid region suffered such miracles of midsummer violence. This one did not last long but when the last trickle died there was no shuttle, no sortie power, and no sentry or live female users. Shards of quartz glittered in the alluvium and, in a crevice ten meters below the surface, the serenity beam continued. Isotope powered, it might continue until the next glaciation.

The user starship, en route to a synchronous orbit, lay beyond the horizon and lacked visual contact when its shuttle was pulverized. Moreover, the starship commanders were already uneasy. On a coastal plain of the southern hemisphere lay effigies drawn on a scale so vast that they were clearly visible from orbit. Animal figures and geometrical shapes predominated on the Nazca Plain, starship-sized and pregnant with possible meaning. It seemed possible that the bipeds had etched the effigies from a sense of religious awe and intended them to be seen from orbit.

But no user ship had ever penetrated this locale and users, with the pragmatism of any intelligent parasite, avoided other spacefaring races. When the starship passed again over the landing site, the evidence seemed to imply climate-control weapons. This was enough, and more: in moments, the surviving earthbound users were abandoned as the starship fled.

The survivors were fortunate in one respect. They had converged on a group of dwellings and beamed the inhabitants senseless before the shuttle was obliterated. They chose adult specimens as hosts. Within an hour, they found their way through the skins of their new slaves to take up residence inside.

For days the people of the tiny settlement wondered aloud at the jeweled airborne motes that had paid them such a painful visit. The inert sortie eggs were all found and smashed. Three men and four women—most of the adult population—complained of various ills as the users investigated their unwilling hosts. The users did not fully recognize their new isolation for weeks, and only gradually realized how their females must have perished.

Lacking instruments, they could pinpoint the serenity beam source no closer than roughly a kilometer and saw that the search would be fruitless without heavy equipment, carefully employed. With their females dead, the seven users would have to bide their time, develop the tools to build subspace distress beacon modules, and stay within the high desert area in the meantime. Perhaps the humans would develop tools which the users could adapt for a beacon. There was, after all, no hurry. Yet.

In time, and after expending many bodies, the users learned to cope. They learned the language—like the people themselves, a Keresan prototype—and learned to use host senses by intruding their own filaments into appropriate nerve bundles. To the unencumbered members of

the tribe, the seven hosts became pitiful husks.
They slurred their words, stumbled, were incon-
tinent. But they never complained, and for an
excellent reason: users ruthlessly absorbed
neocortical tissue. There was no longer any locus
of body control to countermand that of the user; it
was tantamount to brain death.

Once in control of a host, a user typically spread
sensor patches just beneath the surface of the
host's body. In this way two hosts could grasp
hands, the users communicating silently by minute galvanic changes. The users compared findings, agreed that their hosts were slowly dying. It
was none too soon for the naive humans who took
on more of the hunting and cultivation.

In their cruel forays into human physiology, the
users learned that adult humans were simply too
large for ideal hosts. One user guessed that immature specimens could more easily adapt to the
needs of a user. Muscle coordination would also
be easier with a smaller host.

A year passed. Users found that a small child
became an anemic host and that one of twelve or
fourteen must either be artificially stunted, with
unpleasant side effects, or must be abandoned.
One user lived for weeks in a *canis familiaris*, the
short-faced dog that had migrated with mankind
countless years before. The dog deprived the user
of manipulative skills and was too small to last,
but it became part of a successful experiment.
Three users, two in adolescent bodies and one in
the emaciated dog, took a naive ten-year-old into a
canyon.

The dog obligingly bared its throat to a chert
knife. The child lay sobbing, overpowered, his
forearm laid open by the knife. The user flowed

from the dog's bloody tissue directly into the boy, lowering transfer time dramatically. With growing expertise, users could now gain control of a host after the briefest struggle against a child's defenses.

Some of the more subtle problems of the users were more easily solved than were obvious ones. Human leucocytes did not attack the foreign protein since the tiny user cells could surrogate host cell walls without conscious effort. A user took sustenance from the host blood supply easily, but could not dispose of its waste in the bloodstream for long before the human kidneys failed. Eventually, users found it expedient to tap into the host's ureters, passing user excreta liquids into the human bladder to be voided in urine.

The users never perfected the system; bone tumors and tooth impaction were accepted as small difficulties. The host would never outgrow its adolescence in any case, since the user always discarded it when the child's mass neared forty kilos.

The tiny settlement could not, of course, long supply enough children. It would be necessary to obtain new bodies and, with caution, to initiate societal changes more amiable to user needs. Gradually the users surveyed their domain afoot, usurping children as necessary—increasingly male children as they came to know the sedentary role of the local females. Users found tribal societies so refractory to change that it became necessary to build their own settlement. There, new faces could appear without fear of rejection. There, advanced technical skills might be developed without fear of superstitious reprisal.

During the next century, people of the distant

mesa villages, who would one day be called
Anasazi, became aware that their children disappeared too frequently for chance occurrence. Mul-
tiroomed apartments of stone and mud were
abandoned; others were built as cliff fortresses
against a nameless presence. The blistering
three-year drought that began in 1215 A.D. was
thought to be an omen, and Mesa Verde ma-
triarchs came near the mark when trying to keep
their children from wandering: they invented the
legend of the child-stealer.

Eventually a combination of chance sightings
and careful tracking led a party of warriors due
south from Mesa Verde. Nearly a hundred
kilometers away, they found a strange settlement
where small children were enslaved for field
work and deferred use—evidently by a handful of
adolescents. Despite the inhuman accuracy of
crossbows in the hands of the defenders, the fight
was brief, its conclusion foregone. The users retreated down the roof hatch of their kivalike
tower, stoked its fire with dry brush and their
wooden weapons to halt pursuit.

The avenging adults retaliated by heaving
green sage down the hatch, then squatted com-
placently as the smoke poured out. Hours later
they found the short tunnel to the main house.
They never found the child-stealers or the second
tunnel, but they left the site a ruin.

The users pondered long over lessons from
their social experiment. Food production in this
hostile land required most of their time. It had
taken a century to forge a few iron tools and to
admit that they were having little success with
deposition of gold circuitry on ceramic tiles. They
were no more successful with crystal fusion and

other techniques necessary to construct the modules of a subspace beacon. Perhaps the time would come when humans would develop the technology for adaptation—at which the users were experts.

Meanwhile, the users could attach themselves to a settlement large enough to stand against marauding Apache, trading freedom for security. The sinister 'children' were rejected in Chaco Canyon, but had better luck some distance to the southeast.

By an appalling irony, the next drought lasted a full generation, finally forcing the Anasazi south from their cliff cities. Some—especially the children—found a welcome in one settlement. Over two centuries later the settlement was to be named Pueblo San Saba by a user of another sort, Francisco Vasquez de Coronado. Spanish technology of 1540 A.D. was modest, but the users allowed themselves to speculate. Perhaps in time the humans would bring electronic microprocessors within the influence of the serenity beam . . . .

1994 A.D.: he was tall, with the slender strength of a distance runner. His skin was the color of tobacco, and he laid down the camel's hair brush with the weariness, or the care, of a man older than thirty-five. He strode from his excavation to the dented yellow Datsun pickup, wiping dust from his glasses with his neckerchief, and snaked an arm inside the cab to quell the buzzer.

"Raimondo Koshare here," he said to the radiophone. His voice was a slow measured baritone, had a cadence that was not entirely English nor wholly Spanish. It was both, with a touch of Four-Corners Keresan.

His black eyes brightened; he eased into the driver's seat, grinning. "Valerie Clarke? Sure I'll accept the charges, operator." A pause, then greetings that were more laughter than words. He listened for a moment. "Of course I meant it, Val," he insisted, rummaging in his cooler for a beer. "Don't let the formal tone of my letter fool you. Figured you'd need to show it there in Boise to your director at McAdams Center."

Another pause, listening, swilling cold brew. Then: "The truth is, I need the intuition of that friend of yours as much as I need you. Yep, Laura Dunning; but I'm working alone with private foundation money, and I could never justify hiring her. Your master's in Special Ed makes you a reasonable choice to theorize about thirteenth-century disadvantaged children—and naturally I thought your friend could come along."

A longer pause. Through a faint frown: "No, Val, it's legit. Remember that grad course on foundations of theory at Tempe? Yep, old Yendo used to claim you were permanently retarded at the brainstorm level; and then praised you for it. Well, now I understand what he meant. I've got a lot of data that doesn't add up. Maybe it will, for you."

He listened to the reply, nodding absently, then showed strong teeth before responding. "Sure, I still have the knack for touching. It's what makes me a good archaeologist—no, really it's what lets me find things better people miss. But I can't afford to commit that to paper; the next thing to be committed would be me. Psychics had some early success in my field, but these days it's an academic fad to deride the data. All hail to the process and to hell with the product."

More listening. He squirmed unconsciously. "Look, Val, if you must know, your ol' injun guide here is suspicious. Maybe superstitious is more like it; maybe I'm just sunstruck. But I'm touching some very odd things out there. A specialist in, uh, kids with problems might help. Especially if Laura Dunning can do what you claimed. Can she really, and will you help? I need you, Val."

In his blunt honesty, Raimondo Koshare had said exactly the right thing. He brightened further at Valerie Clarke's answer, jotted notes on a clipboard as they discussed details. Gallup and Farmington had closer air terminals, but Boise to Albuquerque was a direct flight. "Besides," he added, "if you haven't shopped and eaten in Old Town Plaza, you owe it to yourself. And I'm buying."

He listened hard, trying to decipher the change in Val's voice, but failed to identify it. As a puebleno who had never quite fitted into Amerind schools at San Saba or Kansas, or advanced work in Illinois and Arizona, Rai Koshare took curious stares for granted. It did not occur to him that Val Clarke's singular appearance had kept men from asking her for dinner dates. He would not have understood why she struggled to talk past the lump of gratitude in her throat. What he did understand was that, at the conclusion of Spring Term, Val Clarke and Laura Dunning would share his quarters for the summer.

He confirmed the date, Wednesday, June 1, then replaced the phone beneath the dashboard and finished his beer in a long, thoughtful draught. There was still time to brush away the

wood ash and compacted dust before sundown, if he kept at it.

The focus of his attention was a firepit in the
exact center of an ancient collapsed room which,
for convenience, he called the kiva. But a kiva had
six, or occasionally eight, pilaster roof supports.
This one had four. It also had no ceremonial
sipap'. As if to compensate for this lack, it did
have some other things. It had a narrow tunnel,
now choked with dust and animal intrusions, that
led to the big house nearby. Another tunnel led
from the big house. Rai had taken bore samples for
days before realizing that the longer tunnel
emerged in a gully a half-kilometer distant.

More: the 'kiva' had a cache of tiles the size of a
thumbnail, more like porcelain than the usual
gritty product and bearing evidence that gold had
once adhered to the fine patterns incised in the
tiles. Ordinarily that would mean a recent intrusion marked 'PROVENIENCE UNKNOWN.' But
Rai Koshare had trembled as his fingertips
scanned the tiles, feeling the message of antiq-
uity—and of warning. The maker of the tiles, he
decided, was one of those children who had built
this riddle—Oshara—before Columbus, even before Niccolo Polo. He was increasingly glad he
had kept the ruin a secret; with every passing
season, evidence mounted that he was wasting
his time on an incredibly well-articulated hoax.
Yet he knew that something more sinister than a
hoax lay behind Oshara, waiting to be understood. The last one who had touched those tiles
had not been an innocent child.

The Oshara site bore every sign of having been
built by children, then destroyed by fire without

effort to save it. And its kiva firepit apparently contained small artifacts of crude steel, affixed to charred fragments that had once been hardwood. He would know more after photographs, notes, and removal of the items to a close-mouthed colleague in Santa Fe. The problem was that he already had carbon dating revealing that this site, which he had named Oshara, had been destroyed in 1260 A.D. give or take a half-century. Dendochronology was even more specific: the few remaining roof beam ends had mostly come from trees felled in 1137 A.D., give or take zero. And that was four full centuries before the Spanish came in 1540. Precolumbian Amerinds did not have iron or steel. Oshara was absolutely and unquestionably precolumbian; therefore it could not have steel.

It had steel.

Surely, surely the mechanism only looked ferrous, or it had somehow been put there by a recent visitor. All of which was goatshit, he thought; his fingertips knew. It was not an intrusion of that ash layer and it was, by God, steel. Not that this was the strangest of his findings. Rai Koshare sighed, adjusted his glasses for closeup work, and continued flicking the tiny brush. The first of June could not come soon enough.

He shifted his weight and toyed with his glasses in anxiety as the passengers disembarked from the Boise flight. A portly Amerind rancher hurried past wearing the equivalent of a Maserati in turquoise; a slight anglo woman with an afro haircut linked arms with a tall shapely blonde girl; a gaggle of orientals in severe suits beamed at everyone, cameras ready; and then he realized that the slender anglo woman was smiling at him.

He knew momentary shock as his vision collided with memories. He recalled Valerie's painfully thin arms and legs, her ears flaring from an abnormally small head with a puckish mouth and great bovine eyes set too far apart. These physical oddities had special terms: microcephaly; hypertelorism. They suggested mental retardation, if one managed to miss the intelligence that gleamed in those big brown eyes. Enough experts had been perfunctory so that Dina Valerie Clarke spent most of her youth in mental institutions. She had been rescued by a brilliant, self-serving interne, Chris Maffei—the same Maffei whose investigation of mental institutions had become an explosive best-seller. From Maffei, Val had learned hero worship and its risks, had finally known bitter disappointment when Maffei later ignored her for finer rags, better bones, a prettier hank of hair.

Rai saw with a rush of intuition that Val had learned subtlety since their casual friendship in Tempe, Arizona. Her ears were now subdued under a full 'natural' haircut, its spheroid of dark blonde ringlets making her skull seem larger. Steroids and a better diet had added a few kilos to her frame so that she might now be termed slender, rather than emaciated. Her coloring was good—but it might have been Max Factor. Wedge heels made her taller, the flowered print of her blouse an added touch of cheer. Val Clarke might never be downright pretty but now, at least, passing strangers did not quickly avert their gazes or quicken their steps. The archaeologist's, "Val! You're really looking great," was only half a lie.

"Good old Rai; still blind as a bat, thank God," she laughed up at him, taking his outstretched hand. Then she turned to introduce her lissome companion.

Laura Dunning's handshake was firm, her, "I've been dying to meet you, Dr. Koshare," softened charmingly by her hint of a southern drawl. She was in her early twenties, a few years younger than Val.

Rai stammered something responsive, awed by the tanned platinum blonde who was almost physical perfection. Yet he saw that her dark wraparound sunglasses masked a wholly eyeless face. Val Clarke had prepared him intellectually for Laura's unique handicap, though a clinician had told him that infants born without trace of eyes almost never survived. Even in those cases eyelids were usually present, being formed from separate embryonal structures. Laura was an exception, perhaps unique.

In short, Rai had been prepared to find that Val had exaggerated. Nothing could have prepared him for the evident paradox of a blind girl who moved as gracefully as a sighted athlete. He recalled Val's phrase, *telepathic vision*, and felt reassured by the label though he knew it explained little. If Val had been accurate in the physical details, perhaps she had not exaggerated Laura's peculiar ability, either. He realized that he was grinning and staring, then reached for Val's overnight bag. "Let's get the rest of your luggage," he said to break his own spell.

The yellow pickup was a crush-fit for the three of them as Rai turned north on University Boulevard and veered toward Albuquerque's Old Town. Val teased him about his choice of an

engine-driven vehicle until Rai retorted: "If you
ever had to haul a pickup out of a drywash with a
winch, lady, you'd know why I don't want an
electrabout with three hundred kilos of batteries.
And," he added slyly, "I hope you aren't trying to
tell me, of all people, to buy American." The
women were still laughing when he parked near
Old Town Plaza.

The visitors were charmed by the colorful mes-
tizo ambiance of Old Town and amused at the
Koshare view. "I'm gaga over the food and turquoise," Val explained to him, grinning, "and
you keep muttering about rusty Civil War cannon
in the plaza."

"Dug up after the Confederates buried them,"
he said, blinking owlishly. "What do you expect
from an archaeologist?"

"Food," said Laura, "and sparkling conversation."

"Not old weapons," Val put in.

"The gazpacho and menudo I can manage," he
grumped, leading them to a renovated adobe res-
taurant. Val's interjection had given him a new
idea about his newest find at the Oshara dig. A
corner of his mind chewed on it as he sketched in
his life for them during dinner.

As a native of San Saba Pueblo southeast of the
Chaco Canyon ruins, Rai explained, he might
have taken the dry, high country for granted. "But
my mother had other ideas. As a niña in the
nineteen-twenties, she'd been taken away by
forced government weaning. She came back from
the white school about 1936, almost a woman.
There were a few kids, she said, who'd run off and
hid, terrified that they were going to be relocated

as far away as Albuquerque. They seemed to think
it was the end of the world. Funny: they all disappeared out in the desert eventually. Kids wander
away from pueblos now and then, but San Saba
has more than its share. . . ."

He paused, an absent glaze in his eyes, then
retrieved his narrative thread. "I came along in
1959, pretty late in mama's life, and I was something of a brat. My papa was casta—uh, part
Hispano—and he didn't stay long. Most Keresan
tribes are quasi-Catholic but they stick to the ma-
trilineal ways; and the 'dobe place was Mama's,
and so were most of the decisions. She wangled a
job teaching traditional cooking at Haskell Indian
School in Kansas about 1965 and took me along. I
never saw papa after that."

"Believe me, I can relate," Val murmured, earn-
ing a nod from Laura. Both women, victims of
their physical features, had grown up as wards of
institutions.

Rai waved one big hand easily. "Hey, don't get
me wrong! My fuel isn't pity, it's curiosity—and
ego, maybe. As long as she lived, mama was
enough parents for anybody." He added details of
his life among the youth of tribes as disparate as
Quinault and Zia during his stay at Haskell. It was
inevitable that he would come to know his
Amerind inheritance more broadly than most, but
not as deeply as permanent San Sabans.

"Then one day at Haskell, a Wyoming Crow kid
got word his papa had died. Later he got a package
he didn't know what to do with; things his papa
had meant him to have. A carved bison horn, a
beaded bag that looked old as Adam, the world's
scroungiest raven's wing—stuff like that.

"Something about it got to me. I snuck back to
his room; he was studying to be a printer, what
would he do with that junk?"

"So you stole it," Val prompted.

The high prominent cheeks flushed slightly. "I
was going to," he admitted. "But just holding that
bag," he began, and paused with eyes closed. He
brought both hands up before him, as if fingering
the steam rising from his food. He shrugged, resumed slowly: "Just holding it made me stop and
concentrate. Like—like forcing yourself to make
chills by energizing something at the base of your
skull. You understand what I mean?"

Laura did; Val was mystified. "I don't, but I've
already got a thrill-chill," she said. "So tell, so
tell . . ."

"You already know the outcome, Val. It was
like being surrounded by presences I'd never met.
Since then I've found that the more people handle
a thing, the fainter a personal signature I get; like
lots of fingerprints obscuring any given one.

"But if a thing's been handled a lot by one or
two people, even long ago, it—well, it's like
dowsing. You feel it. I emptied the bag; it was a
medicine bag, I knew that already. The Crow had
said the bag hadn't been opened since his five-
times-great grandfather died. Some big chief
named Medicine Calf. Well, you know how it is:
everybody's ancestor was five times great.

"I found some lead balls of marble size, a piece
of gem-quality garnet, and a twist of tobacco.
That's all. But when I picked up a lead ball, it was
like a religious experience. I knew instantly that it
was a rifle ball that had been dug out of whoever
owned the bag. He hadn't been a Crow, though;
didn't think like an Amerind, but he wasn't anglo

either. I had a welter of feelings, good-bad, pleasure-pain, and it scared the living frijoles out of me. I fumbled the stuff back in that beaded bag and ran from it to mama's room and hid under my cot."

Rai folded a tortilla and used it to spoon his spicy stew, puebleno style. Val stopped eating and lifted an eyebrow. "If this is a shaggy dog story," she began.

Vigorous headshake of denial as he swallowed: "Uh-uh. Trying to remember when I realized who Medicine Calf was. A year later, I guess, in a history class. Medicine Calf was the Crow name for the black mountain man they adopted: Jim Beckwourth. He died before the Custer pleasantries—about right to be a great-great-great-great-great grandfather." He held up his free hand, fingers spread, and smiled shyly. "Five times great. And he wasn't Amerind, and not an anglo, but he as a Crow chief all right, who'd survived some shootings. That was when I started taking my knack seriously."

All through the sherbet course they argued explanations for his 'knack.' Finally Laura had heard enough. "You two can say it's hydration, very low frequency waves, crystal resonance, witchcraft, or any combination. I don't care; I just know it worked for people like Hurkos. If it teaches Rai how to find Clovis projectile points, it's good enough for me."

"More like the reverse," Rai said. "Look, I'm not all that brainy—I flunked enough exams to know. I got through school because I have this knack, and I can make shadowy inferences that help me map out a dig in advance. It's just a trick. I don't even understand it! Now it's found an unbelievable dig for me and I don't know what to do with it."

"You're being vague," Val complained. "What's unbelievable?"

Rai studied her face as though measuring her credulity before resuming. "Oshara is. It's a small ruin, but it seems to've been populated entirely by child geniuses for about a hundred years."

In Laura's southern idiom: "Is someone pulling your leg?"

"Everything I uncover says aitch-o-ay-ex," Rai agreed, "but *how?* Nope, it's genuine—I think. Sometimes I feel like just backfilling the whole damn' site and forgetting it."

Laura's gentle smile matched her reply. "I wonder if Ventris felt the same way about the way his work on Crete fell into place."

Startled, with new respect: "How'd you know about Michael Ventris?"

"Something we all get in linguistic anthro, Rai," Val chuckled. "People think mostly in verbal terms, you know. And Laura's talent works best when she understands the words as well as the emotional nuances."

"Um. How'd you like to fill me in on this talent on our way to my 'dobe," he asked, shoving his chair away. Laura was willing. They filed out, Rai disconcerted anew at Laura's grace in avoiding tables, walls, hurrying waiters. He would have hotly denied that the found her body fascinating even without the obstacle course.

Rai took the Coronado Freeway, U.S. 40 lancing the mesas under a dying red sun. They would skirt the Malpais lava beds before dark, he promised, but they would see little after that. With good roads, San Saba would be an hour to the north. With New Mexico roads, it was two hours and a rabbit's foot.

By nightfall they were turning north toward Crownpoint, Rai struggling to accept the evidence: Laura Dunning was to some degree telepathic. The proof he asked was easy to come by. When he asked her to describe what he was watching as he drove, she replied that he was focusing on a stone-crater in the windshield. Stunned by her accuracy, he drove in silence as they explained.

As an institutionalized child, Laura had learned to 'see' her world by interpreting the vision of others nearby. Val had found through empirical study that her borrowed vision could even function through animals, after a shadowy fashion. The greater the intellect of her informant, the clearer was Laura's perception of her spatial surrounds. If the informant was colorblind, so was Laura. With no one near enough to see for her, Laura was truly sightless.

The accidental friendship with Val had saved them both: Laura from an endless captivity in a mental ward, Val from violent death. Val was posing as retardate in a private clinic that fronted for a drug ring when she found Laura honing her talent in a desperate hit-or-miss environment.

Val had urged the redoubtable Dr. Maffei to obtain Laura's release but, knowing Maffei only too well, persuaded Laura to hide her unique abilities until they were free of Maffei's influence. Val Clarke trusted no one but herself to study Laura, yet in her limited access to diagnostic equipment she had found no device that could shed light on the mechanisms of Laura's ability.

"I know we're withholding some great potential," was the way Val explained it to Rai Koshare. "It galls the hell out of me; I mean, what if something should happen to the kid here," and she squeezed Laura's hand. "If I thought you were one of those selfish bastards who'd make a media freak out of her, I'd never have told you anything."

Laura smiled to herself. "He isn't," she said.

Rai, discomfited: "Can you read me like a billboard, ma'am?"

"Not quite," Laura replied. "Mostly your emotional loadings; a few clear ideas. I wouldn't have pried—it usually gives me a headache—but that particular question worries Val a lot." She paused, responded to something Val had not verbalized: "Oh, ethics, ethics, that tired old tune," she sniffed.

"It doesn't worry me where Rai's concerned," Val said defensively.

"I know, you like him. *Bags*ful," Laura breathed dramatically.

From Val: "Stop that. How many times must I tell you?"

Rai twisted the wheel to avoid a nighthawk. "Close one," he said.

"Oh? Is it the birds that bother you?" Laura asked it in syrupy innocence. She was rewarded with a whistling slap that startled Rai speechless.

For the next ten minutes, road noise was the only thing Rai heard, or wanted to hear. If *this* was the substance of the women's relationship, he thought, he had made a terrible mistake. He suspected Laura had known the agile nighthawk was

not his sudden concern. What if she had blurted
out his hapless physical response to her? Well,
she had quelled it by a petty misuse of a stunning
talent. *For now, at least,* he told himself.

The headlights swung past the village of White
Horse. Not until she saw the cutoff with its SAN
SABA sign did Val Clarke break her silence. "I
apologize to both of you," she said in a small
voice. "That was no way to end an argument."

Rai mumbled something acceptable. He heard
Laura respond, did not catch the words, but knew
the women had exchanged a contrite kiss in the
darkness. And something about that made him
still more uncomfortable. He would never understand anglo women . . . .

He drove between adobe walls into a great
dust-choked square, broad as a parade ground, his
headlights yielding brief impressions of the low
fortress-like pueblo of San Saba. Now his visitors
forgot their clash and stood very close together as
Rai struggled with their luggage. "Follow the
headlights," he puffed. "The 'dobe isn't locked."

But they preferred to follow him. Rai was one of
the few San Sabans who chose to have electricity
and piped water and, he grumbled as the women
washed in his ancient sink, he paid well for the
extras. "I've got a house trailer at the Oshara dig. It
has an inside toilet." This fact was announced so
proudly that they knew he had none in San Saba.

He directed them to the outside privy and
handed Val a flashlight without hint of embar-
rassment, despite the battered sheet-metal soft
drink signs that formed its sides and top. He heard
Val's, "A one-holer! The story of my life," but
could not fathom Laura's fit of giggles.

When they returned he bade them be at home

amid the *ollas* and woolen rugs, the savory smoke and cornmeal aroma. *Mi casa es su casa,* my house is your house, was a tradition more Spanish than puebleno and neither Val nor Laura yet appreciated the rarity of Rai's outlook. The 'dobe had been partitioned into three rooms, one partition recent and thin. The outside walls were something else again.

The windows, for example, were small and flush with the inside wall, but: "That window ledge looks like a tunnel," Val commented.

"The wall's nearly a meter thick," Rai agreed. "San Saba's big, but about average in layout. Dwellings form a square with common walls, mostly one-story. Back when Navajo were nomads, pueblenos needed a place that'd stop an arrow and wouldn't burn, and had enough insulation to be cool in summer and warm in winter." He patted the whitewashed adobe wall. "The 'dobe is plastered over stone. Believe me, San Sabans intended to stay awhile," he grinned.

The fireplace occupied a corner, with a broad work-surface at the hearth; Val guessed pueblo women had calluses on their knees. Near the ceiling was a high rectangular vent leading to the next room, and rectangular niches were neatly set into the walls for the shelf space. The quiet was almost oppressive, tempered by faint wind-moans at the window ports. Val marveled at the efficiency of the place, and was fascinated by the round roof-beams three meters above the floor. "They sure look sturdy enough," she said.

"The vigas? They are," Rai said. "I ought to bore one to date them exactly; but mama made me promise not to." He went on quickly, "You have no idea how conservative pueblenos are. My

mother was a wild-eyed radical by tribal council
standards. I got council permission for you two to
stay because I'm more help than harm—
connections with museums that buy craft items,
go-between to bureaucrats, that sort of thing. But
don't go strolling around here without me. Especially not this late after dark."

Laura sat up, chewing a full underlip calmly.
"Why not?"

After a pause, a shrug: "It just isn't done much.
You might see the Ogre Katcina." Only his sickly
smile suggested he had made a joke of questionable taste. "Most San Sabans have been asleep for
hours," he added.

"Then who," Laura said pleasantly, "is standing outside there?" She pointed toward the front
door.

Rai was handing supple multihued woven
blankets to Val at the time. He strode quickly to
the door, stepped outside after a moment's tussle
with the rope handle. When he returned a moment later, Val had not moved.

He sensed the unspoken questions, tried to pass
it off lightly. "Always a few radicals, as I said. Just
a kid. The whole town knew you were coming; I
guess he just couldn't wait."

Val seemed satisfied and noted aloud that she
was nearly asleep on her feet. "Coming Laura?"

Laura, sitting at the cold hearth, pulled her
knees together, rubbed her upper arms briskly.
Her chill was obviously internal, but her voice
was steady. "It was not a child, Rai."

"Sure it was, I recognized him. If you saw him
through the window—oh. Sorry." Then, faintly
irritable as he considered it further, he said, "Did
you, ah, see what I saw?"

"It *looked* like a tall slender boy," she agreed.

"It was; a little ladrón named Chuzo Dinay. He's a weird one, I'll give you that, but he's harmless." He turned away.

"Chuzo Dinay," Laura murmured, nodding, moving clumsily because Val's eyes were closed, settling onto the pallet next to Val's. Rai pulled a blanket across the doorway into his study where his usual pallet lay on its platform between a modern desk and rickety book shelves. It was long minutes later when Laura said again, "Chuzo Dinay. Oh yes, he's a weird one, all right."

The limber young body of Chuzo Dinay was a marvelous vehicle for the user. Still, even with contact patches spread across his fingertips, he had heard little with fingers splayed against the door. Rai Koshare's fumbling at the handle could hardly be misinterpreted, and the slight figure sped past a neighbor's beehive oven to disappear into the enveloping dark.

Chuzo ran barefoot toward the commonhouse, half-centimeter callus protecting him from the formidable 'goat head' thorn weeds which Australian sheep had brought to the Four Corners over a century before. He and six others could disdain footgear when silence required it, ignoring the pain synapse from any thorn.

The commonhouse, half dugout, was a low kivalike structure but with two normal doors, modified from pit houses of an earlier time. It squatted in the plaza apart from other structures, overhead lintel carvings its only identification as the quarters of unattached males in the Clown Society. San Sabans held fiercely to ancient clan relationships, indoctrinating children early into

the clans. Of the three users in the prestigious
Clown Society, Chuzo and one other were
deemed old enough to live apart from family
groups.

Chuzo felt his way into the warm blackness,
past the doorway and around the central firepit to
his pallet. A moment later he was seemingly inert,
lying between a sleeping man and the user con-
federate.

The two grasped hands briefly and Chuzo felt
the question: *What of the outsiders, Dinay?* Users
found no difficulty in addressing one another by
host names. Indeed, throughout their racial development a user who owned a host had both
practical and status advantages. Shipwrecked,
abandoned to their own ingenuity, users clung to
the tatters of their own culture. They used host
names as talismans of mutual respect—perhaps
the nearest approach to affection in the user's
lexicon.

Two young females, as we had heard, Chuzo
soothed.

The other, ostensibly ten-year-old Ziu
Tiamunyi, showed his irritation. *One day we
shall kill that casta.* The half-caste label, not
strictly true of Raimondo Koshare, was a common
slur. *Who knows what mischief strangers will
bring to the pueblo? Koshare's own bumbling is
worrisome enough.*

*Be glad he does most of it to the south,
Tiamunyi.* The users were mistaken in presuming
that Rai's interest lay beyond their range to the
south. Rai followed existing roads for convenience, and normally circled southward from San
Saba before heading toward Oshara to the northwest. Rai had told no one of his perplexing dig,

and kept his notes at the site. Had the users even
vaguely suspected that their abandoned settlement was under investigation, tourists in San
Saba would have seemed entirely trivial. With a
naivete he would come to regret, Chuzo Dinay
radiated cheer. *They will be no trouble. They are
only tourists, ignorant of our ways.*

In faint scorn: *Our ways? I truly hope so. You
mean San Saba ways. Are you developing a
weakness for this race?*

*I am as anxious as you to complete the distress
beacon,* Chuzo replied. In this, enslavement of the
human race was richly implied.

Did the females bring equipment we might use?

I could not discover that. We can search later,
was Chuzo's answer, *but why should anglo
tourists have better devices than those we can get
in Farmington?*

Ziu Tiamunyi signaled the equivalent of a
shrug. San Saba was only twenty kilometers from
the southeastern edge of the user range. Gallup
was beyond the southern sweep of the serenity
beam. No user had ever walked the streets of Gallup, would ever do so until the subspace beacon
brought a surreptitious starship with new tools of
conquest. Until then, the electronics parts shops
of Gallup would be safe from user scrutiny.

Farmington, on the other hand, was only forty
kilometers northeast of the spot from which the
serenity beam, as always, emanated. Largely,
users judged the anglos from their interactions in
Farmington when one of their number essayed
hitchhiking trips northward. The users remembered, far better than the oldest human, where to
locate old trinkets and pots which they treated
sensibly enough as treasure. Occasionally anglo

collectors showed up among fiesta tourists at San
Saba, and some of these paid outlandish sums for
old things. Farmington also had its share of roadside museums where a user, in his child's guise,
could vend bits of treasure for lesser sums. Buried
near San Saba was a hoard of pottery to delight
and confuse any modern pot hunter. The revenue
from this hoard had purchased vacuum tube
radios in the nineteen-twenties, transistorized
units since the sixties. Users learned to avoid
mail-order sales after a tribal elder became curious at the anglo devices the children received. In
the fifteen years since programmable pocket calculators became available to them, the users had
accelerated toward success. The subspace distress beacon was now distinctly feasible, given a
bit more time and materials.

Not that the beacon would be a compact device.
It was necessary to emplace forty slave transmitter
modules in a shallow parabolic pattern around
one master module. The array required careful
choice of a site which was both remote from
human meddling, and shaped so that a minimum
of terraforming was needed to obtain the regular
concavity of a parabola nearly a kilometer across.

The requisite landscape had been found thirty
kilometers north of San Saba, on an arm of the
shallow canyon called Escavada Wash. Several
modules would have to be slung at various
heights above the wash from cables which, when
the time came, would crisscross the broad canyon. Power requirements of the modules were
compatible with new battery-powered ceebee
units, the units suitably modified through hand-
assembled subspace translators.

The chief difficulty lay in the module sequenc-

ing, since a three-dimensional parabola in normal
space went through a shape transformation in
subspace. And users were not gods; they learned
at a moderate pace, they had forgotten details
which must be patiently rediscovered, and until
recently they had lacked equipment to quickly
calculate the correct sequence in which the slave
modules must transmit their individual signals.
Without correct sequencing on a rigid timebase,
the message might still be picked up. But it would
be received as random signals both in frequency
and amplitude.

The programmable calculator of 1990 provided
a crucial key to the solution with its internal
solid-state clock timing durations of gaming inputs. For the users, this feature meant that each
transmission digit could be sent from all forty
slave modules in the only correct timed sequence
with precision and synchronization. The alternative would have been to send each digit in every
possible sequence, which is forty factorial, which
is eight-and-a-fraction times ten.

To the forty-seventh power.

The sun would be a cinder long before this
latter scheme could be realized, and the users had
greeted recent models of signal-generating hand
calculators with something akin to glee. Now
the problems were merely those of logistics: more
cable, more parts, more time. And always there
was the possibility that human technology might
further simplify their array which, at present,
called for duplicate modules for reliability. It
would not be the first time they had redirected
their efforts to better effect. Their camouflage in
San Saba was itself a case in point.

Chuzo Dinay disengaged the hand of Ziu Tiamunyi. Their communion had taken only a few seconds and there was nothing more to be said until they knew more about the anglo women who were, Chuzo insisted, no threat. Had users not flourished for centuries among a people much more vigilant than tourists? They had even gathered components from a primitive technology which might provide the subspace beacon within a few months—while attending a pueblo school and managing to seem average children to most onlookers, including the watchful men of the Clown Society.

Chuzo settled his body for the rest it needed and let his user mind play with options. Perhaps they should fill a feed sack with treasures and borrow a car. He had known how to drive for decades, and this body was large enough now. Soon it would be oversized for a user. He had already picked its successor, a sturdy eight-year-old named Hospah Ramirez. Hospah was of the Medicine Society, but no matter: the user knew both clans well, had been a member of them all.

The host exchange was of greater import, with the usual inconveniences of a new smaller body. Perhaps the beacon could be finished before that. Perhaps the users, very soon, could be shouting their message of survival, discovery, and imminent victory across subspace. If they did not do it soon, he mused, the humans had a fair chance to become an interstellar race on their own. Using the beacon, they could stifle that possibility. Only one thing could be worse: human discovery of the users themselves while they were still few and vulnerable. That must be avoided at any cost. . . .

If Albuquerque's oldest structures had fascinated Rai's friends, San Saba mesmerized them.
Under a cloudless morning sky, heat waves already shimmered from the flat pueblo roofs as Rai
squired the women into the packed earth plaza.
Corn, mutton, and dust combined in a pleasant
perfume. They nodded at a boy playing with
twigs in the dirt. He did not look up, but Laura
quickened her steps as if he had spat.

"Careful of the goat heads," Rai cautioned as
they skirted a ground-hugging plant. "They'll go
through a thin sandal." He pointed out the half-
buried kivas and commonhouses erected as San
Saba's population grew through the centuries.
Unlike more accessible pueblos, San Saba lacked
the dozen or so shops where tourists might
browse. A single structure served as tribal council
headquarters, general store, and tourist center. A
brace of dark children bought soft drinks, regarded the strangers with huge serious eyes, and
then wandered outside.

Rai admitted that most of the artwork was imported. "All the way from the Navajo reservation
west of here," he grinned, "and the Jicarilla to the
east. Now this," he went on, indicating a basketful
of potsherds, "is a grab bag." He stirred the as-
sortment with a haughty finger, his face reflecting
distaste and resigned amusement.

"If there's one thing worse than an anglo pot
hunter, it's a San Saba niño. God knows where
they pick up these fragments; they're a buck
apiece. Save your money."

Val studied the fragments, some plain, some
with arcane marks. "Couldn't you tell their source
without looking?"

He met her gaze, saw the friendly challenge, then looked away from the basket as he chose a curved piece, smiling. "Recent," he murmured, putting it aside. Then, "Recent; recent; Mancos corrugated, but anybody could feel that; ah— probably Cortez black-on-white," he said, holding up a cream-colored piece with an angular repetitive black motif. Then he stopped, frowned, looked quickly at the last piece he had chosen. The set of his mouth said it: no more games.

"Oshara," he muttered in disbelief, stroking it between thumb and forefinger. "No, quite recent. And it's Oshara," he added, his frown deepening. "Doesn't make sense." Val and Laura waited, mute with respect for his concentration.

After a moment, Rai fished an Anthony dollar from his pocket and laid it on the counter. The San Saba girl took it without ever glancing up from her comics sheet. He tucket the potsherd into his shirt pocket and spoke to the others as they moved outside. "I swear I'll backfill the whole thing yet," he grunted, squinting at the reflected brightness of the plaza, donning dark glasses as an example to Val. Laura, in public, was never without her own. To change the subject he said, "There's always the church and graveyard."

But Laura shook her head. "Could we drive out to this Oshara?"

Val: "Why not after lunch, and let Rai fix that paper bread he brags about?"

"I'd—I'm just uncomfortable," Laura confessed. "Rai, would you look at the boy who was playing next to that kiva we passed?"

Again Rai was struck by Laura's use of another's vision. He scanned the plaza. "Oh, the Clown

Society commonhouse, you mean," he corrected.
"The kiva's behind it."

"He isn't the same boy you surprised last
night," she hazarded.

"Nope; one of the Tiamunyis. But you've got
the right clan."

"Let's walk near him again, but not too near,"
she said. Val traded friendly shrugs with Rai.
Proximity, she knew, often helped Laura to sense
the mental state of children in their work at Boise.

They strolled back, apparently ignored by the
boy. But Laura's shudder was obvious to Val, who
rubbed her friend's forearm. "Goosebumps? In
this heat?"

No answer for a long moment. They were inside
Rai's adobe when Laura put palms to her temples
and leaned against the tall puebleno. Then, squar-
ing her shoulders and taking a deep breath: "I'm
all right now. Val, last night I got the strangest
flash from that boy outside. Do you remember that
old mountain man in the isolation cell in Boise?
The one they said had killed and eaten those hik-
ers up in the Sawtooth Range? I told you he
thought of people as though they were flies."

"And he was a spider, you said. Don't remind
me," Val answered.

"A crafty old one," Laura persisted. "There was
something of him in that boy, and something else
that reminded me of a true vegetative coma. As
though he were carrying a catatonic on his back,"
she said in exact inversion of the truth.

Rai laid a gentle hand on her shoulder. "The
Dinay boy sure isn't catatonic," he said. "But if
you study the local kids here, you might get in-
sights into some who've been dead for seven
hundred years."

"Maybe pueblo children are just, um—" Val paused to choose a diplomatic phrase, "more stoic than those we're used to. They must surely have a different psychic complexion, Laura."

Laura: "The kids in the store weren't like that. Or were they? I usually wouldn't pay that much attention; why court a migraine? But the one we passed outside: I'd swear he was the Dinay boy if I didn't know better."

"I suppose being raised as a social enforcer could have something to do with it," Rai suggested. "I don't know the secret rituals of the Clown Society, but the Dinay kid and Ziu Tiamunyi are both members. They start early."

"Start what?"

"I'm not sure, I'm more or less in the Scalp Society. San Saba clowns aren't like anglo clowns. They keep folks in line with tricks, or unpleasant practical jokes if necessary, or—well, all the way to broken bones. Think of 'em as police, or as Four-Corners mafiosi, but only when they're in costume. They take it seriously."

A deep exhalation. Then, "I suppose that must be it," Laura said. Clearly she supposd nothing of the sort, yet Laura knew the avoidance garnered by people who worried overmuch at trifles. She offered a tentative smile in Rai's direction: "I wonder if I'll be any earthly use with children who lived centuries ago, but I'm ready for Oshara if Val is."

Val patted her trim abdomen. "As long as this is empty, I'm not budging. All I've had is coffee."

"Can't have anglos on the warpath over coffee," Rai said, deadpan. "The stuff did more to promote peaceful trade than anything else, in these parts." He fixed Val with a comic scowl: "Long as you're going to be that perverse, you can help me."

The good-natured raillery was forced for a few minutes, an unspoken strategem to set Laura at ease. They soon had a mesquite fire crackling under a heavy metal plate in the fireplace, while Rai mixed blue-gray cornmeal paste with a dollop of wood-ash lye. While the steel plate heated, Rai poked among his stored goods.

Under Rai's guidance the women poured zucchini, corn, beans, and a potent mixture of tomatoes and green chiles into an iron pot. Rai added red chile powder and a double-fistful of leftover turkey, explaining that the meat was from local fowl. "Before you whites came, we used a lot of dogmeat," he told them.

Laura, quickly: "I'd rather have turkey than the authentic stuff, thanks."

"Turkey's authentic; where'd you think they were first domesticated, lady?" Then he slid the pot to the rear of the steel plate, bidding Val stir it now and then, and set about making the famed piki bread.

Cornmeal paste, spread thinly over the heated plate, curled quickly at its edges and began to approximate heavy vellum. With a deft sidewise sweep of his wooden spatula, Rai loosened the pungent piki, laid it on a broad—and probably priceless, Val judged—platter of red-on-black. Then he repeated the process. They were ravished by the aroma.

In ten minutes the pot simmered, the pile of piki ready. Laura set the table with modern utensils and soon they were engulfing a San Saba meal, complete with fresh goat's-milk butter. Val, following Rai's example, used a scrap of piki as a scoop. Laura slurred through a mouthful: "Gracious, what *do* you call this stew?"

Rai shrugged. "Stew. Call it sopa Anasazi if you like; it's close to the staple diet of the Anasazi."

"Remind me not to feel sorry for them," Laura replied. "But who are the Anasazi?"

"Navajo word; it just means 'the old ones,' " Rai said, amused at the unladylike attack on his victuals. He went on to say that Keresan pueblos had assimilated cultural bits from their neighbors, but primarily they were descended from the ancient people who built the cities at Chaco Canyon and Mesa Verde: children of the Anasazi. Archaeologists had amassed evidence of an unbroken tradition of occupancy in the Four Corners region that stretched from before 5,000 B.C. to present times. This cultural continuity included the Anasazi and had been dubbed the Oshara tradition, said Rai, who added laconically, "But I really blew it when I named my dig. It's anything *but* traditional. More mysteries than the Balcony House."

Again they pleaded ignorance. The Balcony House, he explained, had been built around 1200 A.D. beneath a sheltering cliff top in Mesa Verde. Its people had moved there from homes on the nearby mesa, becoming cliff dwellers by definition. They had shrewdly constructed the approaches so that no one could enter or leave without a dizzying climb, and passage through a masonry slot that rendered one helpless during that passage. Other ingenious tactics had been employed to create in Balcony House a masterwork in defensive strategy.

"It was a case of sudden, deliberate isolation,"

Rai opined. "Why? There's no evidence of warfare that would've driven them there. But for some reason a bunch of settlements relocated on cliffs about the same time. Balcony House is a statement in masonry: they were hiding from something."

Val: "You mean someone?"

"I think so, yes. Some people insist that since there isn't any proof of organized warfare, we mustn't draw any such conclusions."

Val waggled a forefinger. "Professional caution," teasingly.

"Something I seem to lack," he said wryly. "There's no argument about the tree-ring dating, though. A ferocious drought from 1276 until nearly 1300 forced the Anasazi out of their cliff cities, and they seem to have relocated as Keresans. I thought my dig would add a piece to the mosaic. Datings show that Oshara was built before Balcony House and was occupied until shortly before the drought. Some Oshara pottery looks like degenerations of Mesa Verde stuff. Maybe because it was made by novices; children."

Val's eyes sparkled with surmise. "You think the Anasazi kids left first?"

"Some may have. I found a braided yucca rabbit snare with Mesa Verde knots. Lots of stuff; you'll see. What I don't find are the traditional construction or decoration motifs. Or ceremonial burials. I seem to've found an orphan's home run by the kids, and they didn't bother with traditional ways. Didn't rebuild after it burned, either. Why did they burn it? Or did they?"

Laura wiped her mouth, smacked in childlike pleasure as she sat back from an empty bowl. "If you didn't find any burials, how do you know it was—"

"No ceremonial ones, I said. There are burials, kids dumped into trash heaps just any old way for the next gully-washer to take. No adults. There was one under a ledge in a dry-wash that was missing a forearm and the bone hadn't begun to heal. Couldn't date it but it figures to be Osharan. A boy, judging by the skull, twelve or thirteen.

"Then there's the fingerprints on the pottery. Some of it shows prints of niños only six or eight. Nothing with adult prints, dammit. But I haven't finished the dig yet. It could take another ten years; longer, if I don't get help."

Val finally cleaned her bowl. "So get help," she said. "There must be some bright students who'd love to puzzle it all out under your all-seeing wisdom." She clasped her hands together, beamed, batted her eyes in parody of a smitten sophomore. Valerie Clarke was no schoolgirl, but her satire was compromised by longing. Rai saw it, was flattered, and let it pass. In Laura's presence, Rai Koshare found it hard to consider other women—as women.

The buzzer in Rai's pickup saved him from an uncomfortable moment. "The phone," he said redundantly, and strode outside.

After a moment Laura began to clear the table. Then, barely audible: "I thought you were through mooning over that big Indian."

"Careful with those bowls," Val said in deliberate nonsequitur; "they're museum pieces."

"So is he." Laura made more clatter than necessary.

A sigh, an old dialogue revisited: "I told you a

long time ago, Laura: I prefer men, they just don't return the favor. If you can't accept me as I am, stay out of my head. And never, never take advantage of me like you did last night in the pickup."

"It's Rai Koshare who's taking advantage of you. We're going to waste all summer here for room and board."

"Waste? I hope not," Val argued. "Rai's a rare bird. I do like him, that's a fact. I think you two would get along, too, if you'd give him a chance."

"Is *that* a fact?" The lovely mouth pursed in something that could have been concealed knowledge.

"That's opinion." Val moved to the sink, helped Laura with the dishes, their hips companionably touching. It was unselfishness that bade her say, "One day you'll meet a man and go dipshit over him, and then you'll understand."

"And what will you do when it happens?"

"Applaud. I hope," this last with a flicker of smile.

"No jealousy?"

Val considered. "Maybe. But the more I love you, the more I should applaud. If one of us were male, you and I would have what they call a marriage of convenience. It's more than that, of course," she added quickly, turning as Rai walked in. She missed the subtle relief that, during the past half-minute, had begun to smoothe Laura's brow.

"Snails," Rai said by way of preamble. "Anybody know what a *planorbis* snail looks like?"

Two headshakes. Val: "Fossil snails?"

"Nope; they've been found in Blue Water Creek. Some distance south, but they're hosts to a very nasty parasite. That was a friend of mine on the phone; Jeff Simes, a State Public Health guy in Gallup."

Val let her arms droop, miming helplessness. "Don't tell me: you want us to swim out and—"

"Hold on," he flashed a grin. "Several cases of schistosomiasis have turned up on another reservation. Hope I pronounced it right. It's a twelve-cylinder word for blood flukes. All Jeff wants me to do is convince San Saba elders to let SPH people take blood and stool and urine specimens here." He shook his head in cynical amusement.

Both Val and Laura had too much clinical experience to be repulsed by body functions. "It's not all that bad," Val objected.

A snort: "Try telling that to the tribal council. Jeff knows he'd have to knock this whole pueblo unconscious before they'd surrender parts of themselves to an anglo. Religious dogma; you can't even take snapshots here. I told you we were conservative."

"You can always sneak a stool sample," Laura mused, then donated a gorgeous smile. "You wouldn't believe the clinic slang for that little operation."

"As if I didn't have enough to do. Well, he's sending me some specimen containers, just in case I find some mierda on my boot heel," Rai grumped.

"He's got his nerve," Val said.

"Ahh, Jeff's just doing his best. So am I. But don't either of you try wheedling anything like that from anybody here." Grim lines framed his mouth: "I'm not exaggerating about the Clown Society. I'd probably get wind of it first, but they've been known to whip people out of the area on foot. On the reservation they have the legal right. Just let me do the collecting," he finished.

It was obvious that Rai would go to any lengths for his people, even at the risk of banishment or beating. Laura and Val shared the thought: they would never understand Amerinds . . . .

There were two routes to Oshara, each with roads partway, each with its drawbacks. Rai kept delicate equipment locked in a case in the Datsun, so he avoided the direct northern route with its washboard surface and steep arroyos. Usually he swung far to the southwest in an arc, but this time he chose to cut through Chaco Canyon. They spent a few minutes absorbing the fact of Pueblo Bonito Ruin there, an Anasazi settlement and with eight hundred rooms, literally the largest apartment structure ever on the continent until near the turn of the twentieth century. Portions of the vast four-story sandstone ruin had been rebuilt and Rai made a point of the fact that, in the thirteenth century, the builders had carefully filled in external windows.

"It's easy to assume the Bonitians plugged their windows against the Apache but when a big attack came, the place was overrun anyway. Was Balcony House just luckier? Or were both places holed up against something else entirely?"

Val folded her arms, turning with some asperity. "What's this some *thing* business," she demanded. "That's twice you've avoided laying the blame on *people*."

"Hadn't thought about it," Rai admitted. After a moment of reflection he said, "I could claim I'm being cautious, but I guess it's mama's old stories.

She believed in antibiotics, and in God, and in the Rain Katcina too. And if she believed in good, she had to believe in evil. When she told me to behave and mentioned the Ogre Katcina, I behaved."

Laura, not entirely solemn: "You believed in it?"

"She did; so I did. Most San Sabans still do. The ogre's not a person. More like a ghoul, a huge evil presence that hides and waits for children."

Val nodded. "I doubt if there's ever been a culture where mothers didn't invent bogeymen to scare naughty kids."

"Not necessarily naughty ones in San Saba. It could happen to any kids. You have to understand that just mentioning the ogre was the punishment. When the very *word* is punishment, it gains a lot of potency in a boy's mind."

"Just boys, not girls?"

"Right; maybe because girls are stay-at-homes. It's a very old tradition, and I suppose it's strengthened by the coincidence of San Saba losing more boys than most. Ever wonder why the place doesn't overpopulate? It's a big, hostile land out here. It swallowed up a lot of kids when they got old enough to go exploring. It still does," he murmured, staring across the ancient ruin.

Now Laura was affected. "Will you stop, Rai? I'm already half afraid the place is possessed. It can't be, I know; but—"

"But you don't know it after midnight, huh?" Val prodded her own breastbone with a thumb. "Me too. Let's go on to your dig, Rai."

The thirty-five kilometers from Pueblo Bonito to Oshara took an hour in enervating heat. There was no road across the parched, nearly level valley. Rai followed the windblown spoor his own

tires had made previously. Val, imagining she
would spot the place from afar, was surprised as
the vintage mobile home seemed to protrude suddenly from a depression. She said so.

"A small elevation change hides a lot," Rai
responded. "You don't want to be in a dry-wash
when there's any sign of rain, and you mustn't
take long hikes without water and compass and
beeper. Even then you could walk right around
Oshara and never see it. Forewarned is forearmed,
okay?"

They hauled overnight bags inside, momentarily ignoring the sandstone ruin that brooded a
hundred meters distant, forlorn and time-ravaged
in the same slight depression.

Inside the mobile home was apparent chaos.
Foam packing boxes, specimen drawers, antique
file cabinets, tools occupied every cranny of the
living room except for a path leading to the two
tiny bedrooms. These, too, were annexed for
products of the Oshara dig. Rai had obviously
made herculean efforts to clear enough space for
his guests.

"Well," Val chortled as she eyed a stack of
boxes next to their bed, "it's snug."

The kitchenette represented lip service to
amenity. The refrigerator was half-full of beer and
the utensils were clean. Under the sink was a
cache of canned food and juice, and a plastic
canister on the countertop was half-full of jerky.

Rai opened a beer, took a lath of the jerked meat,
gestured to the others. "I live on this stuff mostly," he said. "Help yourself; I'll give you a tour of
Oshara."

With some hesitation, both women tried the
jerky as they trailed outdoors. Laura grunted,

twisted and tore at her thin slat of meat for all the world like a puppy with a slipper. "Lordy, it's a wonder you don't starve," she said finally.

"Now you know why he looks like a piece of jerky," Val joked. Privately, she admitted, it tasted damned good; salty and wild.

"Just keep chewing," he advised. "A little piece of venison jerky will swell 'til it fills your mouth. With five kilos of this stuff, an Anasazi family could walk from here to Las Cruces. Maybe they did," he ended, guiding them around weatherproof boxes, holding Laura's hand. Val supposed he had not fully realized that Laura did not need the guidance.

Val knew a vague disappointment after the vast pile of Pueblo Bonito. Yet she saw that this small site must have demanded backbreaking labor of its single investigator. An electric barrow, plugged into an extension cord and replenished from solar panels atop the mobile home, squatted on fat tires in the near distance. The barrow had worn perceptible ruts in the hard ground, ferrying tons of earth from the site to a nearby dry-wash. An old tent of buff canvas blended with the bleak landscape, drummed softly under whiffs of hot dry breeze. Beyond the tent lay Oshara.

A yellow cord stretched from a rock outcrop nearby, ending at a metal stake near a crumbled wall. The stake boasted a hand-lettered sign: 31 SJ1989-13. The wall had no true windows, only ventilation slits high on the external face. It had been a single one-story square structure some fifteen meters on a side, with a smaller round house a few meters away to the northwest. Three of the house's four corners were intact, over three meters high; but only the southwest wall near them

had survived centuries of coercion by wind, rain,
time.

Val counted the eight wooden roof beam ends,
vigas, that protruded from near the top of the wall.
They had been as thick as one of Laura's thighs.
Even in death Oshara exuded an aura of strength
and purpose. Unknown, unlamented by man, it
might have dwindled entirely to dust but for Rai
Koshare. Compared to Pueblo Bonito's text of
stone, Oshara was a small question mark in
the lexicon of archaeology.

Val: "What does the sign mean?"

"Site designation," said Rai. "It's on file with
the state. Under the new scheme New Mexico is
alphabetically number thirty-one. Ess-jay is San
Juan County; Oshara's the thirteenth site claimed
in the county in 1989."

Laura broke her silence. "How did you find it,
Rai?"

He waved them westward along the barrow
track. Fifty meters distant, a shallow dry-wash
snaked southwestward from a modest peak that
was visible some fifteen kilometers away. "I was
hiking from a trading post to Chaco Canyon in
the spring of eighty-nine and started following
this wash."

"Why, that was before you came to Arizona
State," Val said.

"Sure; partly it's why I went there for postgrad
work," Rai answered. "But there's no record of
any site like this, and no talk about unpublished
finds like it. I'm not about to publish a word on it
'til I know it isn't another Piltdown Man joke.
Don't ask why: let it sink in.

"Look down the declivity here, along the sides.

Notice how the stones are stacked? That was a check dam."

"Only on the sides of the gully?"

Patiently: "It went across, seven hundred years ago. Every few years, enough water comes down to make it a wet wash. Once a generation, a cloudburst comes through like a monorail express. By making check dams you can capture enough silt and moisture to grow a few ears of corn here, some squash there. Maybe. It was a hard life."

He pointed to the nearside of the slope. "I walked to here before I saw something I'd nearly stepped on. A short digging stick, an antler fork socketed in a hunk of wood. The sinew wrap was long-gone, but somebody had dropped it right there above the high water area. Otherwise the antler and socket wouldn't have stayed together.

"I ran my touch routine; it had been dropped in a hurry by some kid who was overjoyed to drop it. All I could get from it was a lot of sadness and fright, with that brief surge of happy vibes just before it was dropped. From the size of the stick, it must've been just a little fellow.

"Well, people didn't cultivate check-dam plots beyond their personal habitat range, so I started looking around. And there was Oshara, just over the hump in that depression. Well-placed; you can walk right past and not see it, but they built it well away from the wash. Smart, for a bunch of kids."

Rai led the way back to the site, approaching this time from the northwest. Now the circular structure was prominent, rising like a broad cone frustrum. It had once had a vertical story above the present top, making it virtually unique among kivas, said Rai. Other major details failed to tally with the Anasazi: kivas were normally to the southeast of the houses; they never sported turrets; and so on. Rai eventually realized he was overloading the others with data.

"Why don't I show you the radar pictograph," he asked rhetorically, and led them to the tent. "I don't know the first thing about electronics, but I can push a button with the best of 'em."

Radar pictography, a development of side-looking radar, required equipment which Rai had borrowed briefly a year earlier. The transceiver tower had long since been returned to Albuquerque, but the data tape and final computer-generated picture were Rai's own. He unrolled the paper tube, tacked its corners against the makeshift plywood table in the tent. Suddenly, Oshara made sense.

The ruin was clearly outlined from a vantage point twenty meters high, fifty distant. Rai had drawn thin pencil lines on an overlay. When he placed his reconstruction over the pictograph, they saw a ghost of Oshara as it might have looked in the year 1200. Oshara, without exterior doors or windows, had surrounded an inner courtyard. Midway along it on two sides, load-bearing walls had supported vigas at midpoint. Stone slabs had evidently been set as ladder rungs into the walls. That way, Val realized, someone could walk across the flat roof over a solid wall instead of the less-secure adobe overlay.

Rai had found no external traditional ladders, only one inside. On the radar pictograph was a long shadowy pile of debris stretching from the northeast wall. Rai's overlay showed a stone smokestack, rising five meters above the roof.

The kiva had looked like a castle tower rising from its conical base with another stone ladder built in. Dotted lines on the overlay revealed the existence of two tunnels. The short one ran from the kiva to the nearest and largest room of the house. The other ran east from the same room, extending beyond the overlay, sliced neatly by a trench that was obviously recent.

Altogether it was a very sensible plan—and strikingly unlike its contemporaries in many details. Rai suspected that the stone lining of the short tunnel had been added for water storage. "But I seriously doubt they'd have used it as a tunnel when it was full of water," he guessed. "Swimming, especially underwater for ten meters in pitch dark, isn't a common skill hereabouts. That's something you might help me with."

Laura: "Is there some prohibition against it?"

Rai: "No-o-o, but like slackwire walking, it probably wouldn't occur to them. Fish swim, birds fly, people walk. It's that simple."

"It's worth some thought," Val agreed. "Isn't that chimney a little unusual?"

"A *little*?" Rai laughed at the understatement. "You should see the oven it leads up from; a technical breakthrough! The damn' thing has a venturi section before it turns vertical, and the stones on top at that point must've been cherry-red when it was working. They imported some different stone for that section; judging from the stack of spares they must've replaced the top slab regularly."

"Could the glow have been for light?"

"Very good," Rai conceded. "But I doubt it;

there are easier ways like candlewood and oil
lamps—still, I hadn't considered that, Jesu Maria,
you two may be worth your keep!"

"Sire," Val murmured, with an exaggerated
hand-flourish.

"Why don't we build a fire and find out," Laura
said quickly and, Val thought, perhaps competi-
tively. Val fell silent, irked that Laura would want
to compete against Rai. It did not occur to her that
Laura might have been competing against Val
herself.

"We'll do that when I get the smokestack rebuilt," Rai agreed. "Since they dumped most of
their trash in the arroyo, this is like rebuilding a
three-dimensional puzzle with pieces missing.
But we can chalk up the fireplace as another brilliant innovation by the Oshara children."

Rai was also bemused by the long tunnel which,
he estimated, had taken years to complete. It had
not been started as a ditch and roofed over, as
Basketmaker and Anasazi had done for ventilation shafts.

Val: "How can you be sure after all this time?"

Here, Rai was pleased to have some answers.
"My test trench shows the soil above the tunnel
was never disturbed; no crossbeams or slabs
either. Besides, after a few years there's either a
slight mound or a depression where the earth was
replaced. Nope; they went to lots of trouble to be
sure the tunnel didn't show from above."

He was describing an escape tunnel, he
thought; probably the best defense a child could
have against Navajo or Apache raiders. "Of course
it's possible they had some offensive weapons,"
he said, and hesitated.

"Were bows and arrows common here?"

"Fairly. But in Albuquerque, Val, you re-minded me about old weapons; it could tie in with what I took from the kiva firepit recently." He described the metal ratchet with pawl trigger which he had found and sent for analysis. "My expert guessed it was part of an old Spanish wolf trap. He doesn't know it burned about 1260 A.D., and he wouldn't believe it if I told him."

"What else could it be?"

Rai shook briefly with the huh-huh amusement of pueblenos. "Well, yesterday it crossed my mind that it could've been part of a gun. But the barrel would still be there. Anyhow, there aren't any sulphur deposits near. Or nitrates, so far as I know."

Laura, who seldom forgot the most trivial thing she learned, would not let it drop. "Turkey drop-pings have nitrates. And how about pyrite for sulphur?"

A long pause, full of good-humored vexation. "Charcoal's no problem," Rai muttered. "Oh, I suppose—it's—possible."

"But you don't think so."

He smiled. "I don't know what to think. A gun is even more outrageous than," and his brows jerked up with the final, "a crossbow!"

Val, who remembered her English history, thought the crossbow a step backward from the longbow.

"Not as a close-quarters defensive weapon," Rai said. "A child could cock a crossbow with his legs and double the stored energy he could man-age with a long bow." He rubbed his nearly whis-kerless chin. "Maybe I should take another look at my polaroids from the firepit. It's no crazier than half the other things about Oshara."

"Didn't you feel anything about the steel mechanism," Val asked.

"Not a twitch; clean as a lava chunk," Rai admitted. "Whatever I feel, I can't feel it when the sample's been through a fire since it was handled. Which reminds me," he said, replacing the vellum, "let me show you something else."

Presently, rummaging in specimen trays in the mobile home, Rai opened a small box to reveal his rectangular tiles. "Don't touch 'em," he cautioned, as they gleamed white under lamplight.

Val saw the fine lines etched in angular patterns across the tiles, spied a faint yellow sheen, hairthin, in one line. "I give up," she said.

"Me, too," Rai sighed, unfamiliar with etched circuitry. "Some sort of amulet, I think, with gold melted into the lines and melted out again. Absolutely unknown in these parts. But look here," he whispered, turning one piece over with a tweezer. "A little kid made this one."

Before its firing, the tiny hunk of ceramic had been handled by fingers that could only be those of a child; for the whorls of a small fingerprint had been captured, to become vitreous evidence that might last a hundred millennia.

Laura asked Val to keep looking at the piece. "Somehow this makes them come alive," she breathed. "Why can't I hold it?"

"Obscures my feel for it," Rai said, a bit apologetically. "There were adults here from time to time, it seems; for trade, or some ceremony. I gather that because whoever handled this after it was fired was—" He shook his head, a grim frown passing quickly across his features.

Laura stiffened. "Rai, hold it; feel it. Whatever you do, take that tile and do it."

"I was going to say he was an old shaman."

"You were going to lie, then," Laura said evenly. "Unless shamans are loathsome people."

After a moment of regarding her calmly: "Lady, you are really something," he said. "Okay, but let me concentrate." He placed the tile on his fingertips, laid the fingertips of his other hand across it, composed his face.

He dropped the tile at Laura's bleat of terror.

Val moved to stand behind the taller woman, her hands gripping Laura's upper arms in protective custody. Under different circumstances the tableau of Valerie soothing a much larger woman might have been amusing, but Laura leaned back to extend the contact, grateful.

Rai Koshare tried to keep his irritation hidden as he tweezered the little tile away among the others. Rai was not an accomplished actor but, "I'm not sure all this is fruitful," was all he said.

But Laura was nodding, biting carmine lips. "Yes it is," she husked. "Very. I don't know how many people there are like the old devil who handled that tile, but there are two like him at San Saba."

Rai considered this, not fully understanding. "Well, the Medicine Society has a shaman who's nearly a hundred. But he's a decent old fellow—"

"That's not what I mean. Is it possible to live a hundred lifetimes in your head and still be only a child? An evil, inhuman changeling? It must be possible here, Rai. I'm frightened."

"Those two boys in the pueblo," Val surmised.

Laura started to reply, stopped as her chin quivered. She began to whimper almost noiselessly, hands over her mouth, her head nodding in affirmation.

Val murmured condolences, her fingers gentle on Laura's temples, and these attentions had gradual effect in the rear bedroom; eventually Laura slept. Val found Rai Koshare at the ruin, applying adhesive to a stone he had fitted back into the chimney, and offered an explanation that was half apology. There was no point in denying Laura's delicate emotional makeup and Val did not try. She had seen Laura in tears a dozen times while working with disadvantaged kids, chiefly after a stormy session with a vindictive child.

"Think of her as a highly tuned instrument," she told him, "that gets out of whack if you shake it hard. And make no mistake, that experience she felt through you shook her thoroughly."

"Whatever you say," Rai answered glumly. "But if she felt it through me, why didn't I feel just as bad?"

Val squatted, reached to hold the slab in place as Rai sought the next piece in his stone puzzle. "Because she has this double-edged ability to amplify the nuances in our heads," Val said almost sadly. "But there has to be something there to amplify. Tell me: what *did* you feel?"

Rai hunkered back, tossed and caught a stone with the aimless energy of a man who cannot stay idle. "I felt Oshara," he said simply. He started to expand on the statement, then shrugged and selected another stone.

"Don't be cryptic," she pleaded. "We need all the candor we can rake and scrape, Rai. I think you'll be glad we came if you know exactly how things stand. Laura's sensitivity? Sure, sometimes she's—frankly, a pain in the ass; but you take the bitter with the sweet. She's also very special."

Rai did not risk the answer that might reveal his growing concern for Laura. It went beyond physical infatuation. "I'm not sorry you came," he said, knowing it sounded gruff, softening his tone. "In fact I'd like you to read my journals of the dig; and I need to go back to the pueblo for Simes while you do it. May take a day or so, but you'll get a better feel for Oshara."

"Speaking of a better feel. I still want to know what Oshara feels like—and why it upsets Laura so."

Rai had never concretized it aloud, and faltered in the process. The artifacts of Oshara, he said, sometimes gave him an impression of childlike terror and avoidance; sometimes of a cold inhuman ruthlessness that was wise with experience; sometimes both. He had a dozen sets of immature fingerprints on the adobe-like wall plaster, more still from potsherds, some from discards that were never kiln-fired. In one case he could match the print of a frightened child who had made an imperfect bowl and years later—to judge from the expansion of the print—had handled some tiles which had never been completed.

"The same kid because the prints are the same," he said in exasperation. "But someone very old, rapacious, mean as hell, handled those tiles a lot too, without leaving physical prints. I haven't found one adult print on the site. But let's face it, Val, kids don't have that kind of—" He paused.

"Mature, hungry evil," Val supplied. "That's what Laura said before she fell asleep." She picked up a stone, her tongue protruding from her teeth, and wedged it into a space; darted a glance at Rai for confirmation.

"Perfect fit," he approved; "you'll go far. I guess

'mature evil' is a good description of the Oshara feel. But I have absolutely no proof other than my knack, that any adults even visited here. Why did that mature brujo visit," he asked as if to himself.

He went on talking as they worked. Oshara needed a child sociologist to gnaw on analytical questions while Rai completed the reconstruction. With most digs, a few test trenches and a ten per cent reconstruction gave suitable data for a site. Not Oshara. He had found no evidence of trade with shell, cotton, or artifacts to suggest Oshara's connection with any other settlement. He had only hints that Oshara had assimilated Mesa Verde techniques. Since Pueblo Bonito was closer, he had expected cultural connections there.

"I wonder: were Osharans afraid to deal with near neighbors?" Closer to a tactical truth than he knew, Rai changed his tack for a personal reason. "Some of those questions will jump out at you from the journals. Would you be okay alone here for the next couple of days? I'd drive back every night if you like."

With her growing interest in the chimney reconstruction, Val agreed, only half aware of the question. In desultory fashion she even looked forward to scanning the Koshare journals, separated from her familiar world by the sprawling land and the ancient topic.

Three beers and a masonry course later, the shadow of the northwest wall crept across the chimney and Val stepped back to admire their work. Rai chose that moment to complete his request. "It just occurred to me," he lied, "that Laura could help me at San Saba. The radiophone,

checking out those kids; you know," he added
vaguely.

But Val did not know. "I doubt if she'll want to
monitor those boys. You can ask her. Whatthehell," she said.

A grunt from Rai. They trudged to the mobile
home to wash and found Laura alert, refreshed
from her long nap. Val hid her surprise when
Laura agreed to return with Rai, innocently
pleased that her two friends were warming to one
another. The corned beef and cabbage tasted of
old tin can but no one minded. By nightfall, Rai
had assembled his journals for Val, spent an hour
alone at his tiny lab in the kitchenette.

The potsherd he had bought in San Saba, he
found, was indeed quite recent. Clay and temper-
ing grit were typical San Saba ware; obviously its
provenience was not Oshara. And yet—his fingertips queried the piece, and it had the Oshara feel.
He looked up to see Laura's eyeless attention on
him, a wholly unfathomable and lovely face in
repose. He presumed she was monitoring his suspicions about the potsherd, allowed a simple
thought to blanket scholarly matters: *incredible
woman.*

The marvelous mouth composed a smile. He
said nothing, stowed his lab equipment, put away
the potsherd. It had been a good day, he thought;
the best. He would see that tomorrow would be
even better.

Val did not entertain misgivings about her lone
occupancy at Oshara until the next morning, as
Rai transferred instruments from the pickup to the
mobile home. To save time he had elected to take

the rougher, more direct route to and from San Saba. Laura said little but her mood was clearly buoyant. It was, after all, something of an adventure for her to be separated from Val in this country. Val chided herself for a nagging worry, reflecting that Rai would be hardly more than an hour away. Once, Val had been fitted with a mastoid-implanted radio—a temporary and temperamental gadget—but today she would be without any communication device. *Worrywart,* she told herself; *that makes it an adventure for me, too. Smile, dammit!*

"Don't forget the canned ham," she called as Rai helped Laura into the Datsun. She quickly added, "Unless you can't eat it."

Rai leaned from the cab, grinning. "Whatever my colleagues from Brigham Young may say, we're not from the lost ten tribes of Israel. I love ham." He started the engine, waved, then headed southeast.

Laura's wave was perfunctory; a good sign, Val insisted to herself. High time Laura made herself more independent. *Then why do I feel neglected?* She muttered an angry expletive to her inner self, wandered over to the ruin. She would replace no stones without Rai, but it wouldn't hurt to study them before hitting Rai's journals again. In all this solitude she could even strip and get a bit of tanning. Pleased with her idea, she began to shuck her skirt and blouse as the Datsun's dust signature faded.

Rai kept El Huerfano Peak over his left shoulder and ignored his dash-mounted compass, content to run by dead reckoning for a time without conversation. He saw that Laura had left her concealing sunglasses in her shoulder bag and felt honored in some inexplicable way. Laura's was a strange loveliness but, despite the occasional glances he swept toward her—as though tasting her beauty—Rai knew his fascination was the cleaving of like to like. They shared an exotic quality, he with his fingertip intuition, she with her own tacit knowledges. Their internal languages might differ, but Rai deemed them only dialectal differences.

"We're crossing the trail to Nageezi," he said, jouncing with brio through a set of vintage ruts.

Laura, laughing, her hands braced against the dash padding: "It felt like we were dropping into a canyon!"

"You haven't seen Escavada Wash," he rejoined; then in confusion, "Sorry 'bout that—but you *do* see," he ended lamely.

She licked her lips, he found it erotic. "More than you think," she said. *Deliberately* erotic.

"I, ah, was surprised you, you, you wanted to come with me," he said, and immediately wished there were a pauper's home for poor phrasing.

"I felt the same about you," she replied. "Most people treat me like a freak. You don't. I like that."

He angled down a shallow dry-wash, downshifted, enjoyed the sensation of physical and emotional freedom. "Maybe we're freaks together," he said when he had climbed the opposite embankment.

"I meant this," she said, passing her palm across the smooth expanse of forehead above her nose. He saw the gesture peripherally, gave a grunt meant to be one of dismissal. "But you seem to like it," she persisted.

"I suppose I do," he said with an idle one-handed gesture.

Laura reached for the hand, found it, laid it over her face. "There," she teased. "You've been wanting to do that."

He found himself galvanized by this special intimacy. He braked, killed the engine awkwardly with his left hand, shifted to face her. "Damn you," he whispered, "if you know so much, you know what I really want to do."

She allowed his hands to cup her face, placed her own hands over his. "I like that, too," she murmured, and felt his mouth against hers, firm, ardent and inexpert. "Relax," she smiled, her fingers moving toward his hair. Then she gave him an exquisite thirty-second demonstration in kisses.

His progress was remarkable, but: "I have a lot to learn," he breathed, stroking the plentiful pale tresses.

"Val is a good teacher," Laura said amiably. She sensed the sudden reserve in him. "Does that disturb you? It shouldn't."

"Why ask? You probably know already. Does she feel about you the way I do?"

She leaned back against her window, one arm languid on his. "I used to wish she did." Softly, wonderingly. "But I was the instigator, I'm afraid. Neither of us has anyone else who cares much about what's inside us. She's the only person I have ever known whose mind doesn't have 'KEEP OUT' stenciled across it. Until you," she amended.

He laughed, waved a hand helplessly. "What did I have to hide?"

"Exactly. But now you *do*," she said, and suggested that he resume driving.

Rai started the Datsun with reluctance, listened

as Laura revealed the depth of Val's response to
him. Rai, who had accepted a solitary way of life,
took the news with both a glow and a twinge of
regret. He admitted that had Valerie Clarke come
alone, he might at that moment have been making
overtures to Val back at Oshara, and to hell with
San Saba's problems for the nonce. He refused to
pursue the ifs rigorously. Whatever his potential
relationship with Val, in Laura Dunning he had
found both a psychic need and its sweet in-
dulgence. And how were they to bare that to Val?
Rai deferred the query to the one who knew her
best.

"We won't tell her for awhile," Laura decided.
"I think she'll guess, eventually. It's probably the
easiest way." For Laura, it was certainly that. It
was also an unconscious cruelty that she would
not have practiced with deliberation.

Rai's request for Laura's company had not been
entirely disingenuous. For the next twenty minutes he guided her in the use of the phone;
queried her in the collection of stool and urine
samples. Presently they neared an ancient water-
worn scar in the earth, in some places over thirty
meters deep and hundreds wide.

"Escavada Wash, ho-o-o," he sang out playfully, and swung the wheel to make an oblique approach. It was then that he saw the pristine gleam
of a cable, hair-thin in the morning sun, stretching
completely across the wash to the east. Distracted
by the instant glimpse, hardly more than a flash,
Rai failed to see the sandstone slab before the left
front wheel slammed against it. The little pickup
recovered with a bounce and slide, now nosing
directly downhill. Laura vented a yip; Rai eased
onto the brake, regaining some control, and

jounced the vehicle onto flat terrain in the bottom of the ash.

Now a leaden metronome pounded the chassis with each revolution of the tires. Rai pulled to a stop immediately, slapped the steering wheel with the flats of his palms. Then, with a muttered apology, he pulled driving gloves on and stepped out to squat beside the Datsun. The trouble was not hard to find.

"I've bent a wheel with my goofing off," he said, stepping back to unlock the bed cover. "I'll only be a couple of minutes."

The integral chassis jack creaked down with the help of a swift kick; the single-point hub lock was easier. In only a bit over the promised time, Rai had exchanged wheels, re-stowed the jack in its clip, tossed the damaged wheel behind the cab.

Rai stepped to the cab again and squinted eastward up the autoclaved flank of Escavada Wash. He could not see the cable now but a dark speck floated without visible support ten meters above the arroyo floor. It had to be supported by thin cable, Rai knew, and he struck all too near the mark with, "Must be some new communications gear."

"Who lives out this way?"

"Nobody. When Western Electric speculates, ma'am, they *really* speculate!" Then he saw the boy squatting perfectly still in the open, two hundred meters up the wash. "Well I'm damned," he chuckled, and called out in San Saban.

Laura sat quietly, absorbing only fragments of the encounter. Rai's tone was hearty, unruffled. Evidently he had recognized the boy with the dusty denims, heavy handmade footwear and long, full-sleeved shirt typical of the area. The boy

turned—stoically, Laura thought as she monitored Rai's vision—and called out. Presently a
second and smaller boy trudged down from a
concealing outcrop farther up the wash. He cradled a rifle. Rai met them halfway.

The three Amerinds stood and talked; Rai at
ease, the boys less so. Rai asked about the cable
and laughed, the gruff Keresan bark unlike
anglos, when he heard the answer. When the second boy grasped the other's hand Rai was shading
his eyes, peering up the wash. The boy with the
rifle stepped casually to one side, behind Rai, the
rifle swinging up. Then Rai turned back, swept
one gloved hand out in a lightning motion and
plucked the little rifle from the boy's hands, holding its short barrel vertical. The rifle fired once, a
thin report that sent flat hissing echoes from the
slopes of Escavada Wash.

The next interchange was not so jovial. Rai held
the little weapon, muzzle down, with one hand
and ignored the plea of the smaller boy. When he
had emptied the clip of the rifle he flung the
cartridges across the wash, then handed the
weapon back to the boy.

Presently Rai returned to the pickup in a mild
distemper, started the engine. He paid no attention to the boys scrambling up the arroyo because
he could not know of their companion and the
transceiver, hidden among the rocks.

"What did you get from that?" He was perfectly
willing to believe that Laura's ability was bound-
less. The pickup nosed up the other slope like a
bloodhound.

"Not much; you were too far off. What was the
trouble?"

"Couple of San Saba kids. I recognized a red-

on-white clan headband and it turned out to be
Carson Kimbeto. The little one is, um, Hatchi
Leon, I think. They've suspended a bag of rocks in
the air for target practice; Man Above only knows
where they found that cable. Or why they're a
day's walk from home. Browned off at me right
now; they even refused a ride home. They'll be
okay. No trouble."

"Gunfire is no trouble?" Mild reproof lurked in
her question.

A snort, an anglo laugh. He continued his
shorthand speech, concentrating on the terrain.
"Fool kid. Doesn't know how to handle a twenty-
two yet. I saw his finger in the trigger guard;
second nature to keep an eye on the muzzle. Just
an accident. Teach them both a lesson."

Laura sensed no lack of veracity in Rai, considered a reply, then considered again. She was
already on record about San Saba children and
did not want to risk her credibility with fresh
alarums. In any case, they had been too far away
for clear sensations. Perhaps she had simply mis-
translated the Four-Corners mind. For a fleeting
moment, Laura thought, she had detected an impulse toward a cold and casual murder by a child
who was no child at all. Still, Rai had suggested
no taint of evil in the rifle. Laura relaxed; she had
not considered the fact that he had been wearing
gloves.

Within the hour, Rai took custody of a package
brought from Gallup by a priest who lived in
White Horse. This informal express service, he
thought dryly, would last until the day some
postal service nabob realized how badly his system competed against plain rough-country
goodwill. Rai carried the package into his 'dobe,

beginning to appreciate how little assistance Laura needed so long as she could share his eyesight.

He slid a long locking-blade knife from his hip pocket, flipped it open with practiced legerdemain, ran its wicked blade along the glasstape seams.

Laura: "Lord, what a weapon. Aren't switchblades illegal?"

"Yep—and common as clay hereabouts. But this is legal; no spring-loading," he said as he folded it away, "so it's officiall, no weapon." The crossbow image flitted across his thoughts again, replaced by immediate problems as he drew a six-pack of squat flexible jars from the package of a hundred or so. Struggling with a lid: "Can't even open the durn thing."

Laura showed him how. "They're usually sterile until the lid's off; definitely not on the return trip," she smiled. "Identify the donor if possible and make a note of possible contaminants. Analysis could show heavy metal traces, for instance, if you took it from lead-lined plumbing."

This precaution had not occurred to Rai, who was becoming increasingly nervous about the whole operation. He debated the merit of confiding in the few San Sabans who, he thought, might be willing to donate specimens. But they might also talk about it, which would surely eventuate in a visit from the Clown Society. Rai sighed and rethought his original plan: walk around with an absent expression to see where pueblenos casually voided themselves. He would see few if any women or girls at it. A few men; still more boys, probably. Then Rai would—he would—he did not know exactly what. He was certainly not going to commit petty theft from the privies, even if it made a cockeyed sort of sense. The risk was much too great.

After a brief lunch with strong coffee, Rai left Laura in charge of the 'dobe, his pickup parked so near the front door that she could not miss it if the phone buzzed. He strolled over to buy a coke, nodding to this or that person as they moved steadily through the heat like tired swimmers. Mad dogs and anglos, he reflected; he would find few kids playing in this noon sun.

Then he remembered the midden, San Saba's venerable dump where discarded signs and plastics shared space with cannibalized auto bodies. Kids often found or made shade while at play in the huge midden west of the pueblo. He went back to his 'dobe, found an empty mason jar, filled it halfway with water.

Laura lay on a pallet, daubing at trickles of perspiration, content to rest. "You're a coffee freak," she accused from the next room as he poured a bit of coffee into the jar.

"Faking illegal booze," he replied. Sober men might need a reason for touring the midden in such dazzling heat. A half-liter of rotgut in a mason jar would contain its own reasons.

Laura's admiring laugh followed him outside. He adjusted his broad-brimmed hat, walked slowly to the dump a half-kilometer away, idly wondering if he were being entirely fair to Val Clarke. Even on such short reacquaintance, he felt himself more at ease with Val than with any woman he knew; Laura included. If only she had Laura's singular quirk, he might—but Val was what she was. He liked her that way. He carefully avoided thinking of Val in terms of strong affection. With Laura around, that branch of thought would yield bitter fruit.

He turned his attention to the midden, heard a merry shout from somewhere inside it, and knew that he had been spotted by now. He took a swig from the mason jar and sat down cross-legged where he was.

Within ten minutes his backside was baking, but he had glimpsed several children in the graveyard of San Saba artifacts that stretched over an acre of useless ground. Here and there he saw spindletop weeds poking up from debris. High weeds needed moisture and fertile soil. He imagined a momentary rain shower, the rivulets that might sink into the soil where—with occasional shade and fertilization—a resolute weed might prosper.

Applying this fancy to his immediate problem, he stood up and shambled over to the burnt and rusted hood of a once-proud Chrysler. It was too hot to sit on, but he leaned against it and sipped. Human excrement dried quickly out there, and in a day or so would have no odor. Yet he smelled a familiar ripe purulent presence. In due time he found its source. In a narrow cul-de-sac between piles of trash was a spot box-canyoned by weeds. In the center was a placer deposit of human offal—obviously used by several people with regularity.

He leaned back against a protruding wooden post, aware that a small boy, hardly more than a toddler, eyed him in solemn awe from the flying bridge of a decayed Buick, a stone's throw away. He sipped at his tincture of coffee, sat heavily, used his peripheral vision. The child had already lost interest; was already scanning his horizon for imaginary cowboys or asteroids. Rai smiled to himself and, for a moment, wished for Laura's talents.

Rai Koshare refused to dwell on the ludicrous aspect of San Saba's most educated resident in an elaborate charade to pilfer dung from children. After considerable thought on the mechanical operations, he staggered over to the offal; shucked down his denims, squatted; and spent the next furtive moments filling four of the containers from existing deposits around him. Well, he reflected, there are givers and there are takers . . . .

The containers pocketed, he reassembled his clothing. He saw moisture in the curved remains of broken crockery among the weeds, realized someone had urinated there very recently. He removed the tops from his remaining two sample containers and placed them among the crockery, barely out of sight. Then he took his mason jar and moved off thirty meters or so behind a hummock where, without seeming to, he might rest and monitor the area. One thing pueblenos did well, he thought, was wait. Then like a fool he fell asleep.

He would never know what waked him but Rai was suddenly aware that he had been dozing, and that someone was moving away from the open privy. He recognized the Dinay boy, zipping his denims as he trotted into the wilds of the junk heap. Evidently Chuzo had arranged for someone to tend his small flock of sheep that day. Chuzo Dinay's whole body was intent on his errand.

After another minute, Rai inspected his containers and was amused at his own elation. One of them was a quarter full of yellow fluid.

He marked the urine container hurriedly and moved off, remembering to bring the bogus booze.

There might be other areas in the midden to be mined, but he needed more containers. The specimens should be returned to Jeff Simes in Gallup; Jeff had not mentioned whether they had to be very fresh.

En route back to the pueblo Rai thought again of Val Clarke, wondered if she were regretting her solitary occupancy at Oshara; hoped his journals weren't too cryptic. He was struck by the awareness that he greatly valued her opinion.

Laura snored like a puppy on her pallet, beads of perspiration on her face and shoulders, and Rai elected to let her enjoy her siesta while he used the Datsun phone. Simes was out but his no-nonsense assistant said she knew of the specimen collection. She suggested that a second specimen was no farther from Rai than the end of his arm, and could they come for the specimens? Rai offered to leave his six-pack with the priest while shopping in White Horse. It was a common ploy, the priest a waystation between competing cultures.

An hour later, Rai returned from White Horse minus the specimens, with food and a remounted spare tire, to find Laura awake and out of sorts at being left alone. She allowed him to make amends and, perhaps inevitably, it ended on her pallet in a squirming lubricious delight that left Rai spent all too soon. Laura made no elaborate complaint. Her, "I thought archaeologists were slow and methodical," was ambiguous enough.

"We'd better start back to Oshara," Rai said, with guilty concern for Val, and made ready for the trip.

In another five minutes Ziu Tiamunyi squatted

atop the midden at San Saba and watched the Datsun's python of dust writhe northward. "North," he confirmed as he wiggled down into the dugout with the others.

Chuzo Dinay gestured for hand links. Tiamunyi grasped the hand of Mateo Betan on his left and the smaller hand of Naka Flores on his right. With Dinay in their tactile circuit, they lacked only the three who had been surprised at Escavada Wash. As the member slated to make the next host transfer, Dinay would soon be more vulnerable than his fellows. By age-old agreement that made him leader pro tempore.

Carson Kimbeto has hidden the beacon hardware, Dinay reminded them, *but Encino Mangas and Hatchi Leon have not returned from backtracking the pickup. Kimbeto thinks the archaeologist was satisfied with their explanation.*

Then why was he loafing around here today, came Flores's question to worry them anew.

Betan: *The child said Koshare was drinking, perhaps depressed. I did not see him; the child could have been mistaken. It is not Koshare's way to drink that way. Perhaps Mangas should have killed him after all.*

Dinay, who had heard of the confrontation from Kimbeto's transceiver, was no longer certain it had gone well. *The users could not know of Laura's special advantages, considered her as they might any tourist. Perhaps, perhaps. But the anglo woman might have driven off to testify, and then where would our executioners be?*

Flores: *In new host bodies, naturally.*

We cannot squander host children, Dinay replied. *My concern is with Koshare's snooping above Escavada Wash.*

Their transceiver, a small commercial unit with an optional scrambler circuit, lay before them, its antenna patched to a wire leading from the dugout. Now it spoke in San Saban. Dinay answered, alert to tension in the voice from Escavada Wash.

Carson Kimbeto: "Mangas ran ahead of short-legged Leon to tell me the worst for relay to you. The archaeologist Koshare has set up camp at our old place!"

Stunned glances in the dugout. "The burned place?"

"I said the worst! Yes, the laboratory site. I knew we should have erased it long ago."

"Put Mangas on," Dinay ordered.

The piping voice of Encino Mangas labored through exhaustion of a child's body forced to run for kilometers. He confirmed the news: a slender half-naked anglo woman puttered about on the site where the users had worked and planned so long ago. From the look of it, Koshare had been there many times, was amid long and serious study. Mangas ended by saying, "We think the anglo woman is alone. If so, we can eliminate her. I have the rifle."

"Let us confer here, Mangas."

"Let us act here, Dinay. Quickly," said Carson Kimbeto.

The hand link was re-established in the dugout. Presently Dinay flicked the transceiver on again. "Kimbeto, have you enough ammunition?"

"Nearly a boxful."

"Begin by using some of it on Koshare and his blonde woman; they are moving toward you now. You can drive a car?"

"With difficulty. Then we can pick up Leon."

"Exactly—and drive to the old site and shoot

the naked whore. Can you manage that?''

"I am good with guns," Kimbeto promised.
Faintly off-mike, Mangas could be heard, advis-
ing Kimbeto that a yellow car was nearing the
wash from the south.

"Koshare's pickup," Dinay guessed. "Have
Mangas flag them down. If he seems distressed
the fool Koshare will stop to help him."

"And then I do Leon's job properly," replied
Kimbeto.

In the dugout, the users heard the clatter of a
clip being fed into a sporting rifle in Escavada
Wash. Kimbeto was an excellent shot. He could
put three rounds into Rai Koshare's body from
fifty meters before the archaeologist understood
the ruse. It should be no contest.

"We're nearly at Escavada," Rai announced to
Laura over the thrumm and rumble of the pickup.
"Wonder where those kids got all that cable to
hang a target across the arroyo? Cable isn't
cheap."

The sun was near the horizon, glinting through
wisps of high cloud that gave a bloody tint to the
desert. "Let me make a detour; those kids may be
playing with a Western Electric line after all," Rai
said in preamble, then steered the Datsun eastward.

There was no road to veer from; Rai had merely
been following his tire tracks for convenience. He
failed to spot Mangas scrambling along the lip of
the arroyo toward the tracks, concentrating as he
did on his detour. In any case he would not have
seen the canny Kimbeto, who nestled under the
arroyo lip for cover; cover for two kills.

Rai's sudden maneuver took the users wholly

by surprise. Kimbeto could not see and Mangas, ready to mime a broken ankle, stood crouching and inert. To Encino Mangas it looked as if Rai had seen him; was taking evasive action. Mangas and Kimbeto shouted, and Kimbeto whirled to sprint up the arroyo. The pickup must go slowly as it eased over the embankment; perhaps there would be time for a shot through the window. . . .

The yellow Datsun was five hundred meters from Kimbeto as Rai drove along the lip of the wash, eyeing the place for cable anchors or a public utility sign. Kimbeto had hidden the cable anchors well. Rai braked, stretched his head and shoulders outside the cab near the embankment lip for a better view of the terrain. Now Kimbeto was three hundred meters away, his thudding footfalls masked by the staunch little engine of the pickup. Rai let the clutch out, still craning his neck, now only two hundred and fifty meters from the rifle; now two-twenty-five. Carson Kimbeto took three gasping breaths to hyperventilate, stopped, aimed from two hundred meters. Not an easy shot but better than nothing.

Or far worse. The front wheels of the Datsun sloughed over the embankment, dropping the cab a half-meter at the instant Kimbeto's slug moaned through the open window leaving a bright streak across the windshield from the inside.

The report of the twenty-two caliber rifle was almost lost in the noise of Rai's progress, but not quite. Rai ducked back into the cab, saw the metallic scar left by the deadly little slug, made a turn farther to the right, heard the *whap* and whine as the second slug ricocheted from his rollbar. "Get down, Laura," he bellowed, his right hand pressing her shoulder toward the seat.

Subliminally he knew the direction of fire was somewhere behind him. Rai accelerated as much as he dared, slapping the gearlever from second to third, the yellow pickup airborne several times as it crashed over the arroyo bottoms. Now he was angling up the opposite bank, downshifting as he made a snap judgment to clear the north embankment lip without rolling the vehicle.

Two impacts, sounding like the single crack of a dry branch, announced the third slug which passed through the rear window and, on its way out, starred the windshield where Laura's head might have been. For one hallucinatory moment they heard only the crescendoed roar of the engine as the Datsun leaped the embankment lip. Then came the gargantuan *slammm*, the pickup bottoming every spring, a blizzard of dust rising inside the cab.

Rai blinked, no so much from dust as from the huge black fuzzball that threatened his consciousness. He was completely unaware that he had bent the steering wheel with his jaw.

"Stay down," he shouted, unsure whether he was beyond the marksman's range. He had enough wit to upshift by tachometer and fled across the desert toward the shadow of a low butte.

Gradually Rai Koshare came to realize he had put enough distance between them and sudden death, slowed to a pace that was not quite maniacal, urged Laura to an upright position.

To his great relief, Laura was almost calm. "If I had eyes, they'd be the size of saucers," she said, only a little shakily. "Was someone actually shooting at us?"

Rai vented his earth-tremor San Saba laugh despite his sudden headache, elated by the sweetness of life and breath. He drew a forefinger across the windshield, the nail barely registering the inlay of lead on glass.

Laura reached forward, her hand guided as much by incoming air as by Rai's vision, and placed her finger over the hole made by the third slug. The hand flew to cover her mouth.

"That cabroncito Hatchi Leon," Rai muttered, steering a course that would bring him back to Oshara and Val. "No, not a niño; that was good shooting even for an adult."

Laura was no help. "I didn't pick up any vibes," she said, "past yours; and I was trying. Must have been too far off."

"Whoever it was, he wasn't kidding," Rai said, reaching for his radiophone. At the moment, they were passing the user who was called Hatchi Leon. The small figure heard the pickup from afar, lay prone as it passed a kilometer away, then resumed a dragging walk. Leon was without radio or weapon, and could only wonder why the yellow pickup thundered past at such a gait.

In the wash, Kimbeto and Mangas knelt at their transceiver in a defensive dialogue that was passably human. "You were not here, Dinay," Mangas insisted through the scrambler, "and I was! Koshare took a wide detour the instant he saw me."

"And why should he do that unless he feared us," Kimbeto added. "I may have wounded them both."

The reply from San Saba was scathing: "So much the worse! Koshare has a radiophone and has probably used it by now."

"Can you steal a car to pick us up?" Hope was

not a common trait in users, but some of it came
through Kimbeto's tone.

After a pause, in cold implacable anger that *was*
common: "Finish the job, Kimbeto! We cannot
steal a car here. You are fresh; there will be light
from Koshare's camp. Use it. Then you will have a
nice yellow pickup truck to ride."

"That is the consensus?"

"Wait." Kimbeto knew that Dinay, Betan,
Flores, and Tiamunyi would be conferring silently by skin galvanism, hands clasped.

Ziu Tiamunyi's voice confirmed that a group
decision had been reached in San Saba's midden.
"Dispose of the bodies in the old escape tunnel,
Kimbeto. Touch nothing that you do not want to
leave fingerprints on, burn everything that will
burn. Then bring Mangas and Leon here. We expect you sometime after midnight. That pickup
may be a useful tool to hurry the beacon work."

Kimbeto was sullen. "We will need help."

"You would waste time," shouted the voice of
Mateo Betan.

"They are wasting it now," agreed the voice of
their most suspicious member, Naka Flores.

"Call me when you have exterminated them,"
said Chuzo Dinay. "An educated fool and two
anglo *rubias*, blondes, should be within your
capabilities."

The carrier wave winked from existence and, in
Escavada Wash, two users traded shrugs that were
half human.

Rai halted the little pickup, waving into the
dusk as Val Clarke emerged from the trailer house.
"Something's happened," she said. It was not a

guess; she knew the set of Laura's mouth too well.

"Some crazy man playing cowboys and injuns," Rai said with his typical clumsy effort to belittle a problem. He had phoned to tell a deputy about the boys playing in Escavada Wash; laughed at Laura's guess that the two boys had done the shooting. Lugging a bag of groceries into the mobile home, he insisted it had been a fluke, the pixillated rage of some old prospector.

Val inventoried the groceries but paused to ask, "Is that why you were looking over your shoulder just now?"

"The sheriff said to be careful," Laura chimed in.

"Just a deputy," Rai said, patient and slow. "This area isn't reservation land, so I called the county sheriff. Asked them to check out the wash just in case. Those kids could get shot, you know."

Val nodded. "With a hovercraft and night-vision police scanners, I'll feel a lot better." She shivered, hugged her arms despite the warmth of the little dwelling.

"Val," Rai began in a long-suffering monotone, "San Juan County's equipment is twenty years old. They envy a hunter with an infrared scope like I envy Penn State's automated dig hardware. No chopper, no night sorties; they'll fly over in the morning. Next time we'll take the long way around and avoid the problem; okay?"

Val's manner belied her verbal agreement. There was something else amiss, she felt, and covertly judged the interactions between Rai and Laura. She sensed a reserve there, a cautious apartheid as her friends helped arrange the dinner

Val had warmed. They were hiding a distaste for each other, she decided. Either that, or—but she pushed away the alternative.

Val solved the mystery of Rai's sudden headache when she placed a finger on his jaw. The lump, the bruise, and the probable cause led them to stories of stress behavior that lasted through dinner.

Rai had begun comic embellishments on his foray into San Saba's midden heap when he heard the buzz outside. "Sheriff's office, maybe." He was wrong.

When Rai stepped back into the trailer five minutes later, he was the image of consternation. "I know it was Dinay," he gritted, "Dammitall, there weren't any bugs there!"

Laura: "The deputy found someone?"

Rai waved a hand as if erasing a misconception. "No no, that was Jeff Simes, in Gallup. County Hospital has some reagent strips that can test a urine specimen instantly. Stools take longer. Well, Jeff says my own specimen looked fine but the other one was a laugher."

Val: "You mentioned bugs?"

"Specimen was full of protein, which they checked double-quick when they couldn't read my scribbling, didn't know whose it was. And I got browned off after Jeff claimed I'd mashed a beetle in a urine specimen. I got sarcastic, told him I was a stupid injun who couldn't recall who the donor was."

The women were better versed in diagnostic procedures. Was Rai sure the donor had been the Dinay boy? He was positive. "He may be voiding pus in his urine," Val supplied. "That could be serious, Rai."

He leaned against the table, fingering his jaw tenderly. "No, Jeff says they ran further checks and found it was something called, uh, chondroprotein. Which, according to Jeff, is not featured in human urine, exclamation point."

"I don't recall hearing of it," Val admitted.

"I have," Laura said with the bright insistence of the trivia buff. "Chondroprotein is a family of proteins that make up, ah, tendon, cartilage, and something else."

"He said that," Rai agreed. "And claimed I gave him beetle juice."

"Chitin," said Laura in triumph; "*that's* what else! Rai, I think you have to face the idea that somehow the sample was contaminated."

"That, or it came from a bug in a boy-suit," Val teased. Then, seeing his face: "I'm sorry, Rai. Just be glad the specimen was negative for liver flukes or whatever."

Put in that light, it was cheering to Rai Koshare who was childishly glad he had refused to name the donor.

In San Saba this refusal had its repercussions. The users had monitored Rai's open channel, had heard his calls to the deputy and from the Public Health Service. Tiamunyi sat in the midden hideout, facing his fellows as they clasped hands for communion quicker than speech. *If Koshare cannot recall who was fool enough to donate a specimen,* he argued, *we are still safe.*

For how long? Dinay's rage crackled across their synapses. *Who among us knows the limits of their medical techniques, or what traces of us will show in the excrement samples they spoke of?*

The paranoia of their parasitic race surfaced in the suspicion of Naka Flores. *I gave no urine*

specimen! Which of you did—and why did you
betray us all?

Betan worked toward solidarity. The man
Koshare was snooping here today. Why must he
do that if one of us is a traitor?

The central fact, Dinay seethed, is that the humans have stumbled on our trace. For all we
know, there could be soldiers here by morning.

Tiamunyi: When the archaeologist is missed,
they will focus on San Saba.

Flores seemed bent on pessimism. And what if
they took us by force to undergo tests beyond the
range of the serenity beam? Madness and death
for us all!

In the user of Betan ran a strong element of
inertia: You are forgetting that there is a fair possibility of coincidence, he counseled. I propose
that we watch and wait.

I say run, Tiamunyi voted. If we wait, they can
find us.

If we run, they will hunt us, Flores fired back.

Dinay knew the signs of demoralization. And if
we are ingenious, they will mourn us in San Saba,
he interjected. They will reject anglo science more
firmly and we shall be more secure.

The others waited.

It is time, Dinay went on implacably, to man-
ufacture a tragedy. The rest of you are milling like
sheep. I have an appropriate remedy.

Not a change to adult bodies, Flores quavered.

Chuzo Dinay was pleased to savor the moment.
Yes, he replied, and no.

Part Two

As the users approached Oshara under cover of darkness, Rai Koshare lazed in his house trailer, fielding the questions Val Clarke had raised during her lone day at Oshara. From his sketches of the ruin, Rai admitted, his enigmatic Oshara did have some characteristics of a prison compound. Laura Dunning kibitzed as they dallied with conjectures that probed pieces of the truth.

The room with the anomalous fire channel and chimney was dubbed the furnace room. Its tunnel outlets were too conspicuous to be the work of prisoners. The small rooms across Oshara's atrium, however, could have been cells for children. They wrangled over the identity of the jailers, never guessing that ancient users in adolescent human bodies had manned the roof for night guard duty over the children whose bodies they would later expend.

"I'm inclined to toss that whole idea," Rai said at last. "The Anasazi may have kept a few slaves, but why so far from any major settlement? Slaves were a work force for rich tribes. I see nothing that a group of child slaves could have provided, out here in Oshara."

"Hostages?" Laura's eyeless face swept the others as though sighted. "If the kids were ransomed, this might be an ideal place to hide them."

Again, Rai agreed, it was possible. Still they lacked any evidence that adults had lived in

Oshara to enforce a century-long kidnap scheme.
Rai made fresh coffee, argued aloud with himself,
carefully avoided touching Laura lest he reveal
their alliance to Val—which, of course, was a
clear signal to Val, She saw him lean against a
partition away from Laura, studied the flicker of
his eyes as he looked past her platinum mane, and
knew. She knew, no matter that Laura had known
Rai so briefly; no matter that Laura's plangent
sexuality had reverberated against Val herself.

Instantly, Val's coffee tasted of ashes, the itch of
her faint sunburn was an agony. "Getting late,"
she lied, wishing only to sink feet-first into the
desert. "I'll—I'll just take a walk around before
bed." She stood up too quickly, snatched a sweat-
er too abruptly, pulled the door open—and stared
in frozen shock at the figure that knelt below the
steps, half-discovered by light streaming through
the doorway.

She saw Carson Kimbeto, an apparent eleven-
year-old, silently emptying the pickup's five-
gallon fuel can onto parched earth around the
steps. Kimbeto reacted first, dropped the container as he sprang backward into the dark. Made
stupid by self-pity, Val needed a vital second too
long in emerging from her shell. Kimbeto knew
where he had laid the rifle; Val could not know he
had one.

Whirling, Val slammed the door, her back
against it, her eyes grown even larger in fright.
"An Indian boy," she stammered, "just be, be,
below the steps! Pouring fuel," she finished in a
whisper.

Rai reached the door in two paces, wrenched it
open, stared at nothing. He turned toward the
women. "I smell ga—," he began, and his head

snapped around from the impact of the slug. Another harsh *crack!* and flash from the darkness, and a coffee cup exploded before Rai's body crashed into the aisle. The door swung shut.

"What—they're here," was Laura's cry.

"Do as I'm doing," Val hissed, aware that their assailant could hear but not see them as she dropped to her knees. Val locked the door, turned quickly to Rai who slumped with his face against Val's thigh. No sound came from outside. Val gently turned Rai's head upward, saw the purplish wound made by the slug as it exited his cheek.

"Oh my *God*, they shot him in the face," Laura screamed, and then her head lolled sideways against the wall.

"Not so loud," Val insisted, and scrambled to flick off the overhead light. Momentarily blind, she fumbled for the Koshare pulse. Outside she heard youthful voices raised in the puebleno tongue.

"Three of them," Laura babbled into the blackness, lifting hackles on Val's nape. "Old and evil, and Rai is shot! We're going to die," she said as if begging for a denial.

"Pity you couldn't sense them ten minutes ago," Val snarled. "But you were all wrapped up in Rai—hold it." Val's fingers found what she did not dare expect. Whispering: "He has a pulse, Laura." A strong one, at that. "Keep quiet, idiot!"

Crawling, crooning endearments, Laura crawled to Rai as a shout came from nearby. "The keys," shouted Kimbeto in English; "we want only the car keys." It had taken the users five minutes to see that hot-wiring the ignition might take too long, but Leon and Mangas were still at it.

"I don't have them," Val wailed, only half-surrogating her terror.

"Take them from the body," Kimbeto replied smoothly, reasonably, and after a moment added, "then we will leave."

"They're going to burn us," Laura whispered shakily, "or shoot us if we try to run."

Val agreed with Kimbeto, playing for time, then heard Rai's gruff mumble. She knelt, placed her fingers over his lips, roughly shoved Laura's head aside to whisper into Rai's ear. He fell silent, then sat up and fumbled in his jacket. "No, I'm damned if I will," he whispered, the words impeded by the hole through his cheek. "Give me time to try something."

Val, her eyes adjusting to starlight, peeked from a window to see Kimbeto standing, the rifle ready for a snap shot. The pickup's cab light was on, revealing two small forms that peered and poked at the dashboard wiring.

"Stall," Rai urged again, and Val began an altogether convincing display of frustration and terror while Rai struggled upright. She called out that Rai's body was too heavy, that she could not bear to touch him, that she could not find the right pocket. And all the while Rai Koshare worked in furious quiet to remove a roof panel.

Another shout from the pickup, another reply from Kimbeto. Val listened, willing them to go on trading puebleno dialogue forever.

The roof panel swung down and a rectangle of stars was marred as Rai eased himself up, standing on a shelf. Val kept silent, knowing that the solar panels would hide his emergence atop the mobile home. Val heard a metallic scrape from above, burst into another caterwaul. Which key is it, she blubbered; don't hurt me, she wailed; I'm afraid, she said with no exag̅ ̅ration.

Laura's far-ranging senses found employment as she eased her way to Val's ear. "They're afraid to rush us; we're bigger than they are," she whispered.

Another creak from above, another ululation from Val to mask it, another whisper from Laura: "Rai's trying to loosen something big. It's heavy." Laura had not grasped the salient detail of the hundred-gallon water tank which allowed gravity flow to the kitchen. She only knew he thought it possible to tip a massive object over the roof.

Then from the darkness: "Throw out the keys, or I start to shoot. Be nice and we let you alone," Kimbeto finished sweetly.

"Shit, you will," Val muttered.

Rai grunted, ducked down, whispered: "Take the keyring from my pocket. Toss it two meters behind the door, a meter from the wall."

He poked his head through the opening again as Val felt for his keyring. Then she had it, jingled it loudly, silently opened the door a few centimeters. With a prayerful guess, she flicked the keys toward the rear of the dwelling, slammed the door. "Now go away," she stormed, meaning it.

Carson Kimbeto saw the dim flicker of keys, lost his chance for a shot as he heard the faint clatter of metal against the ground. He moved cautiously nearer, shouted in San Saban, lit a match and was dazzled by its flare. But he saw the keys and stooped to retrieve them, unaware that he was visible to Rai from a slit between the solar panels.

Val heard the grunt from Rai, the cascade of screeching metal as the water tank toppled from the roof carrying the solar panel Rai had loosened.

Kimbeto jerked nearly upright before a great black shadow bore him to the ground. He screamed once.

The match might have expired but for the tuft of dry weed it struck as it flew from Kimbeto's fingers. Its glow faded as Rai dropped to the floor inside and bowled over the hapless Val. The tiny flame flickered as the two distant users turned toward Kimbeto's scream, and then it swiftly climbed the weed stalk which fell, its brief moment of glory spent.

The puff of flame fell on earth dampened not by the water tank which leaked slowly, but by five gallons of gasoline. The fireball created a whuffing blow that consumed fumes for meters around. Rai jerked his hand back from the door as the yellow fireball rose around the end of the structure. Val's ears popped from pressure, popped again. With all windows closed, the sigh of superheated gas slapped at the walls but did not come inside just yet.

The forms of Leon and Mangas sprinted toward the fallen Kimbeto, whose legs and abdomen lay under the solar panel. He was face-down, struggling silently, unable to see the heavy tank that had crushed his pelvis.

From inside, the besieged humans saw Mangas race toward his top priority—the rifle, lying just beyond Kimbeto. Rai cursed softly, crawled back toward his bedroom in the uncertain flicker of the blaze that continued to feed from gasoline-sodden earth. The women followed.

Mangas seemed too capable, too well-coordinated, for Rai to rush him, especially through a wall of fire. "I can't believe how calm the injured one is," Laura breathed, flicking her attention from mind to mind, grimacing in fear as she probed the user mentality. "He's giving instructions by touch! The keys—"

"I have the car key," Rai muttered in satisfaction as Mangas arose from Kimbeto, who faced pitiless heat some meters away. A quick handclasp with Hatchi Leon, a transfer of the rifle, and Mangas was running to the pickup.

"They're going to push the debris off with the pickup," Laura said, almost somnolent.

"Not without hotwiring," Rai said, pleased with himself.

A sharp report: Hatchi Leon was slowly firing into the doorway through the flames. "What about the windows in the south wall," Val asked.

"Sandstorm covers, bolted from the outside. And they seem to know it," Rai growled.

Val grimaced as another shot tore through the door. "We sure can't get out the front."

Another shot and a ricochet, fleeing a bell-like clang. "The propane tank," Rai breathed, then, "Yes by God, we *can*. I think. There's an access crawlway under the toilet floor to a storage place up front. That's where the propane tank is."

"Jesus, what if that blows?"

"It'll take the whole interior with it," was Rai's answer, but he was already crawling into the toilet nook. "You have a better idea?"

"The one you talked to—Kimbeto?—is dead," Laura said dully. "No wait, he isn't dead, he's deaf and blind, but he is moving."

"Hell he is," said Val, risking a glance through the window. "He's still as a corpse."

"Head's bursting," Laura mumbled. "Aaaagh, you monster," to something outside. And again with glee, "He knows the car key is not on the ring." As if to endorse her words, Mangas came tearing from the pickup, shucking his jacket off as

he ran. At the call of Mangas, the small form of
Leon sidled near Kimbeto.

Leon, watching the windows now, held the
jacket to protect them from the crackling blaze
that now fed on polymer in the trailer's shell.
Mangas knelt swiftly and drew a knife from his
pocket. Val saw him cut Kimbeto's jacket and
shirt away, gasped as the next sweep of the knife
exposed grayish pink ribs near the backbone. She
could not afford the luxury of being sick and
scrambled toward Rai at his hoarsely whispered
call.

There was now enough light, and some heat,
from the kitchenette, streaming down the hallway. "Floor insulation may help, but it may get
damned hot. But keep going, Val. Me first, to wres-
tle that big propane tank aside and open the forward storage hatch," he recited quickly. "Then
Laura, then you. Okay?"

Rai's was the only sensible sequence, but: "It
figures. At least you remembered me," Val
growled, flames reflected in her eyes.

He reached out with a gliding caress that
stroked her cheek. "Always," he said, and nodded
his chin toward Laura who lay against the wall,
brow furrowed in loathing, teeth bared in rage
against a presence the others could not detect as
she did. "But we two—she needs me," he
finished, and all but dived into the crawl space.

"And I don't?" But Val's reply went unheard.

Val reached Laura in an instant, forgetting to
whisper, urging her to hurry. Laura moved
blindly despite Val's steadfast gaze and insistent
hands. Yet somehow she forced herself to comply,
murmuring information and maledictions as she
monitored the gory business just outside.

"He's prying at the ribs," Laura mewled, and, "Fry, you goddamned animal," as she wriggled into the crawl space. Then, over the sounds of a heavy object scraping in the storage area, "Ah, God, oh, Jesus God, ohh; something's leaking up from the body! It's crawling; it's him, yes, I know who he is, the slime!" Laura panted in a paroxysm of revulsion. Unable to wrench her concentration from the users, dangerously near insanity, Laura lay unmoving in the crawlspace, blocked by Rai beyond her. Val dashed to the window, feeling the heat strongly now, as smoke crawled through the hallway just above her head.

She saw butchery tinted by firelight, Mangas scooping into the cavity he had made, a wound gaping in his own arm as he guided a gelatinous glistening mass toward his self-inflicted gash which scarcely bled. The body that had once been a boy lay blistering in the heat and the kneeling Mangas, she knew, ust have second-degree burns by now. She could not know he was able to shut off the pain; but knew that whatever his vices, Encino Mangas was taking a deadly risk for something beyond himself.

Now Leon began shooting methodically along the trailer house, saw Val's face, took aim as she dropped below the bed pulling the mattress with her. She yelped to feel the slug's impact on the mattress, coughed as smoke descended, saw a wall of flame down the hall, wriggled toward the toilet. Small explosions from canned goods added to the chaos beyond her, but Val saw that Laura's feet no longer blocked the opening. She hurled herself into the blackness of the crawlspace.

It was cool at first, then warm as she worked herself forward, finally agonizingly hot. She ex-

pected every moment to bump against an unconscious Laura, then saw the faint wash of light from
an open access panel. Simultaneously she spied
the propane tank, its copper pipes kinked, and
knew stark terror. She could not go back, might
bake if she went forward. She screamed, closed
her eyes, fought her fear and writhed ahead under
a boiling hot floor.

The hands that tore her from the access hatch
were far from gentle, but they were blessed with
strength. Tumbling to the ground with Rai, Val
would have scrambled away but Rai slapped a
hand over her mouth, forced her by gestures to
take Laura's hand. Together, scuttling low past
the electric barrow, they kept in its shadow and
melted into the night toward the nearby arroyo.

Twice, Val fell while running down the arroyo.
Once it was Rai. They had gone three hundred
meters when a billowing blast lit the sky. "My
propane tank," Rai guessed, stopping to clamber
up the incline. He reported that the pickup was
still intact though dangerously near the fire, the
mobile home's plastic shell in shreds, a tiny figure
circling around the pyre with a rifle at the ready.

The distance was too great for Laura to monitor
them; in any case she was barely coherent. "We're
only draft animals to them," she shuddered.
"They live in—children. The little one was hoping you really don't remember where you got that
urine specimen, Rai."

"Let's go," he said, half-blinded by the glare he
had watched. "If they get the pickup started we're
still in trouble."

"They were certain we were dead," Laura said.

"So's one of them," from Rai.

"No." Val had seen the user's naked substance, creeping from its human integument with clear and steady purpose. flowing into the flesh wound of Encino Mangas. She gave a halting description, heard Rai snort at such a preposterous notion. "I saw it," she insisted.

"Val saw what I saw," was Laura's lackluster comment. "They are very old, very angry that we interfered just as they're about to—to finish their work. I don't know what that means. I know the one from the dead boy was considering your body, Val, as an emergency measure."

"Only he thought I was toasting, thanks to him."

"That, and you were a little too big, and female. Sharing the other boy's body was a last-ditch temporary maneuver; I'm sure of that."

Laura's endorsement forced Rai Koshare to accept the bizarre, at least as a possibility. Besides, he reflected, if they were very old, these sentient parasites might explain much of the Oshara anomaly. "Jesu Maria," he muttered aloud, "it might explain everything!" He stopped, thrilling to the nightwing touch of cool breeze, scanned the cloudless starlit canopy. "Pueblo girls don't mix with boys much, aren't allowed to explore much. Let's see," he said, juggling two trains of thought; "I've got matches, knife; six hours to dawn, and Escavada will be over there . . . ."

Val could not follow his ruminations and said so. It was very simple, he said: he had to accept the idea of hagridden pueblo boys and get back to San Saba immediately. If the San Juan Sheriff's people checked out Escavada Wash at first light, they'd find a signal fire; Rai's. "We can be there in maybe three hours. It shouldn't get very cold," he finished, with fleeting stress on the 'very.'

"You sound dreadful," Val said. "Does it hurt much?"

"Not a lot," he said in wonderment. "The kid let fly just as I was trying to warn you about the gasoline."

At this, Val began to giggle. "Sorry," she gulped; "I just realized the bullet must've gone into your mouth while it was open."

Rai allowed no whimsy in his dismal, "Whee-e."

"I know; but just be glad you didn't smell cheese."

Silence, then a slow rumble, his *huh-huh* of wry appreciation. "I'd need bridgework. Valerie Clarke, you are one weird lady."

"And you're hurting. Shut up, Rai," said Laura softly. He did so.

They struck out eastward. Val had never learned to steer by the stars, was unfamiliar with the dim contours on the star-occulting horizon; she trusted Rai to know both.

An hour later they spotted the lights of the pickup to th south as it sped southwest. They had spent too much breath to squander much on the event—assuming it *was* the pickup,—but breathed more easily when it had passed from sight. If the long trek was a trial for Laura and Val, it gave the archaeologist time to assemble his data. Thanks to Laura's telepathic monitoring, Rai inferred that only a few of the parasites existed. And their concern over the anomalous urine specimen meant that they might be isolated that way. Their communication via touch explained little things, tactile signals he had seen all his life in San Saba.

If they could reject Val as too large, they might need—his mind flinched at the thought but he forced it—fresh bodies frequently. Early in his undergraduate work, Rai Koshare had become familiar with the occasional Anasazi burial of a small body without a forearm, or a foot. If he accepted the testimony of his friends, that now made sense too. Some of those burials had been twelfth century; *and so was Oshara.* The need for new bodies, kept as penned stock and worked as slaves in the meantime, gave Oshara a purpose, and a reason for its unlikely site. Especially did it explain Rai's eldritch tactile sensations of children who became monstrous mature shamans without seeming to grow old.

Yet the trio could not guess the meanings of the tiny, flawed circuit tiles from Oshara—nor could they dream of the rescue beacon toward which the users were working so single-mindedly. The first priority, Val opined, was to get urine specimens that would convince officials in Gallup. Only then could Rai argue his friend Jeff Simes into suspecting that somehow, somewhen, a new species of predator had come to prey on Four Corners people.

Neither Rai, nor Val, nor Laura yet imagined that their ancient enemies were extraterrestrial. Laura's special talent had proven a formidable tool, capable of quickly unearthing facts that had long been underfoot—but she had not been employed fully. Rai was beginning to fear from Laura's depression that the tool might break, might already be strained beyond repair. Rai was in the position of the craftsman, in love with a tool, who might use it wisely but not too well. Armed with only the sketchiest norms of user

behavior, the trio failed to give their enemies
enough credit for lethal ingenuity.

The little signal fire of ocotillo seemed bright
enough at dawn, but Rai was kept busy with his
knife, cutting the burnable branches to keep the
blaze alive as the sun rose over San Pedro Peak.
The patched Cessna, when it buzzed in from the
west an hour or so later, banked steeply and responded to their soliciting waves with a
wingwave of its own before it touched down
nearby.

"Gil Rojas," said the short, square-built deputy,
extending a hand as Rai identified himself. It was
a tough little hand with prominent veins and
heavy tendons. "We talked before, Dr. Koshare."
He doffed his mandatory crash helmet, passed a
forearm across his sparkling dark brow. "Be a
scorcher today," he added as if pleased by the
prospect, then turned to the women. His slate eyes
shuttered at Laura, whose wraparound sunglasses
were now bits of Oshara slag. He glanced at Rai
more closely, clucked his tongue: "Thought you
said nobody was hurt."

"That was before we got shot, burned out of a
trailer house, and robbed," Val begun. "You
won't believe this, but—"

Rojas, a chauvinist of the old casta school, cut
her off. "I could tape your statement after you see
a sawbones," he said to Rai. "Sounds like you've
got a two-bottle yarn."

"We won't stretch anybody's credulity," Rai
said, with a look toward Val that was full of sig-
nificance.

Rojas massaged his graying thatch. "This ol'
Cessna's a four-seater, but she won't lift four out of

high desert. What say we taxi to the Bonito aid station?"

There was no real choice and soon they were moving westward, parallel to the broad arroyo toward Pueblo Bonito; the Cessna's tail high, the engine's drone catastrophically loud, Rojas soundlessly cursing obstacles as he taxied at sixty klicks per hour over the generally downsloping terrain. They ended by deplaning near the lip of the escarpment overlooking Pueblo Bonito, and trudged down between bluffs of tan and bright ochre.

The Park Service nurse had just arrived, a bit late for her eight o'clock opening time, a fluttering brood hen who clucked over the two bedraggled anglo pullets. She seemed dangerously near pecking at Rai after a single close look at the wound in his cheek. "That is a gunshot wound, sir," she pronounced as if spying a weasel in her nest. "Your temperature is normal," she went on, whisking a fever strip from his forehead, "and if you want suturing I suggest you visit Farmington General right away. That could be septic." Her manner suggested that Rai himself was septic, that she had seen Amerinds with bullet wounds survive worse; she dismissed him quickly. Valerie Clarke's slightly blistered palms were things she could treat.

Gilberto Rojas watched it all without a smile or a frown; he had long since lost his capacity for surprise at caste prejudice. "I c'n take you to Farmington," he offered. Rai accepted, prepared to leave Val and Laura to the ministrations of the White Leghorn.

Rai ducked into the nurse's orange-pekoe scented office and promised Laura he would be back as soon as possible, judging that, "You'll be safe and with Rojas I'll be okay."

" 'Sawbones,' " Val mouthed at him over a demitasse cup. "The man actually said, 'sawbones'! I've met some throwbacks, but jeeeeez . . . ."

"Rojas learned about the world from people who seldom get to town," Rai said. "There are some who still bag their venison with black powder rifles."

"And there's worse still, Kemo Sabe." Val indicated her palms. "Take care of yourself." He grinned, nodded, ducked out again.

While walking toward the aircraft, Rai spoke into a pocket tape unit for later transcription by the sheriff's office. He identified the San Saba boys as the pair, plus one, he had seen early Friday. He suggested for the record that the boys had only wanted to steal the yellow Datsun, had probably lost their heads when caught at it. He did not admit that he had deliberately toppled the water tank onto Kimbeto; above all he was not ready to state what, according to the women, had issued from the corpse. Striding up a very real talus slope on a very real New Mexican morning in full glorious daylight, Rai Koshare entertained doubts of his own. Besides, he told himself, his cheek hurt and he sounded like hell. Time enough for those details when he had something to tie them to.

Rojas turned to him as they strapped in. "So there's a body or two at your dig. Mind if we fly over?"

Rai knew the question was pure civility; it would have to be done. He gave the Oshara coordinates. Rojas looked surprised, but not very; there were a lot of things a man could miss repeatedly, flying over a few thousand square klicks of emptiness and shadowed buttes.

The Cessna vibrated and bounced, and then they were banking around Fajada Butte. Rai did not have a helmet and could not follow the radio conversation that began as soon as Rojas plugged into the system. But he knew the sun should be on his right. It was on his left. He leaned forward, pointed north.

The helmet bobbed and Rojas shouted: "Sheriff Hightower's been calling. We got a crash-and-burn west of White Horse. Priority." Rai settled back as the Cessna surged ahead. Rojas made another call, shouted to Rai that a Q.R.U., quick response medical unit, would be en route from Gallup with another deputy. Apparently the accident was on or near McKinley County land.

Between Crownpoint and White Horse lay a cluster of lakes with verdant meadows near the blacktop road which Rai had traveled a hundred times. Soon he saw a smudge of dark smoke scrawling skyward, then a faint orange flicker near the road. He had expected to see an aircraft but saw that it was a pickup, lying on its side just off the road. A human body lay unmoving nearby. Rai Koshare nurtured an awful premonition.

Rojas brought the Cessna in gently, avoiding a pair of horses which took alarm anyway. They passed nearer to a small flock of sheep which continued to graze as the Cessna hurried toward the still-smouldering wreck.

The two men trotted over the blacktop, Gil Rojas fumbling with a hefty fire extinguisher as Rai circled the remains of the once-yellow Datsun. Without a word Rojas handed the extinguisher to Rai and went to kneel beside the youth-

ful body. Rai winced. He had seen the boy grow
from infancy, and knew that Chuzo Dinay would
never reach manhood now.

The tires were still burning. Rai quenched the
flames into smoking embers, squinted into the
shattered remains of the cargo shell, and swallowed against the sour taste in the back of his
throat. The bodies inside were small, too badly
charred for recognition, too jumbled for a sure
body count. Rai felt certain that he could recite at
least two names. He realized Rojas was calling,
moved toward him on leaden feet.

Rojas pointed at the headband: "San Saba.
Know him?"

"Chuzo Dinay," Rai nodded. "There are others
still in there," he added, nodding toward the Datsun. He swallowed again.

Rojas cursed, strode to the wreck, leaving Rai to
stare at the terrible eviscerating slash that had
ended Dinay's life. The body had evidently been
flung twenty meters, but at a ghastly price.

"This was my pickup," Rai said tonelessly.

A quick hard look from Rojas. "Sure about
that?"

"My license plates."

"I smell diesel fuel," Rojas said. "Must'a gone
up like a torch."

Rai nodded, thinking how much diesel fuel
smelled like the kerosense used by many San Sabans. And the Datsun hadn't been diesel; in any
case, the gasoline had doubtless helped the blaze.
Sadly: "I wonder if anybody saw it happen."

"Call-in was from some anglo salesman who
didn't want to be involved. It was burning when
he saw it. We might learn something from up

there," Rojas said, pointing toward the valley ridge.

In the near distance, a flock of several dozen sheep moved in their direction under the urging of a boy and a brindle sheepdog. Rojas put fingers to his mouth, blew an incisive note that curved downward like a scimitar, waved toward the small shepherd. The lad waved back, gave orders of his own. The series of gestures and whistled tones comprised a language that Rai had never mastered. The dog hurtled around the flock, turning its leaders, bunching it as the boy strode away. Rai recognized the boy as Hospah Ramirez, another San Saban; so the dog would be the Ramirez sheepdog, Billichay.

Hospah's route took him past the half dozen or so sheep the Cessna had passed earlier. He paused to look them over, though the spray-painted 'D' on their backs was plain enough; continued walking, giving new instructions to the dog.

Billichay evidently had two settings: stop and hell-for-leather. Before little Hospah reached the road, the dog had bullied the new group of sheep into the main flock.

Rojas shuffled away from Chuzo's body to meet the boy who stopped to survey the wreckage, recognized Rai with a troubled nod. "I wouldn't go any closer," Rai said, softly.

Rojas used the recorder again as he questioned Hospah Ramirez. Yes, Hospah knew it must be Dinay who lay among the weeds. "Chuzo asked me to drive his flock here this morning. He and friends borrowed a pickup to check on some strays; Chuzo said they might be here. We left San Saba about dawn; they left me at the Dinay corral north of here." Hospah glanced again at the wreck where rubber sizzled and metal pinged. "Joy ride, huh?"

Rojas: "Some joy. But did you see it happen?"

A headshake: *no.*

Rai earned a frown from Rojas as he intruded into the interrogation. "Who else was with him, Hospah?"

A long silence, as though the names might have some power to destroy. Then, "Ziu Tiamunyi," he said, staring at the ground. "Mateo Betan; Hatchi Leon, Naka Flores, Encino Mangas."

Rojas sighed, his voice more fatherly than professional. "All friends of yours?"

Even at his age, Hospah Ramirez knew ties closer than friendship. "All San Saba," he replied.

And something else besides, thought Rai. With careful phrasing he asked, "Do you know where Carson Kimbeto is?"

The boy's face was expressionless. He shrugged. On the slope, Billichay barked once. "I have to go now," he said, and turned away abruptly. It could have been his unwillingness to be seen crying, but Billichay stood with ears cocked, and a shepherd's first duty is to his flock.

"Hell," muttered Rojas. "I bet he knows that pickup wasn't just borrowed." He made no move to call the boy back, strolled to squat near the blackened pickup. He jerked a thumb toward Dinay: "Seems like the big kid might've pulled one or two of the others clear."

"With a slice out of him like that?" Faintly now, Rai heard the sound that had alerted Billichay: the thrumming *whop-whop* and whine of a hover-chopper at full speed.

Rojas extracted a cassette, turned a level look on Rai. "Just between us, that looks like a knife slash to me; seen enough of 'em in Farmington. And the body don't look like it was throwed there. But this is McKinley County trouble and they can have it with my blessing."

Rai walked near the body again, studied the awful wound. "But who did this?"

"From what you said him and his pals done, he must've knowed he was headed for juvie correction, Doc. Maybe he done it himself."

"Jesu Maria! With what; glass?"

"More likely a switchblade. You can look around, but don't take anything." Rojas turned toward the hoverchopper, its 'QRU' dark against the shining hull, and waved it from the shuddering Cessna. With stub wings, rotors and internal fans, hoverchoppers had way of blowing lesser craft into the next county.

Rai toed the grass around the body, stooped to pat the pockets of the bloody denims. The knife was there, and Rai tingled as he pulled it free with furtive fore-and-middle fingers. The emotional loadings that thrilled his fingertips were fresh and strong; excitement, elation, hatred—but nothing faintly resembling remorse. The knife was bloody; and so was the mind that had controlled it. An Oshara mind.

The hovercraft settled and Rai thrust the knife back into the pocket, then wiped his fingers on weeds as he stood up.

Rojas was relinquishing a cassette to his McKinley County surrogate as Rai moved near, blinking from the dust. Two paramedics, both anglo, one female, essayed rapid checks for vital signs in Dinay, then prowled into the wreck. They soon managed to pull two intertwined objects, ragged, unfinished-looking things, onto the blacktop. If they had hoped for some miraculous survival, they were disappointed. Nothing human had lived through that inferno.

Rai's cheek wound, the woman judged, was clean. She was tall, rangy, plain-faced, deft. She admitted, "You could use a stitch or two, but cosmetic sutures need a better tailor than I am. We'll lift you to Memorial in Gallup."

Rai agreed readily; he had a lot to do in Gallup. He turned to the blond young McKinley County deputy, whose face showed spots of high color under his Smokybear hat. "If you don't need me—" he let it trail off.

"Don't get out of touch," rapped the deputy, who then turned back to Rojas: "You come down here and hand me five pounds' worth in a two-pound sack, mister! Suicide, hell; let the examiner decide."

Rojas held innocent hands open, shook his head. "Just tryin' to help," he said, and walked away stiff-legged toward the Cessna.

"So I stay here with a half-dozen clinkers until the wagon comes," said the young deputy, kicking a weed.

Rai started to observe that he had driven off an ally, then caught the eye of the husky male paramedic, knew it would be only a goad. "I could use that lift," he said.

The woman took the hoverchopper controls and lifted off without further comment. Rai watched Gil Rojas cajole his old craft over a ridge, wondered how the man would react to the other remains at Oshara. It seemed likely that the nightmare of ancient parasites in small Amerind bodies had been exorcized by fire. Surely nothing could live within those pitiful charred bodies; but if anything could, Simes might find out. Rai's eyelids drooped from exhaustion as he peered from the polymer bubble. The last thing he saw of the scene was a flock of sheep, moving ahead of a brindle dog and a small boy.

Two of the sheep touched noses as they vied for a tuft of range grass; the dog received an idle caress from Hospah Ramirez. Had Laura been near, she might have gleaned scraps of a user interchange.

Do not look back, cautioned the one who had been Chuzo Dinay. *The deputy seems angry and suspicious.*

The ex-Naka Flores answered, *Thanks to you. There was enough time for you to pass between bodies without the old-host incision, had you not lost your courage.*

Had you not allowed the animal to take fright at the fire, was the rejoinder. *We are hidden. So are the subspace beacon modules. What more could you ask?*

The corpse of the fortunate fool Koshare. The comment needed no response. On this point, the users were in total agreement.

An interne at Gallup Memorial probed Rai's cheek with a hemostat, took two sutures with six-oh nylon, finished with synthoderm spray. Ten minutes later Rai had signed a statement and walked from the hospital. His wristalarm claimed it was just past midmorning but his giddiness suggested midnight. He sought his insurance agent in naive optimism. At half-past eleven he was walking down Wingate to the auto lots,

grumbling over delays in insurance payments
and scanning the available rental vehicles. He
chose the first small pickup he found with four-
wheel drive and radiophone, a red two-liter
blown Mitsubishi diesel of middle years, and
showed the requisite charge chits.

Shortly after noon he climbed into the Mitt,
which fitted him like a real one, then made his
first call. The White Leghorn clucked for Valerie
Clarke and, while waiting, Rai wondered why he
had not asked for Laura. "We're wheeled again,"
he exulted, and stopped, aghast at her reaction.

". . . Thoughtless inconsiderate nik-nik," she
stormed, "we were afraid you'd found your Datsun before they found *you!*"

"Uh, I'm sorry, Val. I've been in Gallup getting
sewed up and filling out forms and—"

"And Laura's under sedation and I'm beside
myself enough to be twins! Nurse Milford heard
about a horrible accident an hour after you left,
and then some tourist said it looked like a Datsun
pickup, and finally we got its license number and
by then we knew there were no survivors and
awgoddamitRai," and he sat openmouthed as she
snuffled her way back to an even keel. A long
inhalation. Then, "Thanks for surviving. I could
kick you and hug you both."

"It's a date," he said, then told her what he
knew of the Datsun's last trip, adding, "I want to
talk Simes into doing autopsies."

"Are you going to tell him what Laura and I
saw?"

A hesitant, "I may have to."

"Don't. I was with Laura at an inquest once.
Professionals simply don't believe her—anything
about her, even with proof. That included my old

friend Chris Maffei, an MD who was with us at the time. They figure there's got to be a trick somewhere. Very polite, but you can see pity in their faces. And all you have is our word for what we saw. Pick a story, but tell the truth and Simes will say you're batty as a church steeple."

He had to agree; yet his own sensations, he said, were evidence.

Val: "By all means, tell him about your tactile sense! You'd find yourself looking out of a room with marshmallow paneling . . . ."

"Okay, okay," he chuckled. "May I speak to Laura?"

He could, she replied, if he wanted to hear snores with a southern accent. "Miz Milford broke out her private stock of valium for Laura; the poor kid is completely around the bend about you—as you damn' well know."

Dry mouthed: "How would I know?"

"Don't give me that crap, Rai Koshare, it sticks out like pin feathers all over both of you." A sigh.

Rai changed the subject, promised to call again, rang off to make another call. Simes was at lunch, but was free at one-fifteen. Rai needed no time to decide how to spend the interval; he parked between a sporting good store and a pharmacy, grabbed two candy bars, wolfed part of his lunch as he entered the sports shop in search of something he had always meant to buy: a handgun.

Things hadn't changed much. As a puebleno, Raimondo Koshare could not buy a plinking pistol without hopeless delay. "I know," said the proprietor, a sad-faced latino with wrinkles like a relief map, "the B.I.A. cannot stop you today. But the new law says you must have countersignature by a tribal council. You should have said you were

Mandan; there aren't any councils."

"There aren't any Mandan either," Rai growled.
Then he said half truthfully, "Okay, I'm casta; I
don't live on the reservation."

The old man favored him with a broken smile,
slid a form toward him. "That is a different horse
of color. Fill this out and you may buy the handgun like anyone else—after a seven day wait."

Rai stared at him for a long moment, then
wrenched the wrapper from his other candy bar in
a motion that made the old man jump. Rai took a
savage bite, glared, chewed as though the candy
were a legislator's ankle, turned to leave.

"If you must have it right now, señor," the old
voice cautioned gently, "perhaps you should not
have it." Rai nodded, made a special effort to
leave quietly, and spun the wheels of the red Mitt
as he headed for the state offices, a plastic
pseudo-Taos across town.

The Simes office was on the first floor, protected by a long counter and the stern spinster
behind it. Rai announced himself, heard a familiar voice over a transom. It was dry, resonant,
anglo: "Better let him in, Lucy. He sounds violent."

Jeff had lost a little more of his sandy hair, the
balding temples leaving a vee of short curls. The
vee pointed to a strong slender nose that was just
right, Jeff had once joked, for prying into tribal
business. The hand was like its owner, thin and
nervous and decisive. Rai shook it, flung himself
into an old leather chair. Simes nodded toward
the window: "You snuck up on me; I was watching for your yellow pickup."

"You and everybody else," Rai said, and told
him where it was.

"Good God," Simes breathed and sat back, drumming fingers on his chair arm. "I read about that on the routine printout but I didn't connect it with you." A new suspicion widened his corneas: "Don't tell me it had anything to do with those specimens!"

"Maybe not," said Rai, unwilling to surrender a tactical lever, "or maybe so." He named the boys whose bodies were probably among those in the wreck. "Can we have a privileged communication, off the record? *Any* record," he stressed.

Simes shrugged, then flicked a toggle. "Now we can."

"What if I told you those kids comprised a San Saba gang that were—well, physically different from anybody else?"

Simes leaned forward, placed his elbow on the desk and began to rub his temple. "Different how?"

"Different inside. A San Juan deputy thought Chuzo Dinay might have suicided, cut himself open. Sounds crazy, but I found a pigsticker on the kid. Maybe a very special kid, Jeff. Some mutation, maybe a recessive peculiar to San Saba. I don't know," Rai shrugged. "But different in ways *they* know. Some kind of parasite?"

Simes smiled, the intensity fading from his face. "Schistosomiasis doesn't make secret societies."

"Forget the liver flukes," said Rai, "but remember that urine sample. On my reputation as a trained observer, I tell you that specimen was not contaminated."

Simes watched his fingers fidget, found a cigarillo, chewed its tip without lighting it, his eyes never meeting Rai's until he had composed a response. "I listen to my experts, Rai. Tell me about a pot I dig up and I'll back you. Tell me about chondroprotein in a urine specimen and I have to correct you. It doesn't happen."

"Let's say it's hypothetical. If it *did* happen, and one or more of those kids showed the same deviance, wht would you do?"

Viewing it as a purely intellectual exercise, Simes lost some of his caginess. Autopsies, he supposed, followed by strenuous efforts to get San Saba elders to reconsider their position. "I'd go the route, I guess, depending on what the examiner found."

At that moment a new ploy clicked into Rai's consciousness. He grinned. "And what if you already wanted those specimens anyway?"

Puzzlement: "Hell, we *do!*"

"Keep it hypothetical," Rai said with ponderous coyness. "If autopsies really showed anything at all strange, why couldn't some San Saban with anglo education use the findings and his own superstitions to persuade the elders to do what the anglos want, for once?"

Jeff Simes threw his head back and showed his wisdom teeth. "Now I see it," he laughed, seeing only half of it. "Autopsies often show minor anomalies. You'd present it as some kind of juju."

Rai judged that the moment for perversity had come. He stood, opened the door. "You'd have to convince me—*if* I were going to convince the elders," he winked.

"You'd make some enemies in San Saba."

Rai paused. "I tried to buy a handgun this morning. No dice."

The Simes fingertips drummed again. "If it's purely for defense, try this." He rummaged in his jacket, bringing out a small silver cylinder. "Never know when I'll need it. I sprayed it silver to make it look like a cigar lighter." He handed it over.

The object had the look and the thumb-button of a lighter. Rai saw the safety latch, flicked it off.

"Jesus Christ, not in here!" Jeff Simes waved his hands, only half amused. "It's cee-ess gas."

"As in chickenshit?"

"As in orthochlorobenzalmalonitrile," Simes quoted, relishing the fistful of jargon. "Developed against terrorists, years ago. Imagine tear gas that builds a fire in your lungs, squeezes your chest flat for you, drops you in your tracks,—and leaves no ill effects in a half-hour. It'll paralyze a horse."

"I like it. I can't pronounce it, but I like it." Rai pocketed the cylinder, made a mock salute, nd walked out.

Rai picked up a small recorder and a week's canned goods in Gallup after considering his Oshara losses. His shakedown run to Pueblo Bonito taxed the tough Mitsubishi. The stretch of blacktop near Crownpoint showed some fire damage, bits of glass at the roadside. Rai found it difficult to believe his Datsun had smouldered there only hours before. You had to really work to get it over on its side, he was thinking, and shuddered when he found himself wishing he could have been on the scene for ten minutes before the fire. The accident—if it had been an accident—had occurred at roughly the time that Rojas was landing at Escavada Wash—if you could believe little Hospah Ramirez. Could the boy be harboring one of the—he was beginning to identify users with the Ogre Katcina—the ogres? All of them?

He recalled Laura's datum that two ogres occupied one small body only in desperation. If any
of them survived, how many might now be crawling inside the Ramirez boy? A urine specimen
might yield the answer . . . .

Unfolding from the Mitt's cab outside the
Bonito aid station, Rai spotted Val's bleak features
through a window, saw them transformed in joy.
A moment later Laura burst from the place, running toward him as Val Clarke emerged behind
her.

He clasped Laura's yielding warmth to him,
murmured responses to her sobbed greeting, and
when he opened his eyes he was peering through
the silver-blonde hair at Val who stood with both
hands clenched at her sides, her lower lip caught
between her teeth. Something deep inside him
twisted like a small animal; he knew that Val had
lagged behind, serving as Laura's eyes.

He lifted Laura from the waist with one arm,
grinning foolishly, reached out to Val as he took a
stumbling pace toward her. She eased into the
embrace, laid her head on his chest and hugged
him in silence as he kissed the top of her head.

"We love you," Laura murmured. It was not
clear to whom she spoke, nor did it seem to matter.

But, "I told you I'd try to applaud," Val replied.
"Can't you hear me clapping?"

Rai chuckled to hide the fullness in his heart.
"I'll never understand anglos. Hey, we're wasting
time; lots to do in San Saba."

The women made brief goodbyes to the nurse
and then piled into the Mitt. Rai took them along
faint access roads as he described how Simes had

been duped into doing his part. At the 'dobe, he left them over Laura's objection as she insisted, "Now that we're together, I don't want you out of arm's reach. Ever."

He promised to return soon, and, "Cast your mind around for those little ogres. You never know . . . ."

Waiting, they tidied up premises that did not need tidying. They had already begun to worry when Rai pushed the door open with his familiar, "I'm hungry."

Together they made piki bread again; crumbled it into a salad that might have been scrambled tacos (and tasted better). Laura sensed no lingering alien presence. Val suggested a stroll around the square, just to be sure, after dinner.

To this Rai was amenable. His only worry at the moment, he said, was the Ramirez boy. "I talked to Hospah's folks. His father met him near the sheep pens this afternoon and brought him food. Poor kid was upset about the crash, but his job will keep him occupied. And of course he's got Billichay. Twenty kilos of dog like that are worth a pair of bodyguards."

They disposed of the dinner debris and, at Rai's urging, sat around the new recorder. Their informal depositions might make no difference in the long run but the discussion itself, he said, might clarify their problems. He did not add, though Laura sensed, that such a tape might outlast them.

For an hour they wrangled cheerfully, made erasures, found agreements. Finally Rai flicked the machine off. "So much for facts; now for the wild surmises. Poor Jeff, and almost anybody else,

would think we're on drugs. We can always claim
we're trying to fit facts into some Four-Corners
mystique."

"Mystique," Val quoted, "equals horseshit."
She laughed aloud, tossing her sphere of curls in
remembrance. "That was ol' Professor Yendo at
Tempe."

"Don Yendo," Rai grinned; shook his head in
pretended deprecation. "But he also said, 'speculation between consenting adults is no longer a
felony.' "

Val: "How'd he ever get tenure with such an
outlook?"

Laura was restive, felt vaguely excluded from
the old-school talk. "Maybe they need a gadfly,"
she supplied.

Rai: "Took a good school to know that. Yendo
wasn't oversupplied with tact; he just dared you
to think."

"So let's do it," Val prodded, snapping the recorder on. "To start with, I suspect those ogre
children knew we were onto them, either with the
urine specimen or at Oshara."

"Or both," Laura said quickly. They proceeded
to weave a tangle of fact and folderol, ending with
general agreement that specimens from San Sabans would tell more about those who ran than
those who willingly contributed. It was after dark,
the guessing game beyond its most productive
period, when the buzzer sounded from the Mitt.
Rai went out to answer the call while Val stowed
the recorder on a shelf. She and Laura walked
outside to be with Rai.

". . . Perforated ureters don't mean a thing to
me," Rai was saying in aggrieved tones. "And
bone tumors aren't unusual here."

"No-o," answered a voice the women knew must be Simes, "but they're pathological. Examiner isn't finished but I was standing on his tail until he had something.

"Tumors in two of the burned bodies and in the Dinay boy. Also ureter perforations in four; maybe all six, but the viscera of two were too badly charred to tell."

Rai glanced at Val, made a grimace which she returned, then said to the mouthpiece: "How could they be burned that deeply?"

"I wish this were a scrambler circuit. Heat does funny things to a body, but it doesn't make nice clean incisions. All of those kids probably died of shock and blood loss before the fire," he continued. "Long gashes in the arms of three; the other two had been laid open like a pre-med's cat. Same as the kid who wasn't burned. Tie that," he said. He sounded hopeful.

Pause. "I can't, Jeff. Look; if, ah, I should turn up missing some day, look around my 'dobe for a cassette. It might explain a lot; or it might be sheer—" he winked at Val, "—mystique. Are you going to release anything suggesting homicide?"

"Mine isn't the final word, but I've heard talk about a suicide cult. Touchy subject; I think they'll sit on it awhile."

"Good. I wouldn't have a prayer of getting you here for those specimens if San Sabans felt defensive about multiple killings."

The men agreed that tumors and perforations were the best evidence for the tribal council. One was familiar enough, the other arcane enough, to provoke discomfort among elders. Simes added that they had found no liver fluke damage and, he replied in puzzlement to Rai's query, nothing else that shouldn't be present. Simes said he would accept a call at home, could be in San Saba with his staff in a flash—well, he amended, two hours at most. Rai rang off, then suggested a stroll that would not be entirely casual.

Walking slowly in moonless dark, they kept a polite distance from contiguous walls of residences. At one point Rai pulled his friends to a halt. Softly: "Check this place. Anything odd?"

Laura stood silently, platinum hair falling over one shoulder, a vision of delight to Rai in the soft reflection of deepset windows. After a moment: "You're pretty neat yourself, fella," and then she changed the subject. "I make it two adults, two children. A boy is worried about his sheep; scared is more like it. The girl is watching TV. Ahh, the father, I think—"

"That's enough," Rai said, properly abashed at his prying into other lives. "That was the Ramirez place. The kids are Zana and Hospah. You're sure he's okay?"

"How can I be? But those gory little monsters at Oshara weren't afraid of a lot, much less their own sheep."

"Stay alert," Rai replied. "When we've made our circuit I'll have to leave you again for awhile."

Their objections were useless. There was simply no place for anglo females in Rai's confrontation with even the most liberal of tribal elders. He had the respect of Chamas Tesuque, leader of the Scalp Society, and other ties almost as good. But Tesuque pulled the most weight. The old man had been known to roust his fellows from sleep over a sudden crisis but he was no fool, would not be hurried, might require days to reach a decision. Rai saw the women into his 'dobe before heading

for Tesuque's place across the square. He heard
the unfamiliar squeal of the iron bolt in his normally unlocked door as he moved away.

Two hours later, Rai knocked for admittance
into his 'dobe, visibly irritated that he had been
locked out despite all logic. Val understood, ac-
comodated him with coffee, gently nudged the
dozing Laura and pushed the steaming mug
across the table to Rai. He looked, she said, like
bad news on the hoof.

Rai released a wan smile as he sipped. "Just
wrung out. Old Tesuque has a radiophone to keep
tabs on his broker. Damn if he didn't call Jeff at
home! Very canny gent, Tesuque: asked Jeff
straight out if the boys had been infested with
demons."

Val: "Ah. So a state official had to commit himself to the belief in witchcraft?"

"No, and it's a good thing he didn't. Tesuque
knows the anglos don't believe in it. If Jeff had
claimed to, Tesuque would've known it was all a
shuck. Jeff is canny too—or else it stuck in his
throat to tell such a lie. Oh, Jeff hedged and qual-
ified, and ended by repeating that all the bodies
featured unusual conditions. Inside the boys were
things grimly different from the norm; and if
Tesuque or some loose-tongued archaeologist
wanted to hang a witchcraft label on it, he
couldn't stop us."

Laura, yawning: "And he didn't want to,
either."

"Exactly. Tesuque asked if body wastes and
puebleno blood would help them spot other such
people, and Jeff said maybe, and that was all
Tesuque needed from him."

Val: "Then it's settled?"

"Nope, but it's on an agenda. You don't rush an elder, you let him rush himself. I've had my say. It'd be very bad tactics to ask him about it again. Meanwhile—" He trailed off, sighed into his hands, reached for his coffee.

Laura placed her hand over the mug in gentle reproof. "Meanwhile you need sleep, not caffeine. And stop worrying about Oshara; we'll go with you tomorrow."

Rai nodded and stood, stretching until his joints crackled. He turned toward his study, saw the second pallet arrayed next to his, looked back quickly enough to catch Val's sad smile as she knelt on her own, now solitary, pallet. The huge brown eyes held no anger, no accusation. Val pointedly turned her face to the wall as Laura shrugged lithe and full-breasted from her wrap to lie near him. Rai felt a moment's surge of desire as he switched off the light, felt Laura's hand cool on his cheek. He opened his mouth, paused, felt Laura's lips brush his own.

She asked a provocative question. No response. She asked it again, her tonguetip inquisitive in his ear. No response; he was asleep. After a moment's pique, Laura cursed him softly, smiled to herself. Even for a big man, she reflected, he'd had a busy day.

After breakfast, the trio packed sandwiches and beer into the Mitsubishi. The pueblo pulsed with life; Val misread the cause. "Why so many people dressed up? Have we stirred up a hornet's nest?"

"Not exactly; it's Sunday. The better Catholics went to early Mass." He exchanged nods with one stalwart patriarch, erect and hawkeyed under the bright San Saba headband that matched a woven belt sash. The old man did not pause, but continued across the square. "Not him, though. Tesuque's wearing badges of office this morning."

Laura, murmuring: "He likes you. But not us."

"Quit prying," Val said. Then, "So that's Chamas Tesuque? Seems like he'd stop to chat."

"Not without something important. You have to realize," Rai said softly, "that everybody in San Saba knows there are seven boys dead because of my Datsun—or so they think. They're probably glad the Datsun's spirit was punished, but I was connected with it."

"So the car was a locus of evil, somehow," Val mused.

Rai: "Something like that," as though he half believed it. He swung into the cab, took the direct route to Oshara.

He called the San Juan Sheriff as they sped across the rockstrewn landscape. Deputy Rojas had found Oshara, then directed a vehicle there the previous afternoon. They had taken Kimbeto's body, had made their obligatory holotapes. All the same, said the voice from Farmington, they'd like to talk to Dr. Koshare. Rai sighed and agreed. He was not surprised, then, to find the same sandblasted Cessna nearby as they arrived at Oshara.

Sheriff Rufus Hightower was rufous enough under his stained Smokybear, with orange hairs spurting from an open shirtfront that stretched over his big hard belly; but at Laura's height, he did not tower. His splayfooted stride in rundown cowpoke boots invited the notion of a comic sterotype, if one ignored the hard little blue eyes beneath tufted brows. They would water a lot, Val decided, but they wouldn't miss much. Hightower was alone—if one discounted the long-barreled forty-five and the microvid he wore.

Hightower made no comment as Rai picked his way between limp hunks of glistening glass matt, all that remained of the mobile home's shell after the polymers burned away. The metal chassis protruded from stinking black debris. Rai stooped to inspect a scatter of small objects, groaned to recognize leafy ash as the contents of his old file cabinet.

After a circuit of the burned tent, Val called Rai over. The tent had burned furiously. Rai nodded: "I'd stored fuel in there."

"But it was a long way from the trailer," Hightower said, the gravelish voice ruminant.

"My propane tank blew up."

"Did it, now." The sheriff stumped over to the ruin of Oshara and pointed to the ground. "Did it run your pickup over here, too?"

Rai saw the tracks twining back and forth, then noticed the scattered vigas and stone where a wall had been. He blinked, worked his jaw; somehow, probably with his tow cable, much of the place had been pulled apart. "But why?"

Laura moved closer, eased an arm around his waist as she sensed the ruination of his patient work.

Hightower, offhandedly: "When did the bad blood start?"

"That's terrible," Laura said, facing the man. "Rai couldn't believe those boys were hostile, at first. He liked them!"

A callused hand went up. "Easy, little lady. This is man-talk."

From Val, some meters distant: "Oh, Lord, another chauvinist. Come away, Laura."

The women surveyed the house trailer as Hightower pressed Rai about his dealings with the boys. Rai agreed that the wanton destruction at Oshara was too thorough for a sudden childish prank. Yet they were far from reservation land, said Rai, and asked: "Why do *you* think they were after me?"

"Why," said Hightower, switching on his microvid for its audio, "were your prints on a switchblade in Chuzo Dinay's pocket?"

"Oh." Hightower's drift was clearer now.

"Helluvan answer, doc. The McKinley County folks were hoping for a better one."

"Your deputy said Chuzo might have had a knife," Rai explained. "I checked; he did." He faced the barrelish little man squarely. "I also said that to a man in State Health. And I was in Escavada Wash while my Datsun was burning."

"Best alibi in the world," Hightower said easily, "unless we can figure how you could've got from Crownpoint to Escavada quick-like." He grinned up at Rai: "You don't happen to own a plane?"

Negative headshake. "At least I see what you're driving at." He dared not look at Hightower as he said carefully, "I thought maybe the kids were on drugs. I don't know why they'd go after me or my friends. Or each other."

"Me neither, doc. But I'm tryin'. Do yourself a favor and don't take any vacations. Them either," he said, jerking a thumb at the women. It was his only indication that the visitors interested him.

Rai said Oshara had been intended as a vacation for his companions. Hightower supposed he had no objections if Rai sifted the burned site; but by the way, he wondered, why did state medical examiners want the small body in the Farmington morgue?

Good old Jeff, thought Rai: those perforations had his curiosity aroused. Aloud he said, "Some kind of parasite, I think. I'm just as curious as you are."

The big hat came off; a sleeve mopped the sweaty brow. "No you ain't, and in a way you sure are." Another grin. By this time Rai knew the rictus as a mark of aggressiveness. "In any case, don't let me hear you've decided to pack a gun like you tried in Gallup. But step lively. Could be your enemies ain't all dead."

His hat exchanged for a crash helmet, Hightower puffed his bulk into the Cessna, waved and smiled his re-election smile at 'the ladies,' cranked the old craft into action. They watched until the Cessna turned toward the northwest, its whirr fading into the vastness of the desert. Laura broke the silence: "I hope he's wrong."

"You heard him then," Rai said. "My alibi? Of course he's wrong, you were with me all the—"

"About our enemies," she cut in. "I hope they're all dead."

"Hightower just doesn't want any more trouble on his turf," Val said, adding brightly, "so what can we do about this mess, Rai?"

The archaeologist first checked out the Oshara ruin, which was not hopelessly scattered. The tent was a sad display, though; and the mobile home virtually a total loss. Several maps and many notes had scattered from the tent without burning. They found more papers wind-scattered in the arroyo, more still beyond it, and a few artifacts of stone and pottery blown from the mobile home onto the hard ground. Most artifacts from the site were irreparably damaged or lost, but the dig could continue. Their spirits were soothed by ham sandwiches and bock beer, two hours later.

Then Rai led the work on the tent wreckage, finally moved his water tank. The electric barrow, paint blistered and tires heat-checked, was operable. He levered the now-empty tank onto the self-propelled platform. He avoided stepping on the dark stain near one corner of the solar panel; promised to dig up the bloody dirt and dump it; considered how that would look to Hightower; left the stain as it was.

They left on a note of good humor after Val found that the refrigerator had protected its contents. Upside down, three meters from the trailer chassis, its beer was warm but potable.

All three were whiffy from warm beer and hot sun when Val, enjoying her stint at driving the Mitt, drove past distant sheep pens and pulled into San Saba. Rai saw him first: a youth in his teens, squatting patiently in the shade of the Koshare 'dobe, who revealed a congenitally deformed foot as he stood. Rai hurried to talk with him, speaking in their tongue, then turned back to the pickup as the youth hurried away.

Rai's smile was unconvincing. "Tribal council wants me at my convenience—which means right now. Wait inside." He ducked into his room, returning with a bright headband and a sash belt as Val was unloading their picnic hamper.

As he passed, Val made optimistic noises: "Maybe they're ready to allow the specimen collection."

"Lady, I sure hope so," he muttered, and strode away toward a distant kiva.

Laura took the hamper, stood very close to Val. "He's worried about the deaths," she said, "and whether the elders think he provoked it all."

Without another word, very much aware of their own alien status in this ancient culture, they sought the shelter of a locked door.

The pounding on the door frightened Val, who was dozing over a book; but this time it was the product of Rai's elation. "No more locked doors," he said without preamble. "We won't have to. I just called Jeff to tell him of the decision. Boy, I'm hungry."

Laura stroked his cheek on her way to the refrigerator, withdrew an enormous sandwich, slid it onto the table under his nose, sat down across from him as he continued: "Scalp and Clown and Medicine societies all decided to take the lesser of two evils. Jeff was asleep, but he woke up fast enough when I told him to be here tomorrow morning. I am really hungry for some reason," he raced on.

No one but Rai had spoken since he entered the doorway, and they were amused at the ebullience of this normally taciturn man. He went on, glancing from one to the other. Tribal elders had long pondered San Saba's poor record in raising male children, had kept a strictly oral account of the personality changes that seemed to 'snap' in too many San Saba boys before puberty. Rarely was this noticed in unhealthy children. Often the same conservative boy who had no interest in leaving the pueblo vicinity seemed marked for early death or disappearance. Chamas Tesuque had somberly recounted all this to Rai in the kiva, surrounded by men of tribal substance as they

smoke in firelit gloom and shared bits of some
pulpy food which, Rai said, tended to bite back.

The strong sanctions of the old ways should
have made dutiful followers of normal children.
Plainly, they had not. Plainly, it was time to borrow ideas from the anglos. The sooner San Saba
underwent this new purification rite, the sooner
they might be free of a long-harbored and evil
katcina. Rai inferred that as the tribal argument
progressed, men who most objected to this new
'rite' now tended to raise suspicion in the minds
of the others; if one shrank from giving specimens
it seemed to imply that one had something which
must be hidden. In a way it was poetic injustice:
the crushing weight of conservative opinion turning upon the most conservative—and using the
same social sanctions. It was a coercion they all
knew well. San Saba stood ready to welcome the
State Public Health Service.

"This is all sensitive stuff," Rai added. "I'd be
persona sub grata if they knew I'd told you. But
you'd read it in me, Laura; and why should Val
know less? You know something? I could use
something to eat."

"You could look in front of your nose," Val said
dryly, and laughed as Rai blinked stupidly down
at his untouched sandwich. As he tore into it, Val
wondered aloud if he had been nibbling mushrooms in the kiva. Rai did not know; to him it
seemed unimportant. The important thing, he
mumbled through ham and cheese, was that between Laura's telepathy and Jeff Simes's diagnostic tests they would soon have some evidence
whether San Saba was free of the alien Oshara
influence.

"I only wish you'd seen what I—we—saw com-

ing out of that boy during the fire," Val shuddered. "If it's *that* alien, your evidence had better
be damned convincing."

Laura, head erect as though staring without
eyes at the far wall, nodded. "I'll help, Rai. But
when this is over, I want to leave here. I never
want to feel this—vulnerable—again."

"But this is my home, Laura. Surely a few
months a year?"

"Not a few weeks, not a few hours. I'm not
welcome here!"

"My work is here."

"There must be other places, other work!" She
was clutching his arm now, white parentheses of
strain framing her mouth, her nostrils pinched,
mouth trembling. Laura Dunning did not need
eyes to register desperation.

Rai took her hand and said, slowly, "Well,
there's always a teaching slot at Highlands if I
want it. Las Vegas."

"Even Nevada," Laura said. "Anywhere."

"Las Vegas, New Mexico," Rai corrected her.
"I'm like a lawyer; I have to learn the rules in my
area and practice there."

Laura relaxed slightly, folded her hands,
sighed. "I don't suppose there'd be a job for Val?"

Val had been studying patterns in the rough
planks of the table, but now her head snapped
around. Softly: "You can't be serious, just taking
that for granted. And when you feel secure
enough with Rai, you'll be asking why I don't take
a hike. And I would, too. Only I should be taking it
now." She whispered, half to herself, "Maybe I
will."

Rai saw the great soulful eyes brimming with

tears, the slender shoulders held erect though shaking in some internal fight for control. Val wiped her eyes angrily, refused to look at him as he said gently, "Laura wouldn't do that."

"You know I wouldn't," Laura said, turning to Val, proffering a hand that Val ignored. "I'm not rejecting you; I'm including you."

Proud, defiant, miserable: "Sure you are. You want to include me in your horizontal tango, too, I suppose. You want it all, don't you?"

"If you mean I want to love you both—yes." She found Rai's hand again on her right, Val's on her left. "I don't care if it includes sex pairings or, or treblings, or not; maybe I should, but I don't. Let me hear you tell me why that's wrong."

Val opened her mouth, looked at Rai, found no help there. She managed only, "I don't have an answer for that. But I'm not ready to accept it—maybe I never would be." As her anger segued into remorse, Val essayed a smile that did not quite succeed.

"Isn't anybody going to ask my opinion?" Rai vented his *huh-huh* laugh, brushing crumbs from his shirt. "Not that I have one that's coherent. I've been shot, warned by cops in two counties, zonked by alkaloids, cross-examined by old men, and offered like a bowl of piñon nuts between anglo women. If and when I return to normal, maybe I'll *have* an opinion."

Val had begun to chuckle before Rai's list of intrusions was complete. Sniffling from a previous emotion, laughing through its antidote, she made her peace with Laura by hugs and apology. "That one will bear watching, Montezuma," she said to Rai as she found her pallet. "People tend to forget you're there when Laura's onstage."

"I have that from an expert," he said to Laura, whose response was a penitent smile and nod. He turned out the light and led Laura to the pallets. Her mouth was warm and pliant, and there was no more talk of guilt in their earnest communion. Their physical sharing could have been no more full had they known it would be their last.

They were awakened on Monday morning by repeated knocks, then the cheerful diffident call of Jeff Simes, resplendent in a smock so white it dazzled. A state van, one of the silent white electrics that seemed all doors, shadowed the 'dobe's entrance.

Rai let him in, introduced him between yawns and hid his amusement at the Simes reaction to his guests. He pulled on his boots as he cautioned Simes to 'do' the women of San Saba first.

"Give me some credit," Simes grunted, and drove the van to a spot indicated by Rai. Simes had collated much on short notice: two assistants of each gender, all fluent in Spanish; and automated specimen equipment that ranged from centrifuges to microchromatography and automated printouts. Simes shooed Rai off, perceiving that the pueblo women hung back until Rai left the immediate area.

From his doorway, Rai stared across the square with Val and slurped her coffee. Laura had fallen asleep again, her snores soft in the cool interior. "In-bloody-credible," Val said, studying the queue of silver-bedecked dowagers, sleek-haired young women, little girls. A few began to issue from the other side of the van, holding what appeared to be theatre tickets the color of a tangerine. "He's running 'em through like crap through a tin horn."

He completed a silent calculation. "About two a minute. They'll be ready for the men before noon. And the clowns will be ready for anyone trying to split."

Several men in striking costumes, some naked from the waist and all wearing masks with the smiles of a Sheriff Hightower, cavorted on flat rooftops around the pueblo. Rai explained that the feathers, masks, and the gray, black, and green body paint were more powerful symbols in San Saba than was a copper-buttoned blue uniform in an anglo city. More of the Clown Society men patrolled outside the pueblo walls. They might walk on their hands and mimic the solemn, but they carried blunt staves as well. No San Saban would leave the perimeter without a bright ticket signifying passage through the purifying anglo van. Passage to the pueblo would be strictly one-way until the tally was complete.

"Which reminds me," Rai said. "A few shepherds and husbandry people, mostly kids, are usually out on a given night. They're to be relieved by others who've had the tests, and I want to make sure about—some."

He might have simply specified: Hospah Ramirez. Laura thought the boy unsullied; and he had seemed troubled enough by the tragedy near Crownpoint. But Hospah was also the last San Saban alive who had rubbed shoulders with Ziu Tiamunyi; Encino Mangas; Chuzo Dinay; and others. All ogres. Or janissaries of the Ogre Katcina? Rai's puebleno skin crawled, defying the anglo training inside; he would not relax until the Ramirez boy held an orange ticket. The boy's sister, Zana, was in the queue with her mother—and San Saba mothers were the standard arbiters of child behavior.

They had an early lunch, after which Rai got in line with the men for his own tests, and for the sake of appearances. He lingered with Simes in the van. Yes, a few pathological conditions had turned up: diabetic symptoms, cystitis, anemia, worms. With the males, a slightly different pattern was emerging. Yes, some protein in the urine, especially of the youths.

Rai's heart thudded against his windpipe until Simes added, "But certain types of protein are common enough. We've added a reagent strip for your goddam bug juice, Rai. I feel like an idiot, but I did it. And no, it's uniformly negative for chondroprotein."

Rai thanked him, took his ticket, returned to the 'dobe. He passed the news to Val, presuming that Laura was 'listening.' Why did he not mind that Laura was privy to some of his most private thoughts? In any case, he realized, he didn't mind—so long as they weren't playing cards for money.

As the sun moved well past the meridian, several young people passed Clown Society checkpoints waving orange chits. They left for garden plots, sheep pens, ochre deposits; relieving those who had spent the morning, or the previous night, at some task. Most went afoot. Two young men sped away on electroped bikes, the two-wheelers nearly silent but for the jouncing springs. Halogen batteries made electropeds costly for initial purchase, and the appalling injury index in the old days of engine-driven cycles had prompted the elders to forbid powered cycles

to the underaged. San Saba was far from demo-
cratic, but it fostered unified action.

Presently, Rai stiffened as he spied two small
figures from his single deepset window to the
outside world. He ambled into the square;
watched as Hospah Ramirez trudged to his home.
The dog, Billichay, lay obedient in shade, awaiting whatever his godlet might command. For a
fleeting moment Rai considered Billichay in a
new light, watched critically as the sheepdog
scrambled up to greet Hospah and the treats he
held aloft. As Hospah walked toward the white
van, Billichay swallowed a morsel, darted to salute a dry old watering trough, capered in the
dust, hurried to tease at Hospah's ankle. No, it was
hardly the behavior of a mature evil, Rai judged;
but who could tell what a urine specimen from
Billichay might reveal?

It took the boy a half-hour to queue through the
line. Rai released a long-pent breath as Hospah
Ramirez emerged, stuffing an orange chit into a
pocket. Rai saw him linger with other children,
cadge part of a soft drink, meander back toward
distant sheep pens with Billichay. Then he called
Simes discreetly from the Mitt's radiophone.

Jeff Simes was harried from a long day, his
temper frayed at the edges as he replied to The
Question. Ramirez? No, dammit, the boy was depressingly normal. Diagnostic tests on a goddam
dog were, goddamit, for a goddam veterinarian
and now, et cetera, would Rai Koshare please get
the et cetera off the line?

Rai made the best apology available: he offered
to buy drinks for the crew in Crownpoint that
evening. State expense accounts did not blot up
ethyl alcohol; Simes relented a millimeter,

agreed, and went back to his printouts.

Inside the 'dobe, Rai hugged Laura and Val to him as he beamed that a celebration was in order. Though a few pueblenos needed some social pressure to file through the white van, each of them finally emerged with an orange ticket. It seemed that the nightmare was fading, an ancient evil driven out. Crownpoint's BarBQ Heaven was the nearest approach to formal dining in thirty klicks: would Mlles. Dunning and Clarke do him the honor?

His question was rhetorical in the most trivial sense. They primped in fresh clothes, borrowed from Rai's hoard of heavy silver-and-turquoise adornment. Laura's shining platinum hair against the dull lustre of raw silver made a breathtaking monochrome. Joking, planning their evening, they rode out from San Saba pausing only to show Rai's orange talisman. The two anglos were not, strictly speaking, persons; did not count.

Once Rai tooted the horn and waved to a distant boy, almost certainly Hospah Ramirez, whose dog nipped at determined stragglers in the small herd of sheep that moved toward fresh pasturage. Laura's chin came up, a thoughtful crease corrugated her forehead. Then she put the wisp of suspicion from her mind. From earlier contact, she knew that several ogres would not willingly convene in one small body. With her reliance on telepathic knowledge, Laura had never developed a strong tendency to consider alternatives. It must have been nerves, she decided, and kept her silence as the Mitsubishi carried her out of range of the deadly Oshara minds.

Pasturage was never overabundant for sheep

across most of the Four Corners region. Cattle ranchers fenced and railed against the browsing habits of sheep, which damage grass instead of cropping it neatly. Shepherds had learned long before to keep track of the odd sinkhole, the occasional gullywash, that might offer green forage in unlikely spots one year out of five.

The elder Ramirez had agreed, for a price, to let his son accomodate the needs of the Dinay family since the death of Chuzo. Spray-painted black letters 'R' and 'D' showed stark on the broad backs of sheep that mingled, jostled, forced new dominance patterns as they sought to become one flock. Two of the Dinay ewes touched noses as the pickup droned away, lingered thus.

Execrable planning, complained the user that had recently been Hatchi Leon. He still fumed over his astonishment and shame when the archaeologist appeared at the wreck after they had reported him dead. *And almost as bad to place four of us in female hosts.* The Ramirez rams were importunate.

The reply was no less paranoid than it had been in Naka Flores: *Dinay planned well enough in hiding the antenna modules. I shall forget none of this when I report to the fleet.*

Patience! First we must contact our homeworld; and before that we must take fresh human hosts.

Then, *That accursed dog again,* as Billichay raced toward them, his canine awareness increasingly disturbed at the unsheeplike maneuverings of his new charges. They smelled subtly different; they were not easily frightened; and something in their eyes said more of masters than of sheep.

The boy turned to watch Billichay at work, and

another of the two dozen 'D' emblazoned sheep shouldered next to a ram of the same flock. Noses touched. *You are certain the boy used those words to his cousin? We must not move too soon,* cautioned the user who had been Chuzo Dinay.

The user of Carson Kimbeto: *I have faced exposure more recently and am more wary than you, and I am certain that the white truck has lulled the humans.* The older youth asked if Hospah, like himself, had done with giving of his body to anglo magic. Hospah answered that all the people had given blood, excrement smears, sputum and urine, and that the elders had promised that no more purification rites need intrude upon San Saba.

If only we could interrogate, mused the ex-Chuzo. Physical usurpation was not delicate enough to tap the thoughts of a host before its mind was destroyed.

If all agree, we can take one host tonight and make reconnaisance. I believe you are correct in suggesting our most suspicious member for that task. There was something akin to cynical pleasure in this observation from a user who had nearly died within the Kimbeto boy.

Let us argue toward that end, then. And let us all make the small shepherd work, as planned. He must be worn down in relays. Damn that dog, he finished, as Billichay circled toward them.

They turned away, seeking others with the telltale spot which, before dawn on Saturday, Chuzo Dinay had scraped bare of fleece just ahead of the left ear. In time the users would have come to know one another's ruminant bodies just as they did with humans. Yet they did not intend to stay hidden within this flock for any extended

time. Their confidence in planning and execution
had been sorely tested when Rai Koshare, apparently resurrected, strode from the Cessna near
Crownpoint virtually under the noses of the sinister little flock. The shame of the Oshara assailants
became complete when the once Mateo Betan,
staring from the sheep pen on Sunday afternoon,
identified two women in the passing Mitt as light
haired, probably the anglos. Using sheep eyes at
that distance he could not be certain. Now the red
Mitt had passed again, now the satin sheen of
Laura's mane was unmistakable; and now the
users were certain, angry, restless for the freedom
and violence which new human bodies would
provide.

Objections, supicions, strategems passed
among the users as they moved into a more cohe-
sive fleecy group in gathering dusk. They reached
general agreement that the Ramirez boy must be
taken now, but no consensus on the immediate
action against Koshare and his anglos.

They felt sure that the archaeologist was behind
the specimen program; could not know Val had
observed the rescue of one of their number; felt
certain nonetheless that their future safety de-
pended on the elimination of the three humans
whom they had twice attacked. They had not yet
decided how it must be done; but soon, soon. . . .

Several kilometers to the northwest of the flock
lay a shallow fork of Chaco Wash. In a hollow near
one of its tributary arroyos was a hogan, occupied
only when seasonal seepage encouraged a bit of
forage there for sheep. This year it would be of
scant interest to shepherds, and so its centuries-
old midden heap was an ideal repository for the
beacon equipment of the users. Cable, antenna

modules, water jugs, jerked meat in an *olla;* all
had been quickly dumped from the stolen Datsun
during that frenzied night of destruction, then
covered with older trash. It would be safe until the
users recruited fresh children.

The recruitment of Hospah Ramirez would
have to be without external damage to the small
body. It was a problem, but one with several solu-
tions. The simplest way was to assure that the boy
was bone weary, and to interfere with the flock's
progress to pasturage until the small shepherd
elected to stop on the open range for the night.
There would be choices in terrain, hollows protected from chill winds that wept from distant
blue-gray peaks even on summer nights, bearing
scent of cedar, desert blooms, perhaps of coyote. It
would be then that Hospah Ramirez, lacking
firewood, would ease into a group of his charges,
curling up between them for warmth. He would
fall asleep while Billichay guarded the
perimeter—and while one more ewe settled
against the boy. And under the cover of night,
there would be more than enough time for a warm
sentient wave to glide through fleece to naked
human skin.

The simple solution was executed flawlessly.
Sequestered in the lee of a hillock, the flock of
Hospah Ramirez settled for the night. Frequently
Billichay trotted to investigate the deliberate
straying of Dinay sheep. And once, long after
midnight, the child leaped to his feet to scream
under cold bright stars as he felt the deadly progress of a Thing within him; stealthy, satanic, horrifying and implacable. Hospah took three steps
and fell, first blind, then deaf.

Billichay raced to his master across the backs of

sheep as a child skips over stones in a brook, then stood whining for orders. After several minutes the child's limbs began to jerk, flex; the small voice rasped a command as the user grew adept at control. But Billichay would have heeded that command in any case. Growling, whining, the dog backed away and sped to the other edge of the flock, there to remain for the night. His small human god bore a faint new scent, sour as forgotten cheese, oddly like the troublesome Dinay sheep. It would be easier to perform canine duties while maintaining a respectful distance from this boy who was, Billichay sensed, no longer Hospah Ramirez.

Rai Koshare waited for the vigas to quit spinning overhead in his room, refused the mug of coffee as he struggled to sit up. "Nope, tomato juice," he whispered, and noted without pleasure that the women were faring better than he. The clink of the juice container was a clash of cymbals; its fluid gurgle was God's own millrace in his head. He squinted at the slanting trapezoid of light from a window and warned, "Don't tell me it's noon."

"We won't." Laura smiled, and sat beside him to rub his head. "It's afternoon. By the way; how does one snag?"

Rai heard Val's merry laugh from the dining area but did not understand the question. Laura said, "All the way back from Crownpoint you kept telling us that drinking doesn't make you dance better or snag easier, it just makes you a drunken Indian."

He began a *huh-huh* that hurt, then explained that it was an old slogan at Haskell College. "Pity I didn't take it to heart. I suppose I outraged every-body," he grumbled, sipping juice.

Laura denied it, luring him into her variation on Dorothy Parker's 'You Were Perfectly Fine'— until he realized that he could not have married both Laura and Val without the mandatory delay.

"You takum advantage of poor injun," he rumbled the stereotype, glowering over his tomato juice. Then, "Nice scalp," he added and reached for her as she fled squealing.

In an hour he was mending nicely, able to take the odor of fried food without retching. He made a call to Gallup, learned that Simes had delegated a Navajo medic to begin negotiations with old Chamas Tesuque for treatment of a few San Saba ailments. "You tell a tangled tale when you've hoisted a few," Simes informed him, enjoying the memory of their Crownpoint evening. "But beyond those anomalies in the boys' bodies there's only one coincidence that gets me: why'd they go on such a rampage right after you collected those first specimens? Wish I could get over the feeling that I set it all in motion."

Rai sensed his friend's willingness to shoulder guilt, reminded him that the specimens were their mutual secret, and rang off. He sat in the cab until the heat drove him into the 'dobe, thinking. Their secret was hardly secure if someone else— Tesuque, for example—had monitored their open channel.

But Chamas Tesuque had been a crucial force on Rai's side. No one else in San Saba had sophis-ticated communications equipment, he reckoned. Or did they? If Chuzo Dinay's friends kept such equipment, they would keep it hidden; and that would explain a few things, not all of it very settling to a foggy mind or a fluttery stomach. Rai endorsed Laura's error of the previous evening: he let an awesome possibility go undiscussed.

He felt better after his siesta but nagged himself with memories of the San Saba midden. He had played there himself, years before; had known as a child that some areas were forbidden him by the larger boys. Chuzo, and perhaps others of his ilk, had been there days ago for some unguessable purpose. Maybe a purpose could be guessed by a bit of site investigation. He was, after all, an archaeologist . . . .

". . . Think I'll mope around in the pueblo midden," he said casually, with a strong silent broadcast following his words.

Laura must have caught the warning. She said, "If you're not worried, I'm not," and turned back to shelling corn.

Val put down her book. "Why don't we tag along?"

He needed a stroll alone, Rai said, and Laura chimed in; she'd rather he be bored with himself, for heaven's sake, than with friends.

"You two don't fool me for a second," Val replied, eyes narrowing. "Here it is right up front: the last thing about this place to scare me would be boredom, Rai. I just like to know you're close."

"Then keep the car keys. You know where the midden is; if you get too nervous, drive out and honk."

Val took the keys, tossed them on the table, followed Rai to the door. "Dinner in a couple of hours," she predicted. She would miss the mark widely.

Rai grinned, adjusted his broad hat, felt for his glasses in a shirt pocket, nodded. Long afterward he would recall the innocent irony of, "You anglos try and keep out of trouble."

The user of Hospah Ramirez was no more pleased in his new host than he had been in a sheep; suspicion will always find the dark rationale it seeks. He had walked over ten kilometers under a blazing sun, protected by his tattered poncho, hidden by the uneven terrain, before he reached the San Saba midden. It was best not to be seen, but he could always insist that the flock—a two-hour walk away near the old hogan under Billichay's supervision—was really much nearer.

He skirted the source of childish dialogue from a spot in the midden, reached the dugout un-greeted, found the rifle he had come for. In a few days the pueblo would be back to normal.

The user stood in utter silence, leaning against cool dry earth, and listened again to the prattle of five-year-olds. In all probability, he felt, the coming of the starships would bring an end to the strict necessity of taking these particular small hosts. But the user was thinking less of necessity than of pleasure. He had learned to delight in the consumption of innocents; wondered which of the tiny creatures beyond the next hummock might be next to feed his ravening desires. Even ravishment of a human child by a fellow user brought him a secret satisfaction. In the next few days they could begin to recruit new children. It might take a week. Unnoticed, a runnel of saliva found its way to his chin.

He felt the rifle in his hands, the essential tool by which users could coerce adults, and again 'Hospah' gloated. There would also be pleasure when he, or one of his fellows, managed to find the anglo women alone. The rifle was required to enforce the user plan. The smaller woman might be a marginally acceptable host and, if not, her body would be left in the desert sooner rather than later.

Women held hostage to compel the man Koshare; the man supplying last the essentials of beacon equipment; then all of them in deep unmarked graves. It was a tactic that appealed to the user as he thrust the little rifle under his poncho. The stock came to his shoulder, the muzzle down the leg of his denims nearly to the knee. He would walk stiffly for a distance en route back to the hogan, but the expedient worked. The user was scanning the distant pueblo, ready to move out from the occluding midden, when he saw the tall figure approaching from San Saba. He rejected his first impulse, left the rifle in his clothing instead of bringing it to bear on his enemy, melted again into the midden.

Rai Koshare heard the children playing, smiled at old reminiscence, then realized how little he remembered of the place. He walked nearer to the voices and called to them. A child with the eyes of a Val Clarke poked his head from a dugout and Rai, squatting companionably, traded pleasantries. He turned the topic of the old playground to that of Chuzo Dinay's favorite place while the user, ten meters away, listened with growing alarm.

The damned archaeologist must not be underestimated; who knew what he might discover in the hideout, given time? He might search other middens. The user cudgeled his mind for traces left nearby. If only he could contact the others, this instant—but he alone enjoyed a human host. By the time they were ready to take the anglo females, Koshare might be on their track. Time . . . .

Then as a child led Rai Koshare to the entrance to a burrow that might be damning, the user made his decision. The time was now, *now!* No matter that sundown was over an hour away; if the car and the women were unguarded, he could carry out the entire operation alone, in a single sweeping maneuver. It would not matter what the fool Koshare might find then: it would be too late. Koshare would depend on user promises, because he would have no choice. One had only to make that fact clear.

The user had but one intervening problem: approach to the Koshare 'dobe without answering questions about errant shepherds. He moved off toward the pueblo at a stiff-legged trot.

Few San Sabans occupied the inner square at dinnertime, and none thought to look closely at the small ponchoed figure with the slight limp as it neared the Koshare 'dobe, peered into the red Mitsubishi.

In Rai's dining area, Laura brushed angrily at a crumb on the table. "Why must we fight like this, Val," she lamented. "It's almost as if you were trying to make me dislike you."

"Trying to make you face facts," Val said, stirring at a soup of dubious ancestry. "Everybody has her own fuel, and you run on security. I expect you'll leave Rai when you find somebody else who makes you feel still more secure—only security's a Shangri-La, it's a charming fiction."

"And you're a drab little cynic, jealous of Rai!"

Laura bit her lip, grimaced. "Now you've got me so upset I can't think; I didn't mean that."

"In anger veritas," Val said grimly, and heard the door hinge creak. "Come in, Rai, we're having a dandy time."

Laura dropped a bowl, squeaked in horror. "I wasn't thinking," she whispered, hands to her face.

Val turned, dropped the wooden spoon, elevated her hands as she stared into the muzzle of the little weapon. She tried to smile; it had to be a game, she thought. "Okay, little fella. I hope that thing isn't real."

Laura, breathlessly: "It's real. He's—one of them."

Val stared into the eyes of an ancient evil in a child's face. "Better give me that. Somebody three times your size will be walking through that door any min—"

"I know where Koshare is," said the small voice, its sibilance betraying a mind that was not comfortable with English. "He cannot help you." The muzzle shifted to steady on Laura's breast, but the eyes did not leave Val as he commanded, "Pencil and paper. *Now*."

Val scuttled away, unwilling to shift her gaze from this not-child. She fumbled for her purse, returned and dumped its contents on the table. Her hands were shaking.

The user noticed the car keys as Val found a pen and her checkbook. "Those are car keys?"

Laura, suddenly aware of his intent: "No."

"Yes," Val admitted. "Why didn't you say you wanted the car?"

Car theft had brought them enough trouble, she thought, but maybe he would take the damned car and go. But how could someone his size operate it? Fragments of the truth occurred to her.

"*Cállate*, shut up," hissed the user. "Write, do not print, as I tell you."

She used the back of a check, forced her hand to write as he commanded: *You can buy our lives. Stay in San Saba and joke in public about your old suspicions. Wait for orders.* She shoved the scrap toward him.

He left it there, stepped to one side, gestured toward the door. "Understand that if you refuse one order, I must kill you."

"He wants to! My God, where is Rai?" Laura's self-control suffered from her awareness.

On command, Val took the keys, preceded Laura to the pickup a few steps from the door. The user was close behind, eyes roving, the rifle beneath the poncho but ready to swing up and fire. He vaulted into the cab behind Laura. Val started the engine, wondering if she should try suddenly braking as they left the square.

As if outguessing her, the user jabbed the gun muzzle into Laura's ribs, the weapon held across his lap. "Sit up, arms on the seat back," he said to the cowering Laura. Mewling, Laura did so. "Drive slowly out to the west."

Very slowly the Mitt rolled from the square. They passed two men who did not glance toward them at all. Val shifted into second gear, kept it there. She would use fuel much faster that way, she reasoned as the cold diesel wheezed and clattered. She drove along ruts that led past the midden, suddenly hopeful. If that was his destination—

"Circle wide *a la derecha*, to the right," he ordered. Val saw that she would be forced far from the midden so, as she complied, she took a terrible chance. When the Mitt jounced across ruts she let her forearm brush the horn.

"I couldn't help it," she lied, glancing into the widened, inhuman stare of the user who slid down further, his head below the window level.

He did not pull the trigger. Val searched the rearview; knew she could not expect such an ineffectual bleat to alert Rai; continued her slow detour. She saw no one, did not expect aid now. The user eased his head up, gave a fresh command, glanced from Laura to the landscape and back again. With a last despairing inspiration, Val slid her left foot onto the brake pedal without lessening pressure on the accelerator. Three brief taps, three longer ones, three brief taps again. Then repeated again and again as the safe stolid mass of San Saba dwindled in her rearview. The small decelerations were not noticeable on that terrain, but her slow progress was. Val knew that her captor had all the wariness and intelligence of an adult as he insisted that she upshift. The pueblo faded from view.

At length Val mustered the courage to ask it: "So how did you pass the specimen tests, you little gob of snot?"

No vocal answer but, "He has answers," Laura managed to say without clarifying her meaning to the user. The answers were an overlay on a roiling mass of suspicions within the small demon.

Val continued as if talking to herself. She wondered aloud how many of them existed; if any had been killed; where they had come from; what they wanted.

To Laura some of the answers were gibberish, some vague; but simple concepts were clear

enough. Hardly twenty minutes after they turned
northward, Val obediently urged the pickup
along an arroyo and saw her first coyote, all skin
and bones and wariness, loping out of sight. Finally she reached a turn to the east and then found
herself emerging into a broad sere hollow.

Val saw the penned sheep, dirty buff in the
darker shade of a tumbledown shed of corrugated
metal, before she noticed the earth-tinted hogan
nearby. At the user's command she drove behind
the shed, killed the engine, waited for the user to
exit and trembled with anticipation of his
slightest mistake.

She was disappointed as Laura, terrified that
Val might provoke a fusillade, followed meekly.
Val followed too, noticing with pity that Laura
had wet the seat beneath her. Val left the passenger door ajar. One more forlorn hope: maybe
the cab light would run the battery down. In false
bravado, then, recalling the note she had written:
"You show up to give Rai Koshare an order and
he's going to wring your frigging neck for you."

Perhaps the user's confidence, feeding on success, had grown. "But he would not wring yours,"
he said, the rifle muzzle his goad toward the hogan.

"You little shit, you think I'll follow orders
when that rifle's not pointed at me?"

A steady look, a slow knowing nod.

It was Laura who answered. "You will be their
puppet," she said, aghast. Val thought back to the
moment when she saw a trapped user creep from
one human body to another, and then she knew
how she was to be used. Only Laura's dependence
on another's courage kept Val from screaming
then.

The hideout seemed little more than a children's excavation to Rai, excepting the size of it and the deep recesses with discarded plastic sheeting. His questing fingertips found faint sensations of the Oshara ogres on the sheeting; some of it a generation old, some as fresh as the fleeting moment. Gooseflesh crept along his forearms as he concluded that at least one of them, in the past few hours, had stood where he now stood. To some extent it was fear that drove Rai from the earthen pit into sunlight.

He heard the cold-engine rumble of the distant pickup, waved as it passed; but standing in a small depression he knew he could not be seen. Val drove steadily, rigidly, staring straight ahead instead of searching for him. What the devil was she up to, a joyride? He scrambled along the path leading from the midden, stumbled, heard the single tenor call of the horn, trotted into the open to see the pickup circling wide.

Sunlight streamed through the cab and Rai, whose long-distance vision was average, saw Laura's arms stretched across the seat back. But Laura normally braced herself against the dash padding, he knew; and then he saw the wink of brake lights, a repetitive SOS, and felt certain that Val drove under duress. His hat and glasses fell into the dust as he sprinted for San Saba, thinking of Tesuque's radiophone.

Even as he ran into the square he knew the radiophone could be monitored from inside the Mitt. He could not risk alerting an enemy by a call for help, could not spare the time. He raced past an electroped, then turned back and ripped its recharging cord away. The Mitt had been slow enough that he might catch up. The whine of the

motor rose in pitch as the little two wheeler carried Rai from San Saba.

The pickup was out of sight. Rai's pace tossed
him from bump to bump as he squinted into the
sun, catching a faint trace of dust on the horizon.
Now and then he spied a fresh treadmark in a
patch of windblown sand, and when sunlight
glinted from a moving object four klicks away to
his right, he saw that it trailed a dust-trace. It had
to be the Mitt, now traveling faster than he. Rai
gritted against dust in his teeth and followed.

Speeding northward, he knew that he had been
outdistanced. At every rise in the terrain, he
thought, he might suddenly ride in view of the
pickup, and then he would lose the advantage of
surprise. If only he had stopped to apprise old
Tesuque! He slowed as he neared an eroded butte,
rode near its top, halted the 'ped to listen. Nothing
but windsong and his beating heart; but there at
the bottom of the slope, something moved.

He rolled the vehicle downslope and routed a
single gray opportunist at its gory work. The great
vulture hopped a few times, ungainly with its full
craw, then flapped into the air leaving the carcass
to the interloper and the ants. Rai saw that it had
been a Dinay ewe; judged it had died within the
past day. Little Hospah had run into trouble, he
decided, though he could not guess how the ewe
had died. Rai crossed the dry hollow, turned
northward again.

For a time he saw nothing to promote optimism
until he found fresh treadmarks. One good thing
about a dying sun was the long shadow it threw:
he sped as fast as he dared, a few meters east of the
tracks, catching occasional glimpses of treadmark

shadow. The Mitt had run almost arrow-straight toward a wash that crossed from the east.

He lost the trail as he negotiated the shallow Chaco Wash, continued for a half-kilometer, stopped in frustration. He had just missed the treadmarks, he was deciding, and scanned northward before proceeding in that direction. It was then that he heard the faint rattle of three shots, as fast as a semiautomatic weapon could fire. They had come from upcountry behind him, the reports channeled by the slope of Chaco Wash.

At another time the inside of the hogan might have fascinated Val. An antique kerosene lantern hung on a wooden peg; a rusted bucksaw shared a corner with a pile of ocotillo firewood. The user motioned his captives to one side in the gloom, stirring dust that hinted of leather and smoke of another time. He wrestled a loop of heavy cordage from pegs that helped form a low-slung pallet platform. He ordered the tall eyeless woman to turn around; approached her. The rifle made him clumsy, but knots could be made one-handed.

Val, acidly: "Why tie her up? You can see she's blind."

"She might wander. If she does, there are deep arroyos very near," he said for Laura's benefit. He quickly trussed Laura's hands. Val stared pointedly at the bucksaw, then let her gaze sweep the rest of the place. She knew that Laura was preternaturally acute in memorizing a spatial arrangement, using borrowed vision.

Never at her best under stress, Laura remained as calm as could be hoped. Her breathing became more rapid and shallow as she knelt, permitted her feet to be tied. The user glanced at Laura's face in satisfaction, then used the rifle to prod Val toward the low arch of the doorway.

Most of the sheep had been penned but of course there had been no need to pen the half-dozen 'D' marked user animals. Billichay skulked around them, left to fight any stray coyote and as living explanation to anyone who might have stumbled on the flock. The user of Hospah Ramirez herded Val Clarke to the group, bade her sit, then commenced a rapidfire monologue which contained a smattering of Spanish.

Val's confusion became an icy trickle in her veins as the sheep formed a mixed-sex ring, noses touching. The rifle held under one arm, 'Hospah' knelt, inserted a hand into the focal area without taking his gaze from his captive.

The dog slid on his belly toward the strange little anglo, finally thrust his muzzle into her lap. Val jerked around, saw frank terror and pleading in the honest eyes as the dog prepared to run, then offered her palm. Billichay wagged his tail and caressed the hand with his tongue. When one's personal god has become a demon, even a dog may seek new alliance. Val scratched the burr-encrusted head, keeping the hogan barely in view at the edge of her vision. Then she released a tiny smile before erasing its trace; a flicker of silver moved at the hogan before disappearing behind it. Laura had loosed her bonds.

Billichay lifted his head; some clumsy creature was moving near the hogan and as always, Billichay did his duty. His sharp bark of alarm gave Laura away.

The user raised the rifle, sprang back, instantly saw Laura as he followed the gaze of Billichay.

Laura moved upslope as adroitly as possible
using the vision of Val a hundred meters away.
When the rifle swung toward Laura, Val leaped
into the field of fire.

Billichay knew the firestick could kill, hated its
earsplitting report, concluded that it was to be
used against his newfound friend. He launched
himself at the figure that had once been Hospah
Ramirez. But Billichay was too well-trained and
too affectionate: he could not rip at the arm of a
small boy, even while he held it in his jaws.

Val took a step toward the melee, found herself
smashed to the ground by blunt curled horns,
swung hard to catch one ram across the nose as
she struggled to her knees. The dog rolled to one
side, saw the rifle swing toward him, tried the
best conciliatory gesture he knew: he sat up and
begged.

The blast, three rounds at close range, caught
Billichay full in the chest. He flew backward, a
leaf on a winter wind, and Val screamed. "Run,
Laura; run!"

The user with his rifle had the power and the
voice, trappings of leadership. Val knew the gist
of his piping commands when the sinister group
of sheep backed away and turned toward Laura at
rolling ungainly lopes. The user's face was devoid
of any sympathy for the valiant canine heart he
had burst. As she internalized this fact, Val lost
any hope she may have nurtured.

"Drive the car to the woman," he ordered.

Val made her decision then. She was going to
die: very well, she would take this small ghoul
with her, perhaps at top speed over the lip of a
nearby arroyo. Valerie Clarke straightened her
slender body and marched toward the Mitsubishi,

now in deep shadow as the sun touched the horizon.

The passenger door was still open. She grasped its handle, waited for her captor to precede her. He shook his head, waved her forward with the rifle, risked a glance toward the slopes. For a blind woman, the anglo was making good time. He had not guessed that Laura was using the vision of the user sheep as they neared her.

Val saw the rifle barrel swing within the arc of the door's travel and swung the door as hard as she could. The user was not quite quick enough; he clutched the weapon as the door, with Val's forty kilos behind it, clanged hard on gunmetal.

The door could not possibly have latched. The user planted a foot in Val's midriff as she fell against him, kicked as he levered the rifle like a pry bar. Val bent double. The door flew open again to catch her flush against the jaw, knocked her sprawling and inert.

The user was aware now that he could no longer depend on her fear, could compel her only by brute force, and made a snap decision. He aimed the rifle at her head, felt for the trigger.

And paused, staring. The barrel of the weapon was bent halfway down its length by Val's desperate lunge with the door. He knew it could be dangerous to fire a gun with a kinked barrel and, in any case, the anglo woman lay unconscious at his feet. They could use her later if she were immobilized. He dragged her five meters to a cornerpost of the sheep pen, watched by other wooly captives inside, and pried at baling wire that held two shed panels together. It was rusty stuff and it cut savagely into the woman's wrists as he twisted it tight before attaching it to the post. It would

serve; could not be chewed or easily cut. He left
her face down, his hands sticky with her blood,
and sprinted toward the scatter of sheep that quar-
tered a nearby slope. He took the rifle; it might
still be useful as a threat or a bludgeon.

Rai Koshare cursed as he saw his shadow
lengthen ahead of him, fade imperceptibly into
the sandstone of Chaco Wash. He had little better
reason than blind hope to suggest that he moved
toward Laura and Val. The wash took a bend
southward, then east again, and he paused at a
juncture of tributary gullies. To the right was
nothing but breeze in his face. To the left, nothing,
then something: the low recurrent *baa* of sheep.
He chose the left channel and urged his little
vehicle ahead.

Minutes later he saw the arroyo split into
branches, two broad reaches and several steep
defiles opening into a hollow at the foot of a butte,
its top salmon-pink in the sunset. He saw sheep
above him, light patches against the darker slope
near a precipitous defile, and then saw the small
figure trotting toward them. Nearby were the
penned stock, milling uncertainly away from the
smell of blood and complaining in the process.
Rai could not see the pickup behind the stock
shed, but spied the hogan. Perhaps the shepherd
had seen the Mitt. He stopped the electroped and
shouted for attention.

The small figure froze, jerked around, stared
below him. He identified Rai more by his clothing
and demeanor than anything else, knew that if Rai
had not seen the hidden pickup he might be persuaded to retrace his path. It might be possible for
'Hospah' to excuse himself long enough to smash

the little anglo's head before she could call an alarm. He might even get behind the archaeologist to club him. He traded glances with the nearest ram, called softly that they must find the blind woman who had so quickly found a crevice to hide her. He ran back down the slope quickly; he did not want the man to advance far enough to spot the pickup.

Rai recognized the face of Hospah Ramirez and relaxed. Hospah carried an orange chit in his pocket, even if that little rifle had probably been borrowed from Dinay's friends. Had Hospah seen a red pickup truck or heard anyone else in the past half-hour?

A puebleno shrug, more adult than childlike: not up this fork of the wash, the user lied. However, from the butte he had seen a car to the west, hurrying northward.

Rai wrenched the handlebars around, tears of rage and frustration in his eyes, determined to continue the chase until something broke. A new thought made him pause. The boy might even now be stalked by a loathsome presence, somewhere on the buttes. "Hospah, you've already lost a ewe south of here. You knew that, didn't you?"

A cautious affirmative.

Rai wondered how to warn the boy without unduly frightening him; looked away; and saw the corpse of Billichay spread in its own blood. He moved from the 'ped to the dog, looked back at the user and the rifle he carried. The weapon had been freshly battered. Rai's glance was a silent request for clarification.

"I shot him," the user admitted, and added with inspiration, "He was killing sheep."

Rai shook his head in commiseration; those had been the shots that led him on this fruitless sidetrack. He reached out to run a hand along the angle in the rifle barrel, and the user thought it prudent to let him. Rai grimaced, envisioning the plight of a boy who must kill his traitorous dog, venting his sorrowful anger by wrecking the weapon he had employed.

"I understand," said Rai, not understanding at all as he withdrew his hand. At that instant, the delayed awareness of his fingers flooded Rai Koshare: Oshara evil lay thick as grease on the rifle.

Rai's eyes took on a terrible brilliance in the dusk. To the user he seemed to loom three meters tall as Rai took a step forward, rumbling, "Where are my friends, you dog's piss?"

The user took a step back. "You sound crazy as an anglo," he blustered, then swung viciously with the gunbarrel. Rai ducked under it and then the user was scrabbling toward the slopes, looking for aid. One other user, in the guise of a ewe, was near enough to help. It opted for discretion, nestling unseen into sandstone detritus.

The user could no longer call on Billichay for help. There was a hatchet in the midden cache, and the user fled toward it. He saw that there would not be time to paw through the debris, turned atop the old mound and faced a transformed Raimondo Koshare who had now taken his own knife from his pocket.

"I know you," Rai snarled. "I don't know which one you are, but I know you. Where are the anglo women?"

The user waited until his nemesis was only two

paces away before he snatched the rifle to his
shoulder. With any luck at all, it still might kill.
He pulled the trigger.

It was a painless kill, instantaneous and unerr-
ing. A hissing metallic report accompanied the
ejection of the receiver mechanism as the slug
jammed halfway down the barrel. The receiver, a
tool-steel projectile the length of a finger, flew
backward and the head of the user snapped away
from its impact. Rai had thrown one hand before
his face, saw the body flung spreadeagled like
trash onto the midden. Rai leaped to grasp the
rifle as it clattered on stone. Then he saw it was
ruined, stood over the body of his enemy which
thrashed as an unseen controller found his helm
destroyed. Rai turned away suddenly with an ach-
ing sadness for Hospah Ramirez.

From his low promontory on the midden, Rai
peered through the gathering dusk past the
alarmed sheep in their pen, saw the hood of the
Mitt. Laura and Val could not be far away! He
yelled their names.

Val heard his shouts, but she needed time to
think beyond the cobwebs in her mind and the
pain at her wrists. Rai was already darting from
the empty hogan, calling brokenly, when he
heard her, "Help me! Is it Rai? Oh please God,
Rai?"

He fell on his knees beside her, straining to see
at close range without his glasses in the waning
light. She whimpered as he turned the wire in the
wrong direction, tried to help, and felt the rusty
bonds loosen. He hugged her, kissed the unpro-
testing mouth quickly as he pulled her to her feet.

Val steadied herself, rubbed her bloody wrists,
stammering. "The loose sheep, they're after

Laura. The Oshara people must be inside, Rai."
She staggered into the open, finding her bearings,
flinging an arm toward the butte. "They're searching for her up there but watch out; they attacked
me."

Rai had started for the butte but wheeled with
sudden recall, ripped the little canister from his
denims. "That's a gas projector," he said, and
flicked it experimentally. A thin stream, not of gas
but of a volatile liquid, spurted five meters
downwind. It seemed a useless toy. He shrugged,
laid it in Val's hand. "It may help," he said, and
started on a dead run toward the butte, its sides
wrinkled with black crevices as darkness
gathered.

They both heard Laura scream, a dopplered
"RaaaaI.II," from somewhere above them. He
lifted his deep voice as he ran, and bayed once
more for his lost love.

For a brief moment Laura had huddled behind
an outcrop that was streamlined by age-old
winds, as she strove to make use of the users. The
color vision of sheep, she found, was next to
nonexistent. They scuffled on loose rock, not so
sure-footed as true sheep but infinitely more sure
in their purpose. Her mental vision cleared as a
ram snuffled the air nearby, scanned her outcrop,
turned away. The approaching night brought her
a contrast of grays against black on the slope. She
hurried toward the deepest black, then caught a
clear image of herself as a Dinay ewe confronted
her across the stygian shadow. It baa-ed three
times sharply, flat ugly tones, and Laura knew
that she must flee again even as she heard what
seemed to be a familiar voice on the wind.

The ewe looked away and Laura's heart leaped. She 'saw' the user far below, turning back downslope. Someone stood near the hogan, foreshortened by terrain, but sheep vision did not permit a better view. Since the user was approaching him with apparent lack of concern she thought the newcomer must be another enemy and began to feel her way forward when no vision aided her. Finally she lay prone, blind, waiting. Once she heard a sharp report that could have been a gunshot, and feared that Val was dead.

For long minutes she lay where she was, hoping to be overlooked even in the open if she kept in shadow and utterly motionless. A ram, then a ewe, came near enough to glance past her. Then the first ram saw her clearly, gave the three-element alert, put his head down and charged.

Laura could not use the ram's impeded, head-down vision, dimly sensed the friendly blackness nearby, clawed toward it. Too late, her ears caught the subtle expansion of echo, and she reached back to cling with one arm at the lip of the precipice. The blackness was not a shadowed rock spur at all, but a vertical slice in the butte. Laura slid on the sharp decline, then whirled into nothingness. Her scream began as one name, blended into another, before she was broken on the tumble of sandstone fully fifteen meters below.

A Dinay ewe saw Rai first, turned aside from its upward course and tried, too clumsily for a sheep, to dodge past him. He caught it with a prodigious kick, forgetting the knife he held, and sent it crashing headfirst onto rocks far below. He watched it with fierce satisfaction until his eyes caught a gleam of silver-white in the narrow ravine, not far from the body of the ewe.

"She's down here," he cried to Val, who churned up the flank of the butte across the ravine from him. He pocketed the knife and launched his furious, sliding, leaping descent into the dark cleft.

Val saw the ram before it charged her, triggered the canister into its muzzle as she scrambled onto a chest-high boulder. The animal might have intended the three-element alarm call but never finished it, gasping, choking, writhing on its back. It managed only grunts as it lay twitching under the systemic assault of CS gas. Eyes wide with respect for the handful of power she wielded, Val palmed the little canister and moved upslope again. She knew that her own body was bait, but Val could exult: *this* bait held a formidable hook for the unwary.

A second ram saw her, gave the alarm, and trotted cannily near to await reinforcement. She registered fear, started downslope, then sprayed him as he suddenly ran toward her. He fell on the run, sliding toward her, and as Val turned to the onrushing ewe, it wisely veered off. Val pursued. The third ram approached the one she had first sprayed, incautiously placed its nose to that of the gasping victim for a brief exchange and then suddenly bounded away snorting. It was momentarily blind and Val caught it caroming off a boulder. She sprayed it unconscious. Now it was nearly dark but Val could see that the remaining ewe on the slope had a choice of charging her, or retreating. The user chose a wary retreat. Val caught it trying to traverse the ravine and sprayed it from above. The ewe fell all the way.

Val returned to her foes on the slope, spraying the fleece on their heads, satisfied at last that they

would not recover for some time. Val was no
climber; she approached the vertical drop opposite the place where Rai had descended with great
care. "I've got them all," she cried. She had failed
to keep a close tally; did not see the last isolated
user in a Dinay ewe, creeping away from the body
of Hospah Ramirez. A glistening ruddy mass was
slowly sinking into its fleece.

The drone of a mourning chant arose from the
throat of Rai Koshare, somewhere below. He
paused, calling hoarsely up to Val. "They've
killed her, Valerie," he howled; "*Laura is dying!
They deserve the same,*" he cried, subsiding, and
Val heard him speaking to Laura in a voice that
was mastered barely enough for coherence.

A wave of weakness passed over Val, to be replaced by an awful resolution. She visited the
nearby users one last time, choosing a hunk of
sandstone the size of her head. She could not have
said whether her tears were from chemical spray,
desolation over the loss of Laura, or revulsion at
the grisly executions that were her lot. When at
last she dropped the stone it was at the behest of
Rai, who was making his way out of the ravine's
mouth with the body of Laura Dunning. The path
downward was dangerous, truly no path at all, but
Val cared very little for that.

The Mitt's radiophone brought San Juan
County's only QRU craft from oil fields near
Bloomfield in near record time, and with a full-
fledged physician. He was much too late to pre-
serve life in the body of Laura. There had been, he
said, no real hope from the first. Then the team
sought the small corpse on the midden heap. This
time there could be little doubt that the boy had

died by accident; one eye socket was full of tool steel.

When the hovercraft lifted its pathetic burdens toward the north, its running lights a varicolored shadow play on the arroyo, Rai walked with Val to the pickup. He had done with crying, he told her, after sharing Laura's last moments. Val looked away sullenly. Men, she supposed, could compartment their minds in little boxes—especially when one big box was such an intolerable burden.

The lone surviving Dinay ewe comprised the sorriest kind of vehicle for seven users. Physical control was chiefly performed by the ex-Chuzo, but he could not persuade his fellows to remain entirely in the animal's fleece. With great stealth —indeed, with a desperate valor—the user found two crumpled sheep in the ravine, patiently endured the discomfort of CS gas traces, and in each case found the user more than ready to transfer to a mobile host. Full darkness had fallen before the 'ewe' found its way to the upper slope and, guided by odor, located each of Val Clarke's victims. The users sucked sustenance from the ewe's body while they exuded chitinous shells over those portions that lay within the fleece. Had anyone seen the animal stumbling toward the penned stock, he would have marveled at the patches of gleaming flexible carapace spotting her broad back.

The approach of the QRU with its dazzling spotlights had seemed to suggest military action. The ewe waddled at top speed down the deepest part of the wash and took the path of least resistance. Chaco Wash led to the Pueblo Bonito ruin where other shepherds often grazed their stock. It was a gamble, and the animal's physical resources

would be heavily taxed. But like any other host,
the animal was expendable.

Rai loaded the stolen electroped into the Mitt
while the engine's clatter steadied to a hum. Val's
questions to the not-Hospah, Rai said, had
triggered answers which Laura had passed to
him. "Without a host, they'd lose moisture and
die like any other animal," he said. "And the
entire lot of them were all in Hospah and the loose
sheep. They had a horror of being left in a dead
host on the desert," he said, pleased. "And I'd
rather that happened, than go fooling around up
there after them in the dark."

Val watched the headlights bob as the Mitt
started back along Rai's route. "Laura, Laura; she
never ceased to amaze me. Imagine spending your
last moments like a spy with crucial information.
Guts. It just makes me love her more," she sighed,
blinking away tears.

"Thank you," Rai said, as if in loving parody of
Laura's drawl.

"Unfunny," Val replied, and changed the subject. "Where are we going now?"

"Home, by way of Pueblo Bonito road," he said,
and wrenched the wheel hard to the left, avoiding
a boulder.

Neither of them noticed the ewe which had
stumbled forward, searching for cover, at the
sound of the approaching Mitt. Since there was no
adequate cover, the user dropped into a slight
hollow to one side of the arroyo bottom, unmoving, waiting for the vehicle to thunder past. It
could not react before Rai slewed the wheels into
the hollow. The left front wheel hammered across
the animal's back, rolled it once, and the rear
wheel tore through a yielding mass in its fleece.

"Sorry; didn't see that hole," Rai muttered, and sped on. He was explaining to Val that if the parasites were extraterrestrial as Laura thought, he had some knotty decisions to make about exploiting the Oshara site.

Darkness returned to Chaco Wash as the Mitt rumbled westward, the lights and stink of its exhaust dying away. The coyote lifted her nose on the breeze, followed the scent through dusty bottoms toward a fresh kill. Her cubs would feed well this night, she thought, circling warily around the sheep that still twitched on the stones. She drifted nearer, puzzled by the acid taint, cocked her ears toward the faint susurrus within the fleece.

The coyote waited, indolent, relying on her ears and nose to tell more about this potential feast. Something flowed from the dead sheep; something thicker than blood, moving toward her. She took a dainty step over it, anointed it with precision, and listened as another semiliquid mass dropped from the carcass. Her hackles swelled at the stench. Coyotes had not survived this long by falling on every poisoned carcass tossed into arroyos by men. The coyote spun, kicked grit upon the offering, trotted away for a less malign meal.

The users exuded their chondroprotein as best they could, and waited for the dawn. At sunup they would find that they lay between the sheep and an ant hill. And from the sun and the ants there would be no appeal. It was the land, as always, that triumphed.

Valerie Clarke groaned with pleasure as she emerged from sleep, stretched her arms from the pallet. She had been awakened this way many times by Laura's gentle scalp massage. Then she remembered; her eyes flew open to meet those of Rai Koshare who knelt beside her. "Morning," he said as she sat up. "Thought you might like some breakfast."

"I thought you were—Laura," Val whispered, then put her face into her hands. "Oh, God, Rai; you'll have to give me a minute."

"There'll be lots of time—if you're willing to stay as you promised last night."

"Last night was tequila talking," she said, "and exhaustion. I don't know about staying, Rai. I've taken about as much as I can."

He rumbled gently, "I know that. It's why I'm telling you some things gradually. We—well, I want you to stay. As long as you will." He smiled, a warm entreaty, and spots of red showed over the high cheekbones as he went on quickly, "I'm not very good at this, so let me just blurt it out. We've shared a lot, but not enough; share my work and my pallet. Yep, that's what I wanted to say."

Val leveled a glare at him. "I get the picture. God knows I've watched you paint it! So I throw in with you, and the second I turn my back you'll crawl on somebody else's bones for lagniappe! Well, you can stuff it, Tonto. I won't play that way, and I won't have a man that does."

"Laura isn't just somebody else. She's part of us both." A hesitation, almost a quote: "More than you think, Val."

Val turned agonized eyes to heaven, shook tears aside angrily. "Now you've become an expert on Laura in a week's time."

"More like a few minutes," a voice replied. It was the gentle rumble of Rai Koshare, and simultaneously it was not. "Be nice, Deenie; this isn't easy for him either."

Deenie: diminutive of Val's first name, Dina, and used only by Laura Dunning in moments of endearment. The accent, the intonation were both Laura's. Weak with confusion, brittle with something akin to fright, Val stood. She was at rigid attention. "Don't do that," she begged. "Please, if you have any compassion—"

"It's already done, Val." Rai again. He reached out and she came to him, unresisting but enervated, very near collapse. He swept her up, eased into a sitting position to hold her in his lap, doll-like.

She laid her head on his shoulder, the tears streaming freely now. "You don't understand how that sounds," she sobbed.

"I know exactly," he said. "I'm hearing it too, you know. It's a depth of sharing I never expected to know, and I'm—forgive me, Laura—I'm not comfortable with it yet. Val, just listen. Please."

He felt her listless shrug, took it for agreement, went on. "I felt that Laura was dying back there in the ravine. In a sense, of course, she was. But I was right about my tactile sense somehow matching Laura's telepathy. It did, literally. When I cupped my hands around her poor fractured skull, it became a two-way channel. Maybe it could only happen under extremes; maybe—I don't know.

"I couldn't bear to lose the essence of her, not physically so much as internally. Her memories, hopes, willingness to share; her love of life—and of you, Val. Then we realized we were sharing her mind, all of it pouring into me. And I asked her to come in and stay if she possibly could."

Slowly, in a disbelieving haze, Val straightened to stare into his face as Rai—but again it was no longer Rai's voice pattern—went on. "I was in such pain, Deenie," said the drawl-soft voice. "I know I took advantage of him, but I was so awfully hurt, so terribly afraid of dying.

"And suddenly it seemed that I could invest Rai with myself, I don't know how else to say it. He asked me to come in, and here I am. Most of me, at least. There wasn't time to share everything, so I left some of my childhood behind." A platinum laugh, entirely Laura: "I traveled light, so to speak."

So to speak: another of her pet phrases. Yet it was no longer an irritant, but validation of the seemingly impossible. The awesome fact of Laura's presence within Rai Koshare was almost beyond Val's grasp. She placed trembling fingertips on his face, and she did not realize that she was smiling past her tears. "You always did enjoy taking a dump in somebody else's drawers," she murmured. "Now you've made Rai a schizo. Bitch," she added tenderly, the smile becoming a grin.

"I don't think it will go on like this," said the Laura voice. "I hope I can settle into being a part melded into Rai. But I can't tell what you're thinking anymore, and I miss it. Tell me."

"Go to hell," was Val's artificially gay response, the tough shield by which she had learned to protect her tenderness. "A little privacy might improve our relationship."

Now it was undeniably Rai speaking: "I thought I'd be complete, with Laura sharing my awareness like this, Val. You know, it might be an advantage not to need anybody. But it only makes me need *you* more. For what it's worth, I'm afraid I—love you," he said, tasting the phrase as though

it were his first experience with cream sherry.
"Will you give me time to prove it?" He started to
go on, stammered, said, "Be fair, Laura. She can
make up her own mind," and fell determinedly
silent, his gaze on Val.

Val Clarke drew on reserves of strength from
some hidden wellspring, stood up, walked to the
fireplace and turned to study the swarthy strong
face. "I don't know. I don't know if I could juggle
two double-handfuls like you both in one package." She began to pace, stopping twice to stare
at Rai, each time resuming with a half-snort,
half-chuckle. Rai sat placidly, hands on his knees,
patient as only a puebleno can be patient. At last,
Val strode to him and placed her hands on his
shoulders. "What was Laura going to say to convince me?"

His flush was barely detectable before the headshake. "I'm running my show," he said, im-
penetrable.

Val nodded. "Good. But you can give me a
hint."

The prominent Koshare nostrils flared momentarily; a smile threatened to break out. All he
would say was, "It had to do with making love."

"Uh-huh! I knew it, Laura. You figure I'd be
crazy to refuse the best of both beddy-bye
worlds?" She waited, expecting to hear a response from Laura.

Rai clamped his lips, burst out laughing at some
internal dialogue, recovered. "She knows how to
take advantage," he said to Val, and added to
something within himself, "If you don't shut up
I'll slap my face."

At this, Val raised her hands helplessly. "Listen
you two: if you think I'm going to spend the rest of

the day, much less all summer, with a bisexual
schizophrenic I'm ditsy about, and who knows
how to turn me every way but loose on cold
nights—you are absolutely right, damn you. I'll
give it a try, for my own selfish reasons. No promises beyond that; I'll try not to go bonkers.

"I wouldn't agree, Rai, if it weren't so obvious
that you've got my sex-sodden lady friend under
control. Just keep her that way and maybe we'll
last through the day."

It proved to be a long summer, with unseasona-
bly chill nights in the remote high desert country.
Valerie Clarke was rarely moved to complain
about the weather—or about Raimondo Koshare.

POSTLUDI

The social behavior of the ants after consuming
the users.

Attempts to worship the Ogre Katcina as San Saba
gradually becomes overpopulated.

Tyende, the Navajo clairvoyant. His sensing of the
serenity beam as the Song of the Female Other.
Tyende's cult and its success in reclaiming that
spot from the desert. The squatters.

Gradual recovery of some of Laura's powers, and
Rai's objection in behalf of Val. 'Divorce' of Rai
and Laura; reconciliation.

Val's brief return to Chris Maffei; Maffei's genuine
empathy and aid. Contact between Maffei and
Laura at Mesa Verde ruins.

DEVIL YOU DON'T KNOW

Maffei, brushing at his cheap suit, produced his papers with confidence. They were excellent forgeries. "I dunno the patient from whozis," he said. "Will she need sedation? A jacket?"

The receptionist was your standard sanitarium model: stunning, crisp, jargony, her uniform a statement of medical competence as spurious as Maffei's authorization. "Dina Valerie Clarke," she read. "I did an ops transfer profile on her. If I may see your ID, sir?" It was not really a question.

Both driver's license and psychiatric aide registration were genuine enough. Neither card hinted that this stocky aide, Christopher Maffei, was also MD, PhD, and in his present capacity, SPY. To stay in character he rephrased his question while surrendering the cards. "Will the kid need restraint?"

"It doesn't say," she murmured, returning his ID. "We can sign her over to you after your exit interview."

"My interview? Lady, I'm just the taxi to some clinic in Nebraska."

"It's only a formality," she purred, fashioning him a brief bunny-nose full of sexual conspiracy.

Maffei avoided laughing. In three years of residency and five of research, he had observed enough morons to be a passable simulacrum on his own. "I never done that before," he lied. He had listened to these sales pitches only too often. "Can I use your phone? Dr. Carmichael can talk to you from Springfield . . . ."

"Sign here, please, and here, and there," in ten-below tones.

Maffei smiled and signed. *You're beaten by invincible ignorance*, he thought. *Maybe we should start a club.* He straightened and looked around, realizing that the receptionist had buzzed for Val Clarke.

She came toward him slowly at first down the long hallway, made smaller by her outsized luggage. It was very expensive luggage, the guilt-assuaging hardware a wealthy parent would provide for an unwanted child. Chris still chafed at what it had cost him.

As Val neared him, he saw that her hair had been shorn almost to the scalp. Lice, probably. Her height was scarcely that of a ten-year-old. The frail angular body, still too large for her head, was yet too small for its oddly misaligned and bovine eyes. She wore the same white ankle socks, slippers, and trousers she'd had when entering Nodaway Retreat two weeks before. Her smiling gaze swept up to his, then past, and she broke into a stumbling skip toward the entrance.

"You must be Valerie Clarke," Maffei said with forced gaiety, catching gently at her pipestem wrist.

The vacant smile foundered. A silent nod. No more skipping; the girl stood awaiting whatever this vast authoritarian world might dictate.

"Let's get you to an ice-cream cone," Maffei said, letting her bring the suitcases. He maintained the running patter while strapping her into his electric four-seater and stowing the luggage behind. "I bet you'd like a Frostylite, hm?"

Tucking his slight paunch under the steering wheel, Maffei whirred them toward the automatic gate. It slid aside, then back, as they emerged onto the highway. Val Clarke slumped in her seat with a lip-blubbering parody of released tension. "Oh come on, Val, it can't be that bad," Maffei smirked.

"Not for you it can't. It isn't your screwed-up implants, pal, you try running an inside surveillance with an intermittent transceiver short sometime and I'll patronize you."

He glanced from the road to her, reached out to her tiny skull and gently stroked behind her ear. "No swelling. If it were a mastoid infection you'd know it for sure."

The girl shrugged upward in her seat, barely able to see over the battery cowl ahead. "I'll survive. Well, what do you make of Nodaway Retreat?"

"Typical ultraconservative ripoff," he mused, barely audible over the hum and tire noise. "From your reports I make it one staff member per twenty patients, minimal life-support for everyone concerned except for the up-front crew; one honest-to-God RN and a pair of general practitioners who look in once a month from Des Moines to trade sedatives for fees."

"I've seen worse. Remember Ohio?"

Maffei nodded sagely. Val Clarke had scarcely been admitted when her transmissions began to read like a bedlam litany. Rickettsia and plain starvation, a 'bad ward' where three children of normal intelligence were chained, and a nightly victimization of youthful male patients by the staff. "That's what my survey is about; to change all that. It was the worst I ever saw," he admitted.

Val flicked him a quick glance but Maffei intended no sarcasm. He had seen two staff members wearing masks of outraged innocence, and strap marks on Val's thin calves after the general warrant had been served—really more raid than service, brought on by Val's moment-to-moment account via her minuscule implanted transceiver. In the space of thirty-six hours Val had seen two compound femur fractures on a girl who had jumped from her high window, and a gang assault of one profoundly retarded child by besmocked thugs. The worst Maffei had seen in Ohio was not precisely the worst Val Clarke had seen; but then, Maffei bore no stigmata of retardation.

It was Valerie Clarke's tragedy to have been born with an autosomal dominant inheritance which was instantly diagnosed as mental retardation. The astonishing width between her eyes had a name of its own: hypertelorism. It explained nothing except that Val's great brown orbs were set a trifle too far apart to please a society which, paradoxically, distrusted eyes set too close together. Her lustrous roan hair normally covered a skull which, from its small size, also had a special stigma with label attached: microcephaly. Her ears flared a bit, particularly noticeable now that her hair was shorn, and at twenty-two, Val Clarke passed for twelve even without her training bra.

Any competent specialist could adjust to the fact that Val's intelligence was normal, her motivation superb—a recipe for 'genius.' The unadjusted expectation was something else again. Val, an early victim of maldiagnosis and parental rejection, knew the signs of a good sanitarium from the inside because she had experienced enough bad ones in childhood.

When Val was thirteen, a suspicious young interne named Chris Maffei taught her basic algebra and the scatology of three foreign languages to prove his point. After that, her schooling was more formal if not exactly conventional. Any girl who patterned herself after Chris Maffei could junk the word 'convention' at the outset, with the obvious exception of medical conventions where Chris read scholarly papers and pumped for any grant money he could locate.

Now Chris was a year into a fat HEW grant to study the adequacy of private mental homes; and if he had not actually suggested that Val volunteer for commitment in these places, he had not omitted oblique hints at the notion. Nor turned down her offer. It was a symbiosis: Maffei had his spy, Val her spymaster.

"Hey," she said. He looked around and, briefly, laid his hand over the one she offered palm up. "Thanks for reeling me in so fast."

One corner of his mouth went up. "Had to. That short was interfering with my favorite live soap opera."

"Schmuck," she said tenderly—Maffei had never entirely managed to socialize her language. "Speaking of soap, you could introduce Nodaway to the idea."

"I'll note it when I debrief you after supper. I was in the army with a geepee near here. If I know Farr, he'll do an Onward Christian Soldiers when I send him my notes on the place."

"Fine. And by the way, good guru, you just passed a Frostylite. You p'omised," she added, expertly faking a vocal retardation slur.

"First things first. We need a battery recharge to make Joplin tonight."

Startled: "Why Joplin, of all places? That's south."

"Because I have you scheduled fo a scrub-up and transceiver check there tonight. And because after that we're going into the deep south."

She was silent but he lip-read her response: *Oh my God.*

After the Joplin stop, Maffei's little sedan hummed on barrel tires toward Mississippi. Val failed to concentrate on Durrell's *Clea.* The source of her unease was not the September heat, but the fact that she had slept at the clinic in Joplin. Chris lavished care on her as he would on a rare and exorbitant device, but she did not delude herself on the point. Val needed a secure relationship and physical human warmth. Very well then: he shared motel rooms with her. She also needed passionate attention, as anyone might when in constant proximity to a beloved. Chris dutifully pleased her when, on rare occasions, she was insistent enough. The one thing Valerie Clarke could not elicit from Chris was his desire.

Durrell's velvet prose wasn't helping Val's mood. She studied her reflection in the car window. *Ms. Universe I'm not. If I expect this sex-object of mine—okay, twenty pounds overweight and why shouldn't he be?—to come fawning over my Dumbo ears I'm worse than microcephalic, I'm scatocephalic.* She traced a tentative forefinger along the pink smoothness of one ear.

At least she had perfect skin. "Chris, why do you put me out before making the transceiver check if you don't make an incision?"

He yawned before answering, flexing strong hands on the wheel. "We do, Val. Those antennae are so fine I can run 'em just inside the dermis, on the fossa of your helix—uh, inside your ear rim. A microscalpel does it; almost no bleeding and it heals quick as boo. But I have to keep you abso-bloody-lutely still. Same for the X-ray check on your implant circuitry. It's a whole lot bigger in area than it might be, since I wanted it spread out for easy maintenance."

"You didn't cut down to the mastoid?"

"No need to fix the resonator; I just incised a tiny slit to your circuit chip. It was a hairline circuit fracture, just right for laser repair. Total heat doesn't amount to a paramecium's hotfoot, using the miniaturized Stanford rig. See, you don't *have* to hurt the one you love," he grinned.

"I'll remind you of that after supper."

He clucked his tongue in mock dismay, still grinning. Message clear, will comply, out. She returned to Durrell as the kilometers hummed away.

The supper hush puppies in Vicksburg were a pleasant surprise, not by being in the least digestible but in their lingering aftertaste. When she and Chris vented simultaneous belches later, her fit of giggles might have caused a lesser man to make war, not love. All credit to the Maffei mystique, she decided still later, as she lazed on the motel bed and watched Chris attack his toenails. "You never told me how you got those mangled toes," she murmured. "We beautiful people are repelled by physical deformity, y'know."

He looked up, preoccupied, then grinned. "Same way I got this," he rubbed his finger over the broken nose that gave him a faintly raffish look. "Soccer. Did I ever tell you I once played against Pelé?"

She fetched him a wondering smile. "Wow; no."

Deadpan: "Well, I never did—but Lord knows what I may've told you." Dodging the flung pillow, he went on. "You'd best save your energy for tomorrow, Val. We'll be delivering you up to the graces of Gulfview Home around noon."

Retrieving the pillow, she placed it in her lap and hugged it, eyes half closed, dreaming awake. "A view of the gulf will be nice. I hope this is a clean place—and please, God, air-conditioned."

"Don't count on it. It's forty kilometers from the gulf; how's that for an auspicious start?"

She shrugged. "It figures. But why this place? We're kind of off our itinerary." She wriggled beneath the covers, hiding her thin limbs.

He put away his clippers and reached for the lightplate, waving it to a diffuse nightlight. "A tip from HealthEdWelfare," he said, swinging under the coverlet. After a long pause he added, "You'll have a contact inside: a Ms. May Endicott. She won't know about you, but she knows something, I guess. And an insider's tip is a good place to start. Better the devil you know, and all that. I'll find out what sent her running to HEW after we commit you. Most likely a snoopy old dowager with fallen arches and clammy handshake." He grew silent, realizing that Val's response was the softest of snores. Chris Maffei fell asleep wondering if Gulfview and old Ms. Endicott would fit his preconceptions.

Gulfview Home squatted precisely in the center of its perimeter fencing; held its white clapboard siding aloof like skirts from the marauding grass. Viewing the grounds, it was hard to imagine much organized recreation for patients. Chris identified himself to the automatic gate, then rolled his window back up to escape the muggy air. In silence, they pulled up before the one-story structure.

Their expectations followed earlier studies which, since the 1950s, had always shown higher per capita need for institutional treatment in the southeast—and lower per capita effectiveness. The region was catching up; but, in 1989, still lagged. To Chris it was a problem in analysis. To Val, stumbling up Gulfview's steps with her luggage, the first problem was a dread akin to stage-fright. It always was, and as always, she hid her fear from Chris. The air conditioning was a relief but a new fear sidled up to Val when they found the receptionist. She was, and wasn't, old Ms. Endicott.

Chris saw that Ol' Miz. Endicott had very high arches for such small feet. He stood watching as May Endicott ushered a vacant-eyed Val Clarke from the reception room. A waist he could span with two hands, but la Endicott hourglassed to very nice extremes. Rather like a pneumatic gazelle by Disney, he judged.

Endicott boasted thick brown curls. "Dye-job," was Val's whispered aside as she stumbled, entirely in character, with her luggage. But Chris was not listening.

The Endicott woman returned in moments, to help Chris complete papers placing Val Clarke squarely in the hands of a private jail—or asylum, rehab home, whatever it might prove to be. "We were expectin' you, but the senior staff are busy at the moment. The child's history seems well-documented," she remarked in a soft patrician drawl. "Do you think she might be a trainable?"

Chris hesitated. A trainable might have free run of the place, or might be closely watched if it were more of a prison. Suddenly he remembered that May Endicott was, after all, a potential ally. "Depends on how good you are, I guess," he said. "I'm told you're concerned for the patients."

"We try—I think," she said as if genuinely pondering.

"I mean you, personally."

A flicker of subtlety in the dark sloe eyes. "I can't imagine who . . ."

"Just a friend in the discipline," he said easily. "Henry E. Wilks. How's that for a set of initials?"

"I don't . . ." she began, and then she did. "Well," she said in a throaty whisper. It set Maffei atingle. "And what are all the Wilkses doin' these days?"

"Waiting to hear from me," he replied, enjoying the respect in her oval face. "And I'm waiting to hear from you. I don't need to meet the staff just yet."

"I'm in the book. M.A. Endicott, in town. Perhaps this evenin'?"

He nodded and continued with the forms, pointedly sliding a blank set into his disreputable attaché case. As he rose, he noted that May Endicott's hands trembled. Anticipation? Fear?

Chris made a leisurely trip into town, bought a sandwich, then found the Endicott address. It was after five PM when he parked. He began to study the commitment forms—the fine print could sometimes raise hackles—and remembered the barbecue sandwich. During his third bite he remembered Val Clarke and fumbled for his comm unit. Although the major amplification and tight-band scrambling modes were built into the car, they also enhanced the signal to and from his pocket unit. Without the car, his range was perhaps two kilometers. With it, over thirty. Val, behind high fencing and well beyond the town limits, should be within range. But you never knew . . . .

He thumbed the voice actuator. The cassette, as usual, was recording all transmission into the system. "Val? How'sa girl? I haven't heard a peep." *Nor thought about one*, he told himself. He waited for a moment and was about to try again.

"i gave up on you around suppertime," the speaker replied. Implant devices did not yet rival conventional transmission. Val could receive a voice with fair fidelity but could only transmit by subvocalizing. With lips parted slightly she could transmit almost silently and as well as, say, a tyro ventriloquist; but bone conduction and minute power sources had their limitations. Val Clarke's nuances of intonation and verbal style were sacrificed for the shorthand speech of covert work. In short, she sounded very like a machine. Maffei would have denied that he preferred it that way.

"I was doing errands. And it's only getting to be suppertime now," he objected.

"not when you're running a money mill," Val replied. "it's on cassette. these people use patients to serve meals—and to cook 'em, from the taste of it. yuchhh."

"If you're bitching about the food you can't have much worse on your mind."

"yeah? try thinking of me in here on an army cot, and you outside with miz handy cot."

"Endicott," he chuckled at the mike. "I'll review the tape later. What else is new?"

"i'm in isolation 'til they figure how to use me, i think. two males, a female, all young and retarded, doing chores."

He thought for a moment. "Good therapy for 'em, unless the chores include lobotomies and group gropes. Who's in charge?"

"you got me, chris. and i wish you did, this doesn't smell right. quiet as a tomb in my room with very soft wallpaper and no view at all. when i say isolated, i mean locked away. but the kids gave me a toy."

"Something educational?"

"a rubber duckie, swear to god. well, they're nice kids."

"Look; I have some reading to do, and a session with the Endicott lady so we can plan. I'll check with you later. Don't eat your duckie."

"same to you, fella," in monotonic reply. He smirked at the speaker but no answer seemed very useful. He pocketed the comm unit and returned to his sandwich and forms.

Although commitment forms varied, they generally claimed almost total control over their wards. Chris Maffei had doctored Val's record to assure that she would not be subjected to insulin shock treatment, surgery, or unusual medication. The forms implied that Gulfview could damned well amputate her head if they chose, but there were safeguards against such treatment. For one thing, Val could transmit her plight and get help from Maffei. Or, if it came to that, she could simply admit her charade. In sixteen previous investigations, she had never blown her cover.

Maffei was munching a pickle slice when he saw the steam plume of the bus, two blocks away. It slid past him a moment later, slowing to disgorge the unmistakeable form of May Endicott. She had a very forthright stride, he decided, and admired it until she disappeared into her apartment. The pickle disposed of, Maffei crammed the forms into his attaché case and grunted, sweating, from the car. Val was right, he'd have to watch his weight.

At his knock, the door whisked open. May Endicott tugged him in by a sleeve, darting quick looks over his shoulder at her innocent shrubbery. She shut the door just as quickly and jumped at his reaction. "Gentlemen don't usually laugh at me."

"They should, if you treat 'em like jewel thieves," Maffei grinned. Beneath the makeup, he saw, she was quite young. "A poor beginning, ma'am. We really don't have anything to be furtive about, do we?"

The faintest relaxation of erect shoulders, and: "I'm not sure, Mr. Moffo."

"Maffei; Dr. Christopher Maffei, Johns Hopkins, to be insufferable about it," he said, getting the expected response. "Can we sit?"

She had a merry musical laugh of her own, waving him to a couch between stacks of periodicals. He saw several journals on abnormal psychology and special education. Idly he checked the issue numbers as they talked. His first goal was to put this talent centerfold at ease, simply done by asking her to talk about herslf.

May was agreeable to the low-key interrogation. Modestly raised in Montgomery; a two-year nursing certificate with notions of an RN to come; parents retired; summer work in a state hospital. "I don't know if I have a callin'," she finished, "but I like to feel I'm bein' used well."

"You will be," Maffei said cryptically, and flipped back the journal he held. "Thought I might find myself here. Just a small reference," he added with exaggerated modesty.

She saw him referenced by another author and looked away. "You embarrass me, Dr. Maffei; I should've recognized your name."

"Hey, none of that," he laughed. "I'm Chris and you're May, if you don't mind it. You seemed jumpy and I wanted to reassure you, that's all. Want my full ID?"

She sat back, relaxed, strong calves crossed fetchingly as he glanced through his cards. Maffei had a rising sense that this would be one of his more pleasant investigations. "Understand, May, I hope you're wrong about your job. As you know, private homes run a long gamut from excellent to atrocious." She nodded, beginning to pour an apertif.

"I can't survey every asylum in the country, but the HEW agreed to pick up the tab for a little—" he searched for an Endicott trigger-word "—chivalrous snooping. I have no official standing beyond what the AMA lends me, which is vague enough, God knows. But soon I'll have a fair sampling of the virtues and vices of private sanitariums. Who's mistreating patients? What staff training is most needed? Where should the gummint step in? Not exactly cloak-and-dagger stuff, May, but not the questions your average institutional exec likes to hear." He did not add that the book from his research might be a muck-raking bestseller.

"So you don't ask out loud," she prompted.

"Right; I try to find someone like you, and whisper in her ear."

Rising smoothly, she purred, "Well, now I know you're really a doctor. Developin' your bedside manner." Maffei realized his gaffe too late and refused to admit it was accidental. "Let's say my Freudian half-slip is showing and let it go," he said. "I mean, no, dammit, that's not what I meant." A pause. "Do you have this effect on everybody?"

She stood quietly, reaching some internal decision. Then, "It's a problem," she admitted, with a sunburst grin that took Maffei by frontal assault. "Physician, heal thyself."

"It may take some patchwork," he chuckled, "but bear with me."

A nod; slow and ageless.

"Professionally, I need you to check on a list of things. You reported that the last receptionist had no specialized training, was lucky to have the job, but seemed anxious to leave. And when she left, she did it in style. Expensive car and so on."

"A Lotus Cellular, no less," May put in. "And I know Lana Jo Fowler's family and they couldn't support that kind of spo'ty habit."

"Maybe she had sugar-daddy support?"

"That's how she let on," May said, "but she wouldn't say that if it were true. I think she was bein' paid off. I don't know what for, Lana Jo was no dumplin', and no brain either.

"Then there's Dr. Tedder," she continued, "I mean both Drs. Tedder, Lurene and Rhea." It did

not escape Maffei that she named the woman first.
"They live on the ground and I don't see him
much, but he isn't my idea of a doctor, more like a
wino, and she—is—a—sight; a proper *sight*," she
finished, rolling her eyes melodramatically.

"You haven't mentioned the honcho."

"Dr. Merkle? Rob Merkle is unmentionable,
maybe that's why. Those soft sausage hands; but
when he keeps 'em to himself he's competent. I'll
say this, he knows where every penny goes."

"No doubt. Well, I need data like, where Merkle
and the Tedders did their residencies, what's the
cost of boarding a patient, the sources of referrals,
types of therapy, type and dosage of drugs pre-
scribed and by whom, dietician's schedule . . ."

"Whew," with lips pursed in kissable fashion,
Maffei thought. "That's a tall number."

"I haven't begun," he said sadly.

"We both have," she smiled. "I smell cheap
barbecue sauce on you but could you use a shrimp
salad anyway?"

"A small one. Need help?"

"It's woman's work," she said, surprising him
again by her atavism. By the end of the evening,
May had a long list of Maffei's professional needs
and a sketchy idea of his personal ones. Never
once did he mention Valerie Clarke. He could not
have said exactly why.

Val awoke to depressingly familiar voices, muffled by the padding on her walls. It was not the
timbre of a remembered person but the quasilin-
guistic chanting of mentally retarded children
that she recognized. Aware that the staff might be
watching by monitor, Val lay on her musty bedding and played with her fingers. She recon-

structed the ward's morning by inference from the subdued noises. A parrotlike male recited a holovision commercial with astonishing fidelity: one trainable, sure as hell. Footsteps, peals of animal glee, angry hoots in their wake; horseplay, probably unsupervised and therefore dangerous. A bucket dropped (kicked?) hard and a howl of dismay; some poor MR klutzing his cleaning chores. Every few minutes, shuffling thumps at her door. Val gave up on that one and lay back to give her fingers a rest.

Her door swung open so quickly that Val jumped. It was no trick to register a fearful MR grimace. The heavy door seemed a trifle to the dray horse muscles of Dr. Lurene Tedder. The pale deepset eyes flanked an aquiline Tudor nose, and Val sensed great stamina in Lurene Tedder's hundred and seventy pounds. Yet the most striking feature was hair, seemingly tons of it, a cascade of blue-black tresses spilling over her shoulders, an emblem utterly female crowning the stocky woman.

A voice fortified with testosterone: "Hello, Valerie. Time for us to get up." A practice smile fled across the face, to be replaced by a gaze that promised to miss very little. "Do we understand?"

Val waited a moment to nod assent, then stood, hands at her sides.

"Can we talk? Dr. Lurene, can we say that? Dr. Lurene," the big woman crooned.

My, but she loves the sound of that, Val thought. She nodded.

"Then *say* it, you . . . try and say it, Valerie."

Val said it in unfeigned fright. Lurene Tedder's ignorance of MR training was so blatant that Val wondered momentarily if she were being baited

by a patient. "Docta Luween," she said again,
dully, and again.

Lurene Tedder nodded, again treated Val to a
smile; but this time it lingered: "I think we're
gonna work out fine."

And the operative word is 'work,' Val thought.
She risked a hint of a smile with eyes that begged
for acceptance. Only half of it was pretense.

Lurene Tedder motioned Val from the cell and
Val, scurrying to comply, nearly collided with
May Endicott. Thrusting a folder brusquely at
May, the Tedder woman produced an expensive
hairbrush and, sweeping it through her one glory,
hurried off. "Find something therapeutic for this
one," she flung over a broad shoulder.

May, placing a gentle hand on Val's arm, called,
"Were you going to do an assessment?" Her tone
implied that Tedder had merely forgotten.

"Oh sure, yeah," as the big woman sailed on
from the ward, her voice booming louder. "Send
her to, uh, our office about three."

Thick steel-faced fiber doors swung to and fro
in Lurene Tedder's wake. Val looked straight
ahead, half-fearing that eye contact with May Endicott would reveal too much. May aspirated a
bitter sigh, then brightened as she turned to Val.
"I'm goin' to introduce you to some people, Valerie," she promised. These were the first friendly
words Val had heard and, almost, she began to
forgive May Endicott her splendor in gender.

May did not hurry, nor ask questions of Val, but
maundered, talking easily, from one patient to
another down the row of beds. Val noted the
linolamat floor approvingly; you could fall on it
without harm, yet May's virginally white,
whorishly spiked heels left no indentation. Why

must the woman flaunt it so? The floor's barely
perceptible slope led to a small drainage grate in
the ward center; Val thought herself petty to hope
a highstyle heel might catch in it. She let details
register without quick eye movement, indexing
data with mnemonic tricks Chris had taught her.
This was Val's metier and, doing it well, she out-
paced her fears for the moment.

But: *Why doesn't she slip me the high sign,* Val
thought. She and Chris always chose a fresh code
word for ID and a general all-is-well signal, but
May Endicott had not used it.

May broke into the reverie: "Is there anything
you'd like to see especially, Valerie?"

After a long pause for pseudoserious pondering: "Chitlins?"

Val privately admitted that the Endicott bimbo
had a nice laugh. "Well, not today anyway. We're
havin' a fortified soup—" as if to herself adding,
"what else?"

Val pointed to a patient May had ignored. "Big
Boy," she slurred.

May smiled again at this wholly understated
description, then walked to the end bed. Val
stepped near and gazed upon a mountain of flesh.
It was alive, in a way.

"This is Gerald Rankine," May began. Doubtless, she did not expect Val to understand much,
but persisted. Rankine was eighteen, an enormous smooth-faced cherub in cutaway pajamas.
Severely retarded, he would vegetate in a clinic
for as long as his body might function. May
guessed his weight at four hundred pounds and
Val saw, with an old shock of recognition, that the
great body was asymmetrical. The limbs and even
the head were distinctly larger on the right side.

"He can eat when we help," May ended, "and we give him medicine so he won't hurt himself."

Hurt himself? If this great thing was subject to seizures, Val opined silently, he needed better accommodations that these. She wondered if Rankine had bedsores; and if he felt them; and if it were more ethical to maintain him or not to, under the circumstances. It was hopeless to feel assured at any answer. She was saved from further speculation by May's greeting to someone approaching from the ward kitchen. Val knew better than to turn on her own volition.

"Laura, honey," May said happily. "We have a new girl; I think she might be a help." And then May pulled Val around, and Val swept her eyes up a slender girlish form to meet—no eyes at all.

Laura Dunning was in many respects a lissome sixteen. She moved well, spoke with a charming drawl, dressed neatly, with pert nose and an enviable rosebud mouth. But the high forehead continued down to her cheeks with only faint, shallow depressions where her eyes would be in a more rational world. Val cudgeled her memory for a similar case, could find none. And somehow, inexplicably, Laura Dunning was very beautiful to look upon. Perhaps her animated speech helped; an old theorist's prescription for superb speech performance was an intelligent female with good hearing, blind from birth.

Val expected a fleeting fingertip inspection of her face, shoulders, arms and hands by the blind Laura. Instead, she offered her hand to be shaken. Another discard from an embarrassed family, Laura was obviously no more MR than was Val, herself.

As Val took the proffered hand, May seemed to shift roles and excused herself. "I'll go double-check the darlin' soup," she said in pleasant sarcasm, and Val was left with the blind girl.

Laura began talking, talking, eliciting brief answers now and then from Val, evidently deciding what chores Val might be willing and able to perform. Disturbingly, the blind girl studied every answer with satisfaction—or was it secret amusement? When Laura turned to lead Val to the ward kitchen, she did so with balletic grace. Val was no stranger to the blind—but in some way, she felt, Laura Dunning was extraordinarily sighted.

Under close supervision, Val had no chance to give a detailed reponse when Maffei transmitted before noon. She cut in only long enough to respond with their code word. Anxious to begin his paper chase of senior staff documentation, Chris elected to leave Val on her own. "We can count on Endicott," he assured her. "I'll leave the comm unit recorder here at the motel; you can report when you get the chance, even if I'm out of range."

Again Val muttered their code word, loudly enough that May, hovering supportively near, chuckled. Satisfied, Chris keyed out.

Lunch was passable, kitchen chores simple, her three o'clock assessment a misnomer. Val left the Tedder office at suppertime, squired by Laura Dunning and too angry at the Tedder couple to trust herself in an immediate report. Laura, her every gesture as assured as a sighted dancer's, wangled fresh bedding for Val in a ward bed next

to Laura's own. Val waited a half-hour, pulled her
pillow over most of her head, and began to transmit.

"... and then i realized they never intended
legit tests," she recorded, nearing the crux of her
message. "assessment? i scrubbed their deleted
floor! rhea tedder's stoned on something;
middle-age, middle-size, middlin' scared of docta
luween. he'd make a great spy, you can overlook
him so easy. i expected him to float up to the
ceiling when he wasn't grabbing for my goodies.
no sweat, lurene handled him. but they had no
motor skills hdwe., no nothing for m.r. tests that i
saw.

"the rankine boy could be hell on square wheels
if he is epileptic. can't tell from laura if it's grand
mal, akinetic, myoclonic, whatever. i can hear me
asking!

"caught sight of merkin—see merkle's goatee
and you get the connection. fifty, hefty, soft
mouth, dead eyes, voice like the bottom note of a
pipe organ. bad-liver skin i'd say. treats lurene as
peer, maybe something going there between 'em.

"drug dispensing: weird but may be ok. there's
a lot of it. the blind girl—her you have to meet—
does the work and i swear she's efficient. gets
dosages from the staff. boy does she empathize; a
girl had a petit mal seizure tonight, laura's ears
must be like tuning forks. stopped dead, turned
toward the kid shuddering. lucky me, i got to help
clean the beddypoo. laura says she doesn't mind,
helping the helpers. some help: profound m.r.
and epilepsy.

"and what's with miz bandicoot, haven't you
told her i'm me? and whatthehell keeps you out so
long, can't you xmit? sure leaves me out on a long

string and if you infer i'm strung out, you're improving.

"i suspect merkle uses drugs as babysitters; no organized play beyond what laura fixes, they all love her. 'course, some get enough exercise working. i think they do it for laura and i also think lurene knows it.

"nutrition: ok i think. hell of a good modern kitchen with equipment they don't need to make soup. m.r.'s keep the stainless shiny. tons of soy flour; so what else is new? tedders and merkle set up meals after lights out, i can hear 'em in there now. merkle doesn't seem the type for menial work but that's his voice.

"and i ache all over from charlady chores. drop me a postcard some day, i could use good news." Sleep came easily to Val after that; the lax operation at Gulfview had given Val a breadth of insight that ordinarily might take weeks. Surely, she felt, Chris would wrap this job up easily. It was a lullaby thought, a beguiling diversion that left her utterly unprepared for the morrow.

Val tried to doze through the ward's early morning chaos, failed, and feigned sleep to query Chris Maffei. Instantly his reply began in her head. She felt the elation of contact trickle away as he continued.

"Hey, Mata Hari, we're making progress," he began. "I'm transcribing now at, uh, two AM. Got back from—uh—an interview to the comm unit late and just finished your tape. Great stuff, hon." Val needed one guess to identify his late evening interviewee.

"Nothing on the Tedders yet," he went on. "But data retrieval isn't all that good here in town, I can

get to a records center in Biloxi if I'm up bright
and early."

*So he's already hull-down on the horizon from
me this morning,* Val thought.

"Keep your eyes open for indiscriminate use of
phenobarb, valium, zarontin, all the old standby
zonkers. You recall the drill: valium's the same
size pill regardless of dose, it's the color—well,
you know.

"I haven't blown your cover to May . . ." The
barest of hesitations, then the surname added,
". . . Endicott because what she doesn't know,
she can't reveal. What she already knows is in-
criminating enough. Merkle might be tricky—or
worse.

"The rundown on Robin Terence Merkle
looked okay at first; bona fides from med school
and AMA. But no special work with MR; he went
into pharmaceutical research with a chemical
company from seventy-one to eighty-three. Took
an enviable vacation then until starting Gulfview
in eighty-five. On a hunch, I dropped in at the
local cop shop and asked about the last receptionist before Endicott; Lana Jo Fowler, a local
girl. And there's a missing persons sheet on her.
They found her nifty Lotus abandoned in a Hat-
tiesburg parking lot and she'd been dropping
school-girl hints about hitting it rich. It occurred
to me that maybe something rich hit *her.*

"The desk sergeant said they'd done their
number on the Fowler girl, a plain sort who got
her popularity the only way she knew how. One of
their many blind leads was a gentleman who'd
recently paid for her visa and hovercraft fare to
Cancun, down the Yucatan. A very proper professional man. Rob Merkle.

"The police aren't disposed to worry about it but the girl's family is. Which leaves me with hunches. If any of 'em are right, Merkle knows where Lana Jo Fowler is, and she knows where something expensive is. Mexico? Ironic thing is, I'm in a better position than a small-time police department to spend time on it.

"In case you wonder: I'm not sidestepping to pursue this little mystery. I suspect the Gulfview operation should be shut down, but I don't want to pillory a guy who may be doing his half-assed best." His yawn whispered through Val's head. "If you're as tired as I am, you'll thank me for not waking you. I'll get a few hours' sleep and then head for Biloxi. 'Night."

Val struggled to avoid a sense of being discarded. Told herself that Chris had given so little new instruction because she had done so much, so quickly. Took it for granted that Chris was seeing May Endicott at night, and rationalized that he had no better way to confer with the woman. Val's intuition said that Chris was lagging at his forte, the massing of inferences from paperwork. *He's floundering for once, poor love,* she told herself, then felt the gentle touch of Laura Dunning on her arm. She could arise easily enough, but must remember not to shine.

The blind girl seemed pleased that her new retarded helper wanted to accompany her everywhere—even to the bathroom, where Val affected concern that she was made to stand away from Laura's stall. Val sensed no supicion when Laura allowed her to help dispense the morning's dosages in the ward. Again there was that rarely felt response in deeply retarded patients to a special person. Laura dispensed as much tender loving care as anything, but one oddity began to form a pattern. The more obvious the retardation in a patient, generally the less assured was Laura's deft handling of capsule or liquid suspension. The great vegetative Rankine took a Shetland pony's dose of dilantin, the cream-yellow suspension given by syringe directly into his slack mouth. Yet Laura fumbled the simple task.

Val was congratulating herself on a complete survey of all-too-heavy ward drug dosage when: "Did we miss anyone," Laura asked.

Val thought, *How would I know, with an IQ of 40*, and only smiled in answer, a gesture totally lost on Laura.

Laura persisted, "Did we have any medicine left?"

Perspiration began to form at Val's hairline. The questions could be innocent, but they were perfect tripwires for an unwary actress. Val chose the most equivocal response she knew, a murmuring whine that begged relief from stress without imparting any linguistic content. "Mmmmuuhummmaaaahh," she sniveled.

Laura's laugh was merry, guileless. "Well, I guess not." She straightened up from the silent mass of young Rankine, and her hand unerringly found Val's head to pat it, once. "You're a great help. Thank you," she said, and permitted Val to follow her to a holovision set at the end of the ward. Laura, Val found, could enjoy the audio even if she could not receive the images; and she enjoyed company.

Val squirmed as she watched the holo. Suspicions caromed through her head, leaving hot sparks that would not die. It was barely possible that Laura was equipped with some incredibly effective stage makeup and could see—but that seemed wildly unlikely. It was more possible that she had been briefed by the staff to test newcomers for hidden intelligence. Or perhaps Val had somehow conveyed something to this child-woman, something that Laura's sensitivity would respond to, without knowing what that something was. It was also quite likely that Val was overly suspicious; but Valerie Clarke had learned the folly of easily accepting the comfortable answer. She began to hum a repetitious tune from a holo commercial in what she hoped was suitably MR until a male patient shushed her.

Val helped at the noon meal, serving two patients who were unable to eat by themselves. Laura kept one hand on the patient's chin; the other she laid lightly on Val's wrist, until satisfied that Val could complete the chore. The meal and its inevitable cleanup served to lessen Val's ennui while Chris Maffei chased his papers—but Val was not to be idle for long.

The afternoon quiet was punctuated by the skritch of scrub brushes on linolamat as Dr. Robin Merkle made his rounds. Val, part of the work force, entertained a faint hope that Merkle gave adequate attention to his charges. Merkle propped a clipboard on his substantial belly to make occasional notations. The inconspicuous Rhea Tedder cradled more clipboards as he followed behind. Several times the smaller man spoke—Val thought, a little diffidently. Merkle smiled, or did not smile, behind the goatee but only shrugged in reply. Lurene Tedder stood before the great locked double-doors of the ward, preening her dark tresses with her brush, watch-

ing her minions scrub. With stolid calm, scrub-
bing more quietly, Val crept within earshot of the
men.

Tedder eased up to exchange clipboards with
Merkle. "Lissen, Rob, I could really use a hit," he
wheedled. Val paused, addressed a speck of detritus with a trembling fingernail. "Just a little
one," Tedder insisted.

Val kept her face down, trying to be invisible,
and was rewarded. "One more request," Merkle
said in his quietest pleasant basso, "and you get
none tonight. We want to be on top of our cycle for
tonight's delivery, don't we?" Val thought, *Now I
know where Docta Luween gets that 'we' crap.
Really grooves on Merkle.*

New hope surged in Rhea Tedder's voice.
"Then after tonight, again tomorrow with supper?"

A long silence. Val could almost taste the as-
tringent look from Merkle.

"Just checkin' on my cycle," Tedder said.
"You're the expert."

An avuncular laugh from the portly Merkle.
"Yes indeed," he bubbled, "and we'll be friends
then, will we not?"

Tedder joined in the laugh, a neurotic *henh,
henh* that Val knew from a thousand holo
stereotypes of dirty old men. Rhea Tedder was
nominally harmless, she thought. *Unless you
weigh eighty pounds like I do.*

A crackling slap from across the ward drew the
men's attention. Val began to scrub away from
them. She could hear, but not yet see, Lurene
Tedder at her specialty: corporal punishment.

The victim was a young man perhaps twenty-
five years old, a quiet one with teeth ruined from

habitual gritting together. Val risked a view from
her vantage point behind Laura Dunning's bed.
Laura sat, knuckles pale as she gripped the coverlet, facing away from the scene.

"You act like a dog, you get treated like a dog,"
the Tedder woman said in derision. One hand still
holding the hairbrush, Lurene Tedder clutched
her other hand into the young man's tangled hair.
She was plainly pleased that he struggled as she
forced his face into something on the floor.

Merkle raised his voice slightly in reproof:
"Lurene . . ."

She released her hold with a shrug-and-grin
display, satisfied with her punishment of any patient who fouled her ward floor with his excrement. Val mused that it might actually be possible
to train a patient away from such pathetic lapses,
in the manner of a Lurene Tedder—but at what
cost to the patient? Then she saw what the others
missed: the youth rising, arms windmilling craz-
ily as the woman looked away. He fell on her
without warning. His hands were fouled, too, and
while he dealt no serious blows, Val thought his
repayment apt.

It was no contest; neither of the male staff tried
to help and in a moment, repeated slaps reduced
the youth to a cringing serf at Lurene Tedder's
feet.

She then applied further discipline.

In all, the hairbrush hammered only a dozen
times; but Val shuddered each time it fell. She
realized that Lurene Tedder was not using the flat
of the brush, but the far more damaging bristles, a
thousand dull needles seeking passage through
the coarse fabric of the youth's ward smock. Seeking, and finding.

The woman paused for breath. Merkle stepped
up, took her hairbrush gently, his face a study in
mild pique. He ignored the sobbing wretch at
their feet. Rhea Tedder, shuffling near them, was
the only member of the staff to notice the real
victim. He managed to get the young man to his
feet and hauled him toward the distant bathroom,
and Laura moved in swift silence to help.

Val followed. She paused at the bathroom entrance to survey the ward. Some patients were
unaffected by the beating, but others contributed
to a pulsing obbligato of fear and misery. Over it,
Rob Merkle soothed his dear friend Lurene, who
had now taken her brush. It was faintly stained
with blood but unheeding, she brushed away her
waning fury and punctuated each stroke with
curses. Merkle knew his patients; he drew Lurene
out of the ward with practiced aplomb and a
promise of gin.

In the bathroom, Rhea Tedder had relinquished
the youth to Laura, who peeled the filthy smock
from the patient with infinite care. Val remembered to make a low repetitive moan without
words, though the words were dangerously close
at hand. The youth's back, neck, and arms oozed
bright red pinprick droplets. The physical damage was only moderate, Val saw as they bathed
their charge in water hot enough to be soporific as
well as cleansing. The damage to a muddled
psyche would be impossible to assess.

When Laura Dunning asked for synthoderm,
Tedder grumbled, but he got it and applied the
healing spray himself, mumbling all the while.
His complaints were all variants on the "Why me,
God?" theme, but he was at least willing to give
minimal aid and for this, Val was grateful.

As he left them, Tedder paused an instant and Val felt a grasp on her buttock. It was untimely, covert, somehow more prank than overture. *He's easily pleased*, she thought. Laura would have to wonder why Val chuckled.

But: "Yes, it's too much, Charles Clegg," Laura said. This was the first time Val had heard the youth's name. "She just doesn't know. But," Laura added opaquely, "she will."

Valerie Clarke puzzled over this prediction. Laura, withdrawn into herself and for once less than agile, enlisted Val's aid in getting young Clegg dried, reclothed, and back to his bed. Drugs were again dispensed to some of the patients after supper but, this time, Laura rejected Val's help. "Go and see the nice holo," she said in no-nonsense tones, and Val played the obedient child.

Alone for all practical purposes, Val signaled Chris Maffei while she watched the distant Laura move among the beds. As she expected, Chris was still out of range. She spoke to the remote cassette. ". . . haven't seen any of the staff since then," she said, completing her account of the ward violence. "didn't see your sweetiepie at all. she too sleepy today?

"dental care: have i mentioned it? some m.r.'s need caps and there's caries everywhere. and something about laura has me on edge, something i can't specify. yes i can, too; she isn't on merkle's side but maybe not on ours either. i guess she's just on her own side and i can't blame her.

"i gave you rhea tedder's conversation with merkle verbatim, and if he's not on a drug mainte-nance schedule i'm an m.r. for real. and his sweet wife needs a leash; her ordinary interactions are

patho, can't guess why merkle keeps either of 'em.
maybe you can tell me what delivery merkle ex-
pects at night; my guess is, it ain't pepperoni
pizza. i get the feeling i'm holding a basketful of
cobras and no flute. how soon can you reel me in?
i really can't justify a mayday but, i mean, how
much do we need to learn beyond this? well, it's
your show. just get back to me, ok? all i have to do
is play with my fingers and hope the evening
stays nice and dull."

Presently, Laura slipped into a tattered seat
near Val. Fidgety at first, the blind girl soon began
to relax and Val guessed, incorrectly, that Laura's
quietude was a pure effort of will. They watched
the holo for hours, becalmed with the surrogate
window on a trivial make-believe world. It was
quite late when Val heard the staff in the nearby
kitchen, and later still when the screaming began.

Val, semientranced before the holovision set,
started up violently. The ward lights had au-
tomatically cycled off at nine PM and only she and
Laura lounged before the holo. Vainly she peered
down the ward to identify the noise that had
aroused her. Was there a spasmodic movement on
one of the beds? Val darted a glance at Laura,
whose shadowed face and inert form suggested
sleep. With the barest whisper of her clothing, Val
snaked out of her seat and into the ward's center
aisle.

The next moment found her unable to cope. The
noise ripped through the ward again; a hoarse,
unsexed and dreadful mooing from the nearby
ward kitchen. A bombard of metal gongs told her
that something flailed among the huge kitchen
metalware. She could hear Merkle shouting, and

now his voice held tenor overtones. As the terrible lowing segued to a gasping scream, Val recognized the voice of Lurene Tedder, muffled by blows.

Val glanced quickly toward Laura and had the nightmare sense of duality, two places at once, cause and effect in one. At the same instant, the kitchen door emitted stark light that flooded the ward, followed by the struggling forms of Merkle and the Tedders. Rhea hung from one of Lurene's arms while Merkle pinioned the other. Lurene Tedder's prized hairbrush fell at their feet as the men steered her toward the cell where Val had spent her first night. Valerie Clarke crouched motionless in the aisle, alone and desperately vulnerable—but unseen in the tumult.

Lurene's feet seemed willing enough to follow Merkle's staggering lead, yet her arms strained convulsively for freedom. Val ducked between beds, saw Rhea Tedder lose his grip for a twinkling. Lurene's arm thrashed once, catching herself squarely on the chin. She sagged at the blow and her husband regained his purchase. The big woman subsided into breathless sobs as the men led her into the cell. The cell door remained ajar.

Val saw the vandalized kitchen through its open door. Dark ovals of blood shared spots on the floor with a scattering of white powder that Val supposed was sugar until she heard the voices in the cell.

"I can hold her," came the deep voice between labored breaths. "Get the hypospray and a cartridge of cytovar from my office. Wait: first grab her damnable security brush and toss it in here, it might help. Can you do that much?"

The brush lay two meters from Val. She sank to

the floor. A pair of feet shambled near and she heard Rhea Tedder in an old monologue as he retrieved the brush. He stood erect, paused, gave a huh? of surprise, and Val gave herself up—too soon. Rhea Tedder strolled back toward the cell, oblivious of the struggle Val could plainly hear in the cell.

Rhea Tedder paused at the cell and tossed the brush in. He spoke calmly, detached. "What about the shipment, it's all over the floor in there. Hell of a waste . . ."

"LATER," Merkle boomed. "Or do you want to hold her?"

The smaller man hurried away from this threat, pausing only to unlock the doors at the end of the ward. The big room was awash with light, the cell door still open, a patient moving uneasily in her bed nearby, and Rob Merkle only meters away with a madwoman barely under control, when Valerie Clarke crept to the kitchen door. She held a discarded paper cup pilfered from a wastebasket, and in one scurrying pass she scooped a bit of powder from the floor. Then she was in darkness again, frenziedly duckwalking in deep shadow toward the holo area.

Val thrust the wadded cup far down into the seam of her seat as she settled down beside Laura Dunning. She opened her mouth wide to avoid puffing as she drew lungfuls of sweet air and waited for her adrenaline to be absorbed. She had no pockets, no prepared drop, no confederates— and no delusions of well-being if her petty theft were discovered. She bit her tongue as Laura spoke.

"I've been bad, Valerie, but so were you." The sweet voice scarcely carried between the seats.

"We shouldn't be here, we'll have to sneak to bed." With that, the blind girl swirled up from her seat and in an erect glide, quickly found her bed near the kitchen-lit center of the ward. Val trailed her in double-time.

Then: "Pretend sleep," Val heard—or did she imagine it?—from Laura, who took her own advice. Valerie did not, for several minutes, recover enough presence of mind to call Chris Maffei. Instead she lay facing away from the cell where Lurene Tedder lay moaning, tended by Merkle and, at his shuffling return, Rhea. Val was certain that Rhea Tedder had neither the inclination nor the guts to attack his sturdy wife. She wondered how and why Merkle, the only other person with Lurene, had chosen to punish her. Valerie had not yet grasped a shred of the truth.

"chris, oh god, chris, be there," Val transmitted her prayer of hope from halfway under her pillow.

The response was an intercept code promising live dialog after a short wait. Then abruptly, with great good cheer: "Hi, Val! I'm working late, believe it or not, but I have a little time . . ."

"you have a mayday, too." Val rushed through her synopsis of the past few minutes, adding, "you wanta come get me? i don't know what's in this cup but it's part of the shipment—and it bothers this little addict more'n his wife does. if you hurry you might be able to figure what they're up to in the kitchen and storeroom."

After a long pause, Maffei replied. "I don't think Merkle will have time to worry about you tonight. You can slip your sample to May, I'll have her stop by and see you tomorrow."

"tomorrow?" The word was bereft of hope.

"Look, Val, these people are fumbling something; I've only just realized what it might be. You're my eyes and ears while they do it and you could pick up something a whole lot bigger than either of us ever bargained for."

"e.g., rigor mortis . . ."

"Don't be melodramatic. I have a make on the Tedders; he's a pussycat. Doctor Tedder, all right. Doctor of Divinity from a diploma factory in South Texas. The old mail-order business, he may pray you to death but he's a harmless fraud. His wife's a reject physical ed teacher from a girl's military school, with some experience in a chemical plant—curiously, the same company Merkle worked for. My guess is, they're matched pair of technicians Merkle can count on."

"for what?"

"You ready for this? Sleet! A refrigerated cocaine derivative the feds turned up in New Orleans last year. It avoids most of the side effects of snow—ulcerated sinuses, convulsions, stuff your higher class of cocaine addict will pay to avoid. Potent and highly addictive. Sleet was concocted by somebody pretty bright; pure snow processed with a powdered enzyme and protein. You take it with food, the enzyme comes up to your body temperature, and your stomach lining lays a swell little hit on you when the three components interact."

"you think they're cutting it here?"

"I think Rob Merkle could be the capital S source. You say soy flour's abundant there? I damn well bet it is, to keep fresh batches of enzyme going. It'd have to be slurried and centrifuged, dried—but hell, once you had the process and the enzyme, your only problem would be keeping the secret and maybe fighting off your buyers. Merkle may have caught Miz Tedder sneaking some."

Val coded a 'hold' signal and emerged slowly from beneath her pillow. She could hear Lurene Tedder speaking with the men, her enunciation mushmouthed but steady. Val employed cloze procedure to mentally fill in the words she missed and listened for several minutes, mystified. When she burrowed under the edge of the pillow again, she brought a new loose end with her. "something's not meshing, chris. merkle's asking lurene what happened and she can't tell him; doesn't blame him for anything. as if the invisible man lambasted her." It was a much closer guess than Val knew.

Maffei used her simile to press his earlier point. "It's *all* been invisible until now. You have a chance to see things I couldn't even get close to, and . . ."

". . . and you can't see past those big boobies." The wrong moment, she knew; but there it was.

Chris answered *sotto voce*, as if to a male friend, and Val knew that May Endicott was within hailing distance of him. "If it'll make you feel better, she, ah, puts up a good front."

"i swoon with delight, you bastard. you could have the good sense to lie about it."

"My work is too important for lies between us, Val."

"But not too important for lays with miz ran-dycu . . ."

"Val!" In dulcet reasonable tones: "A certain—relationship—can enhance motivation on the job." Too late he saw the sweep of that truth.

"don't i know it. but the job isn't a clean scholarly paper, the job is people—a boy who doesn't know the hurt is because nobody cares that his teeth are rotting—a lovely girl with smooth flesh where eyes should be, piecing her world together alone—kids that might be curable if anybody cared."

She could hear anger rising in Maffei's answers. For years she had used that as her motive for retreat. "And the first step is just what I'm doing, Val."

"my my, do tell me all about it."

"We're doing! You know I include you."

"when you think about it." Her tones, she knew, were flat; her words harsh. She should be pleading, begging him to complement her love and need, but Valerie Clarke could not cling this time. "look, you have things to do and i don't need this. send—send may around."

"Right, I . . . you're transmitting oddly. Rhythm's off or something. Trouble?" He rapped out the last word.

She was glad Chris could not see the runny nose, cheeks glistening with her tears. "i'm—jumpy, i guess. forget it."

"Well—if you're sure you don't need bailout." His intonation asked, instead of offering, reassurance.

Despite her growing fear, choking back a reminder that she had clearly sent a mayday, she replied, "i'm sure. go 'way, lemme sleep—please, chris."

For a full half-minute Val lay still, commanding her small frame to stop heaving with sobs that might wake Laura. It was easier than ever, now, to empathize with children who could not expect help from Outside.

Then: "Val?"

"yeah."

"Are you really sure? I'm worried; you don't sound right."

"you want a framed affidavit? i said i was."

"I just sensed . . . as if someone had tied you up and forced you to say it. Give me the word."

"somebody did, a long time ago; and chitlins, goddammit, chitlins!"

Then the channel was silent. For a long while, sleep evaded Valerie. Self-doubt shored her insomnia. She was both losing Chris Maffei and throwing him away; the hard facts militated against her when opponents were violent and massive; and somehow, she knew, she had been witness to more than she could absorb. Sleep came while she searched for a neglected detail. She should have analyzed them in pairs.

If Valerie Clarke awoke sluggishly, she could take comfort in the notion that the staff had managed even less sleep than she. The kitchen was spotless and Rhea Tedder, not Lurene, superintended the breakfast. When May Endicott appeared in the ward to help him, Val noted the shadows under those seductive eyes and enjoyed a nice mixture of emotions.

Twice May found Val's gaze and twice Val treated her to the briefest of enigmatic smiles. Under Laura's tutelage, Val fed two patients and there was no secret way to retrieve her problematic sample, much less pass it on. Immediately after the cleanup—always necessary with patients who fed like caged creatures—Val made her way to the holo area. May could not know Val's intent and soon followed in a manner much too bright, forthright, and amateurish.

May's greeting was tentative and too loud. Val replied in a mumble. "Beg your pardon," May said, leaning near.

"Quit calling attention to us," Val murmured calmly, "and sit down and especially, *pipe down.*"

May sat as if felled. She was blushing as she studied the holo. "Dr. Maffei said tell you his communication set is damaged," she said finally. Two other patients, sitting near, ignored their entire exchange. "But he's getting it fixed now. And he trusted me as courier. You do have something for me to bring him?" The naive brown eyes radiated concern.

A nod indistinguishable at any distance. "When I leave, it'll be in my seat. For God's sake get it out of here. And get me out, too, as soon as you can. Don't delay."

A winsome glance from May. Val wished the woman weren't so likeable. "We say 'dawdle' in these parts." Then after a long pause, in kaffee-klatsch cameraderie: "I had no idea he was usin' you like this."

"You're even stealing my lines," Val muttered the multiple entendre with relish. To soften its impact she continued, "That goddamn comm set! What's wrong with it?"

"I don't know, Chr—Dr. Maffei said he must've hit it with his heel."

Val examined this datum for a moment. Only the scrambler module, a recent addition, was mounted in Maffei's car where it could be struck by a foot. And then only by someone in the passenger's side by kicking upward with one's toe. But with the heel . . . ?

The heel. Right. Val turned her head with great

deliberation and, despite herself, a twitch on her
lips. She said nothing, only looked volumes. And
saw a furious blush mount the Endicott features as
May realized her gaffe to someone intimately
familiar with Maffei's car. Suddenly shamed by
her meanness, Val arose clumsily without a word
and wandered off. She had found the bit of paper
cup by blind fumbling and let it drop into the seat
in plain sight.

Val adopted a shuffling gait as Lurene Tedder
entered the ward doorway with a tray of medication. The big woman did not notice Val's spindly
person, so intent was she on something at the far
end of the ward. With prickly hot icicles at the
back of her head, Val knew that Lurene was studying the holo region.

Quickly the woman stepped out to the hallway
and keyed a wall intercom. "Dr. Merkle, Dr.
Merkle," she called in smug parody of a hospital
page, "you are wanted in the ward. Right now,"
she added with the assurance of a drill sergeant.

The intercom replied but Val could not hear it
clearly.

"No I can't, buddy-boy, I just caught me a
stasher and I ain't gonna take my eyes off her."
Another faint answer. "You come and see. I'll give
you a hint, lover: this makes two in a row. I could
be wrong, but can you chance it?"

Lurene Tedder marched into the ward again
and, without conversation, relinquished the tray
to Laura Dunning. The woman never took her
stare from the end of the ward and Val, playing
finger games for camouflage, studied the square
Tedder face. Under the telltale gleam of synthoderm the entire face was puffy, facial planes
indistinct under localized swellings. Like collo-

dion of old, synthoderm tended to peel around the mouth; the naked skin that showed was freckled with tiny scabs.

A chill scuttled down Val's backbone; Lurene's punishment had been a terrific hiding across her face with her own hairbrush! The eyes glittered even more deeply beneath swollen brows and Val knew that Lurene Tedder was fortunate to retain her eyesight. Yet she could be civil to Merkle—who strode into the ward at the moment Laura chose to begin dispensing dosages.

Val shuddered with relief as the pair moved past her. She hurried to Laura's side to take her 'instruction' in dispensing the drugs. A backward glance revealed that Merkle and Tedder, talking quickly, were converging on May Endicott. Val wondered whether May had the good sense to think of a cover activity, and guessed against it. As she saw her guess confirmed, Val began to hope that May would brazen or physically force her way out.

From the first moment, May's fear was emblazoned on her face. The dialogue rose in volume until Laura paused, her head cocked attentively. "She's the only good thing that's happened here," Laura said quietly, "and now she'll be gone."

May exchanged glares with Lurene while Merkle, much the tallest, looked down at May. For a second he craned his head to one side at May's cleavage, then thrust one hand into it in a lightning maneuver. May jerked her hands up—too late. Merkle stepped back to examine his prize and Lurene Tedder moved to intercept May's desperate grab.

While May darted anguished looks around her,

Merkle studied the scrap of heavy paper and its contents. Brusquely he gave an order and fell behind as May led a procession toward Val's end of the ward. It seemed that they might pass outside until Merkle, with a silent thumb-jerk, indicated the isolation cell to Lurene Tedder. Val considered, for one instant, the possibility of a diversion. Flinging the tray; anything.

No one was prepared for Laura Dunning's reaction. Screaming, "She doesn't hurt anybody," Laura dived past Val and upset the tray as she flung herself at the sounds of combat.

Merkle spun to catch the lithe girl while Lurene grappled with May. He took no punishment and, with a backhand cuff, sent Laura squalling to the floor. The blind girl, hopelessly unequal to the fray, moaned as she rolled aside. She nursed her right shoulder as, still sobbing, she found her bed and lay back.

Val knelt in the spill of drugs, terrified and inert. She had never felt so vulnerable to physical violence, and almost transmitted an open 'mayday' before remembering that Maffei could not receive it.

May's body was not fashioned for the rough-and-tumble of a Lurene Tedder and, after a brief struggle, May was flung into the cell. The door slammed shut, locked under Tedder's key.

Merkle ignored Val, the drugs, and faint pounding from inside the cell, patting Lurene in the manner of a coach with a favored athlete. "You were right," he grunted. They were three meters from Valerie Clarke. "Where did she get it?"

Val hefted a bottle, wondering which skull to aim for, somehow remembering to keep her jaw slack and her eyes slightly averted. An eternal moment later Lurene hazarded, "Must've hidden it down by the holo someplace. You'll have to ask her when."

"You anticipate me," Merkle said jovially, urging Lurene to the ward entrance. As he paused to lock the ward doors, Val heard him continue. "She has to sleep sometime; it'll be simple to find out then." They receded down the hall, and Val heard a last fragment. "No shortage of time, or of scop. I told you this setup would be ideal for it . . ."

A youth began to take interest in the strewn capsules and Val scooped up the mess quickly before taking it to Laura. A corner of her brain marveled that Merkle could simply stride away from an addict's array of downers, knowing that any of the patients might ingest any or all of the drugs—or simply lie down and wallow in them. She sat down heavily on the side of Laura's bed and leaped up again at Laura's quick gasp.

"Don't, oh, don't! My shoulder," Laura moaned, and Val realized that her small mass had jarred the bed. "Valerie?"

Val answered guardedly. She could call no one, trust no one; Laura might suspect, but had no proof that Val was equipped with that formidable tool, knowledge. On the other hand, May certainly knew. And if Merkle employed scopolamine on May Endicott, he would soon strip the imposture bare. Val sat on her bed, trembling.

It was clear that Laura could not dispense medication. Val judged it was half-past ten, and thinking of the chaos of a dozen interrupted medication schedules in an unsupervised MR ward, she administered the dosages she recalled. Nor was she really out of character: idiot-savant retardates had been known to demonstrate a memory far beyond that of normal people.

The docile Rankine was one of her failures. Laura had evidently stepped on the big needleless syringe which she would have used to administer his whopping dose of dilantin suspension. Val wasted half a bottle of the stuff trying to pour it past his lips, then gave it up. Rankine was not disposed to help take the dosage by this unfamiliar method; very well, then. He would simply have to bear it with several others whose dosages Val could not recall.

Val lay back on her bed, vainly transmitting to Chris Maffei every few minutes. Interrupted by a low sobbing from Laura, she suddenly considered the remaining drugs. Surely a yellow valium, only five milligrams, couldn't hurt. She found one in her leftover cache and laid it to Laura's lips.

Laura took it greedily with an attempted smile. "Not enough," she confided. Val stiffened, then relaxed. Even recognizing the drug by taste or shape, how could the blind Laura know a white two milligram pill from a potent blue ten? But perhaps even ten would not be too much. If the scapula were broken, Laura's pain was surely intense. Val administered another yellow pill and lay back to narrowcast another blazing 'mayday' to Chis Maffei.

Two patients scuffled briefly. Another yodeled for joy. Val studied the narrow clerestory windows, knowing that even her very small head would not fit, presuming that she could smash the glass tiles. And if she tried to signal May, only meters away in the isolation cell, the staff could easily pick it up via monitors.

Laura breathed more regularly now, the valium taking its effect. Lying full length on her bed, Val found satisfaction in her act of loving kindness. Then, without preamble, a delicious lassitude washed through her body as through gauze. Val saw that her right hand was stroking her thigh. Eerily, it did not respond to her next command. "Stop that," she said aloud. She felt a presence not her own; it was purest intuition to reply.

Val composed another message. Deliberately unformed, not vocalized but simply broadcast thought, a cloudy montage of unease and avoidance. No effect, but her left forearm nuzzled her bud of a breast before she could stop it. On an instant surmise Val thought hard of a putrid slime, mentally smelled it, pictured it. Holding the thought, she felt something slip away. It was like a fever breaking, a fever unannounced but somehow benign, that now began reluctantly to loose its hold. Quickly Val visualized a smile; the smile she valued most, the dimpled puckish leer of Chris Maffei.

Then, despite her effort to halt it, her right hand patted her left wrist, twice. She watched her hands intently, a sham catatonic, for many seconds. Whatever it was, it had withdrawn. To where?

Across from Valerie Clarke lay the girl who was prone to mild epileptic seizures. Charles Clegg, the youth who had taken the hairbrush beating, stood near the girl, pointing, laughing. Below a certain level of socialization there is little empathy, and Clegg's amusement stemmed from the girl's loss of control. It was over now, at any rate, with no harm done.

Val told herself she had her own gooseflesh to ponder, then in a fresh surge of adrenaline, mentally connected the events. Lurene Tedder did not know the source of her flogging. And Val had a lucid flash of memory during *that* event: the epileptic girl had jerked on her bed while Laura Dunning, otherwise inert before the holo, sat and pounded her hand on her chair arm. Suddenly Laura's subliminal hand movement was meaningful.

Just now, the MR girl had suffered another spasm, while some unseen presence bade Val to caress herself. Who had reason to thank Val? She rolled over, lying now on her side, and faced Laura.

"What do you need?" Laura spoke soothingly, in deep repose. Val had said nothing.

All thought of keeping her cover vanished, Val answered, "You said you'd been bad, Laura. Did *you* make that woman punish herself?"

"I'm not sorry."

Good Jesus, I'm hallucinating. This isn't real. "And you thanked me just then—a minute ago?"

"I *am* sorry for that," was the contrite reply. "You're normal, you didn't need it like that."

Another thought whirled in Val's head. "I don't even have to talk out loud, do I?"

"Better to talk. Thoughts are so fast they're confusing sometimes. And it hurts sometimes."

"You don't know your strength," Val confided. "I believe you trigger those seizures the others have."

Laura could not weep tears, but she could cry.
"Sorry. Sorry. Sorry. So much pain and confusion, I try to help. I'm sorry."

"You do help," Val said. "You can help now if
you can listen in on those miserable sonsofbitches
to see what they're up to."

A long pause, then: "Too far away. I have to take
medicine to make people do things. I steal it. Can't
be sure when the power will come, sometimes it
doesn't. Sorry, sorry," the blind girl wept, her
high forehead furrowed in grief.

Val soothed Laura, kneeling next to her, thin
fingers on the girl's wrist. A rattle of keys at the
ward doorway, and Val eased back onto her bed.
Merkle came in first, Lurene next. They held the
doors open for Rhea, who wheeled a gurney into
the ward. Val realized then that they did not intend May Endicott to walk out of the cell, and
subvocalized a prayerful plea to Maffei. Nothing.
Kicked it with your heel, you turd, she raged.

There was no desperate speed in the prepara-
tions. Val guessed they had simply tired of waiting for answers, and had elected to overpower
May Endicott before drugging her. "Laura," she
whispered, "can you help May when they open
that cell door?"

"It's not coming," Laura breathed, as the cell
door swung open. The trio stormed the pathetic
May and slammed the door.

Val flew to the cell and cursed herself for not
having checked the lock mechanism earlier. No
use in any case: without a key, she could not lock
them in, and she went jelly-kneed at the thought
of entering that cell with anything less than a riot
gun. From the muffled noises Val knew that May

was going under sedation. Merkle's bass reso-
nated in the cell but wall padding strained it of
content.

She ran to the ward doors. Metal-faced, sec-
urely locked, as was the kitchen. But with enough
mass piled on the waiting gurney, it might just
possibly be accelerated down the ward to smash
the doors. And smashing the wheeled metal cot
itself might slow them in getting May from the
ward. Val did not need a legal opinion to con-
clude that, with every additional step a fresh
felony, the staff of Gulfview might welcome pre-
meditated murder. Whatever might have happened to the Fowler girl, Val did not relish seeing
it repeated. She tugged at the gurney, wheeled it
up the center aisle toward the holo area. Perhaps
the chairs would serve, if she could pile them on,
or enlist patients in her enterprise.

She could get no one to aid in her little game.
Patients strolled over to watch, slack-jointed and
empty-eyed, as Val managed to tip two seats up
into the gurney. Whimpering with the effort, she
pulled the vehicle near the ponderous holovision
set, all of a meter wide and massing perhaps a
hundred pounds. She reached to disconnect the
wiring, but at least one patient knew what that
meant. He wanted his program, and the skinny
girl with frightened eyes wanted to pull its plug.
He screamed, face twisted in sudden ferocity, and
thrust Val away.

Val raced to the side of Laura Dunning, who
seemed asleep but for the mobility of her features.
"Laura, is valium the medicine for your power?
Could you make some patients help me smash
those doors?"

"Dilantin's the only thing that works," came the soft reply. "I only discovered it recently. Do you have any?"

Val whirled to her cache of unused drugs beneath her pillow. They were gone. Disoriented for the moment, she looked up to see young Charles Clegg. He held capsules in one hand while trying to bite off the safety cap of the dilantin bottle. He had seen people drink it; maybe it would taste good.

Valerie Clarke did not know she could leap so fast, with such hand-eye coordination. She flashed past Clegg in a two-handed grab and the bottle was hers. Clegg was between her and Laura, but Val thought to circle around behind beds across the ward. It was at this juncture that Dr. Robin Merkle emerged from the cell.

He scanned the ward, saw Val, and then spotted the gurney filled with furniture. He looked almost pleased. Val saw it in his face: her cover was blown.

Val held the crucial dilantin and Merkle, the advantage. He also wielded the hypospray, which could accept pressure cartridges of anything from saline solution to curare. While he could not know Val's intention, Merkle obviously proposed to take her into custody here and now. Their eyes locked. Neither spoke. Lurene Tedder hurried to cut Val off from her narrow corridor between beds and wall.

"Easy, Rob," Lurene cautioned, and Merkle stopped to listen. Val took a step back, poised. "This li'l thing didn't get here on her own, somebody Outside will be askin'."

"If we wait it's a sure bust," Merkle rumbled as if reasserting an old position. "On the new

schedule, we can process another, oh, say eighty
pounds of protein." He beamed at Valerie. "Thirty
hours or so at twenty-three celsius."

At this, even Lurene Tedder blinked. "We're
gonna process these two?" Val first saw the flicker
of revulsion in the woman's face, then realized
what it meant to her, Valerie Clarke, and had to
steady herself against fainting.

"For more enzyme. Matuase doesn't care what
it feeds on," Merkle said, pleased at his logic.
"These ladies will complete a perfect irony. Part
of the operation, as it were."

Sickened with loathing, Val fanned a faint
spark of hope that Lurene would rebel. The lump
in Val's throat forbade her any speech; the pounding of her heart was physical pain. Then, with a
great sigh, Lurene said, "Well, it's better tactics
than planting 'em, like you-know-who," and
closed in on Valerie Clarke.

The thought of herself as finely ground fodder
in some unknown enzyme production phase
nearly robbed Val of consciousness, but the approach of Lurene and Merkle was galvanic. Val
spun and ran for the gurney, hoping to get it un-
derway before they could stop her. A quasi-female
laugh followed her like a promise of extinction.
Val collided against an inert patient, reached the
gurney, began to thrust it ahead of her down the
center of the ward. Even as it began to roll, she saw
that she was simply too small for the task.

Lurene danced almost playfully out into the
aisle, hands spread before her to intercept the
loaded gurney. Val grabbed the thing she held in
her teeth and hurled it at the woman, then was
aware of her mistake. Val's missile connected
against Lurene Tedder's forehead, but the soft

plastic bottle had little effect and Lurene diverted
the gurney between two beds. Val saw Merkle
stoop to retrieve the dilantin bottle as it skittered
near him. The bottle went into his pocket. She had
literally hurled her last hope away, and in a
stumbling panic Val fell over the huge form of
Gerald Rankine, looming in his bed near the holo.

Rankine stirred slightly and opened unfocused
eyes. Val scrambled over the great form and into
the holo area, now devoid of its two heaviest seats.
Lurene Tedder bawled for Rhea, who trotted up
the ward for his instructions.

As Val cowered behind the holovision, mind-
less with terror, Lurene waved Rhea around while
she herself took a frontal approach. Merkle moved
to cut off any escape behind the beds; and the very
proximity of the three triggered Val as it might
any small and cornered animal.

Val flung herself into Rhea Tedder as Lurene
crashed against the holo set in pursuit. Rhea
found himself grappling with a small demon, all
thin sticks and sharp edges, that spat and clawed
as he held on. Recovering, the sturdy Lurene
thrust herself away from the holo, already totter-
ing on its stand from her impact, and then Lurene
tackled Val in a smothering embrace. Merkle had
time to laugh once as he saw Lurene's clumsy
success, but he did not see the holo as it toppled
onto the silently staring young Rankine.

Lifted aloft by the big woman, Val caught a
glimpse of the holo set. It leaned drunkenly on
Rankine's midriff, its great window facing his
eyes, its picture transmuted into bursts of flicker-
ing light by the rough handling.

Val took two fistfuls of hair and wrenched, trying to tear it from Lurene Tedder's abundant mop. Val's throat was too constricted to scream and Lurene only snarled. From down the ward, then, floated a dreamlike, ecstatic moan. "Ohhhh, it's a *lovely* one," cried Laura Dunning, borne into an orgasmic flood of silently thundering energy.

Because Merkle was most distant from the melee, he was first to catapult himself down the aisle. Val felt muscular arms relax and, kicking furiously, vacated Lurene Tedder's shoulder. Lurene staggered, nearly fell, then began to accelerate down the center of the ward after Merkle. Rhea Tedder tried to follow but tripped over Val before he began to run.

A welter of impressions clamored in Val's head. The holo, crashing to the floor as young Rankine jerked in the throes of a truly leviathan epileptic seizure. Howls of helpless terror from Merkle and the woman, bleats from Rhea, as the three found themselves sprinting harder down the ward. Laura Dunning's cooing luxuriance in a stream of almost sexual power was lower-pitched, but Val heard it. Valerie Clarke splayed hands over her ears and blanched an instant before Merkle impacted against the great double doors.

Merkle, with a hysterical falsetto shriek, never even raised his hands. He slammed the metal door-facing with a concussive report that jolted every patient, every fixture. Headfirst, arms and legs pumping, driven by two hundred and sixty pounds of his beloved protein, Dr. Robin Merkle comprised part one of Laura Dunning's battering ram.

Lurene Tedder's last scream was entirely

feminine; she managed to turn her head to one side as she obliterated herself against the sheet steel.

The doors, bent under Merkle's hapless assault, flew ajar; a lock mechanism clattered into the corridor beyond as Lurene fell into the opening. Rhea Tedder, ever the rear guard, called his wife's name as he hurtled into the space. One shoulder caught a door frame with pitiless precision, hurled the door wide as the addict ricocheted into a corridor wall. Val, leaping to her feet, saw Rhea disappear down the corridor, lying on his side, still pantomiming a sprinter's gait on the floor. He did not stop for moments afterward; Val could hear the tortured wheeze of his breath, the ugly measured tattoo of his feet and arms beating against the corridor floor and baseboard.

The patients were shocked into retreat from the violence at the ward doorway, and none seemed tempted to approach it. For one thing,—*two* —the remains of Rob Merkle and Lurene Tedder sprawled grotesquely in their way.

With all the caution of a nocturnal animal, Val rifled Merkle's lab smock. She found the hypospray intact and felt armed; then she hefted the dilantin bottle—and in a moment's reflection, realized that she was doubly armed. As she faced her puzzle, odd pieces began to warp into place and, for the first time in many days, Valerie Clarke knew what it meant to smile in relief.

Quickly, gently, Val checked for vital signs. She saw the ruined, mishapen head of Robin Merkle and knew why he had no pulse. Lurene Tedder lay dying, insensible, extremeties twitching. In the hallway lay Rhea Tedder, unconscious from

shock and fractures, his breathing fetid but
steady. She judged that he would live. Her small
joy in this judgment was proof that Val could still
surprise herself. It was true that Rhea Tedder
could answer crucial questions—but it was also
true tht he could ogle a homely girl. She made a
note to tell Chris Maffei: *Blessed are the easily
pleased, for theirs is the kingdom of Earth.*

The corridor intercom needed no special key.
She punched Outside, idly musing at the close-
ness of help for anyone who could reach the corridor. In moments, a policewoman was taping her
call.

Two minutes later Val reentered the ward. She
opened the isolation cell with Merkle's keys, once
again tense almost to the point of retching with
thoughts of what she might find inside. May Endicott lay sprawled in fetching disarray on the cot,
drugged to her marrow but apparently unhurt.
That enviable body would decay one day, Val
thought; but not today, at twenty-three degrees
celsius. She could see from a distance that Gerald
Rankine had passed the tonic stage of his seizure,
and was well into the clonic, his body jerking
slightly as the effects of the monstrous seizure
passed. She moved to Laura Dunning's side. It felt
good to smile again.

Val wondered how to begin. "I have news for
you, Laura," she said gently.

Laura was awake but, with the valium, quite
mellow. "I know. I did it without the medicine,"
the blind girl said proudly.

"Well—yes and no. It's seizures by other people
that bring on the power, Laura. No wonder you

couldn't tell when the power would come: *it isn't your power!*"

Confusion wrinkled Laura's nose. "But I make people do things."

"Can you ever," Val agreed, "but not alone. You're a—a modulator, I suppose. Rankine did not get his dilantin today; and that could've brought on a seizure by itself. You see—oh, excuse me—you understand, whenever you stole a dose of dilantin from Rankine or that young girl, the patient who needed it was in danger of an epileptic seizure. But the surest way to bring on a seizure is a strong blinking light—and that holo set zapped poor Rankine into the grandpaw of all grand mals, thank God."

"My," Laura murmured with a secret smile, "but it was good. But you mean, I never needed the medicine myself?"

"It probably impedes you. You need a carrier wave from some strong source, and you manage to modulate it into commands. You know what electroencephalography is? Anyway, a real thunderation seizure comes with the damnedest electrical brain discharge you can imagine, far more intense than any normal discharge. Of course, that same intensity raises hell with the higher centers of that same brain. Like trying to send morse code through a flashlight, using lightning bolts." She raised her hands, then let them drop in frustration. "All I know is, you've gotta be sensitized in some way to modulate other people's brain discharges ino commands. Normal brain activity just doesn't feature such power; those huge discharge spikes are characteristic of epilepsy. All this is simplistic but I haven't time to detail it now." Nor *understand it yet,* she thought.

Laura sought Val's hand with her own. "You know something about these things? You'll stay with me?"

The idea settled over Valerie Clarke like a security blanket. "I've learned some from a man. I need to learn more." This astonishingly gifted girl needed her, Val realized. Her smile broadened as she stroked Laura Dunning's brow. "I'm going to claim Rhea Tedder went berserk and stampeded the others into that door. It's a weak story, Christ knows, but it'll accommodate the facts you can see." The ethics of her decision disturbed Val until she remembered Rhea Tedder holding her for the processing team.

A sigh from Laura: "I wish I really could see."

"Don't you? Through other people?"

As if showing a hole card, Laura said, "Kind of." Her hand gripped Val's desperately. "If I could do it better. I could help some of my friends here a lot more. Some of them are trying to climb walls in their heads, to get out to us."

It was possible, Val admitted to herself. And who would be a better tool than an honest-to-God telepath? With a machine-generated carrier wave, could Laura reinforce improved behavior patterns in a trainable MR? The possibilities were untouched, and staggering. Chris Maffei had spoken of Gulfview's problems as the devil he knew, but Val smiled at a new thought: *the devil you don't know may be an angel in disguise.*

"Who've you been talking to at night?" Val realized that Laura had, at the very least, known of the transmissions at her end.

"Dr. Christopher Maffei," Val answered. Curiously, it sounded flat. The name no longer held its familiar emotional lift. She considered this further.

"Can he help us—me?"

"Us." Val's correction was an implicit promise. "Yes, but he's a proud man, Laura. He'll want to make you famous." *Because it'll make him famous,* an inner voice added.

Slowly, Laura replied, "I don't think I want that."

"We may be more useful without it," Val agreed. "But I know Chris, and he has strong opinions." She grinned at a sudden unbidden thought. " 'Course, you could always run his opinions off a cliff—and I'm kidding, by the way."

After a long pause Laura asked, "Do you love him?"

Since Laura could probably sense a lie anyway, Val resolved to use utter candor. "Yes." With a starshell burst of insight Val added, "But now I don't think I need him much. Does that sound harsh?"

"Your thinking isn't harsh. And Dr. Maffei: does he need you?"

Put in such blunt terms, the questions brought answers Val had never formalized. They hurt. "Yes; but you see, he's never loved me much."

"*I* love you." Laura's admission was shy, tentative. "But I don't think it's the same, is it?"

Val chuckled. " 'Fraid not. But it's enough. Was it Vonnegut who said the worst thing that can happen to you is not to get used?" A new resolve sped Val's answer. "In a few minutes a whole raft of people will be here to turn everything upside down and set it right again. You're sedated, baby, so you be goddam good and sedate! Keep your ability to yourself, don't force any automatic behavior on anybody, don't even hint about it—until I come for you. And I will."

The hand tightened again over Val's thinner one. "You have to leave?"

"For a while. Weeks, maybe. But you and I will figure out how you tick, and we don't want Chris Maffei diddling with your metronome so he can compose a bestselling ditty with it. Later, maybe. And maybe not. The trick is being used properly, isn't it, Laura?"

"You're the boss," Laura said meekly. And listening to police beepers in the distance, Valerie Clarke knew that she was, indeed, ready to assume the leaden mantle of decision-making. She wondered if Maffei's scrambler unit was repaired yet. It was the simplest of matters to find out, but Val could wait. There was plenty of time for her to put Maffei to use.

PORTIONS OF THIS PROGRAM . . .

"At first the child lives in the present like the animal; however, he gradually breaks this fetter and learns to anticipate the future inwardly and to grope back into the past."

—Louise Taichert, 1973

"And you thought you were so cleverly metaphorical . . ."

—Miriam Deshong, 1992

Miriam Deshong sat cross-legged on the lab carpet, aware that the child was just behind her. Dish was certain that five-year-old Merry Mohr wanted her therapist to maintain the game. Even when she heard the faint familiar clatter of objects in her handbag, Dish denied herself the luxury of looking backward. That was why she could not see Merry approach, swinging the sharpened nail file.

Dish heard soft fleshy impacts but was not alarmed; an autistic child often chooses strange hand-games. Besides, Warren Lamar, behind the one-way mirror, was her backup. The senior pathologist would warn Dish if tiny platinum-blonde Merry Mohr were in danger.

Lamar had left his post for perhaps ninety seconds. He was pouring coffee from their battered percolator when Dish's anguished cry reached him. The pathologist dropped his cup as the steaming brew sloshed his hand. His first step was onto the fresh spill, which spun him onto the tile floor still holding the percolator. Slipping and cursing, he failed twice to rise before scrambling toward the observation room on hands and knees. Under different circumstances even Lamar might have laughed.

Dish didn't scream the first time Merry slashed her. She felt only slight pain, her blouse absorbing much of the damage. Before she could turn, the nail file connected again, scraping across her rib cage. Dish yelped, rolled away, and avoided Merry's next blow. Then she grappled with the slender girl. Merry, slippery with her own blood, slid easily from Dish. She then resumed her little game, rhythmically stabbing into her small blue-veined wrist. She made no move to avoid Dish until the therapist grasped her weapon. Again she squirmed away but this time Dish had the nail file. Dish hurled the makeshift stiletto into a corner, half-expecting Merry to explode in the hyperactive chaotic rage of the autistic child. The temper firestorm did not come.

Warren Lamar burst into the room to find his assistant crooning through tears of pain and frustration, trying to carry the tiny girl from the room. Blood was seemingly everywhere.

Merry sat inert until Lamar tried to snatch her up. Dish saw—could almost *feel*—the rare return of Merry's awareness as the girl mewled and fought him. "Get her to the sink, Dish," Lamar rapped out, rushing off into the lab. "I'll call Matson!"

Dish heard Lamar's rapid-fire exchange with Matson's secretary. As institutional research director of the university, Dr. Charles Dana Matson rarely played the M.D., but it was nice to know the bastard had his uses.

As small as the lab sink was, it made a bathtub for little Merry. Dish cleansed the small ravaged hand, fighting shudders at the sight of the open punctures, while Merry focused with calm intensity on splashing her free hand in the water. Dish felt Lamar's presence at her elbow and glanced around. "Matson coming? And," she flared, "whatthehell are you smirking about?"

"Relax," he said, reaching for alcohol swabs. "Himself is on the way. And sorry, but check your face in the mirror there, and then look at Merry's."

Dish saw her own features, framed by the luxuriant bronze mane. Basically a good thirtyish face, firm mouth with a slight tartar tilt to the gray eyes. But she was squinting and her lips were pulled back: classic pain behaviors. Merry Mohr's silvery-blonde hair was blood-matted, but her face was wholly composed, lovely, intent on her play. With an effort Dish reshaped her own expressions. "I can't help it, Warren. She may not hurt but *I* do," she muttered.

Lamar nodded and applied a swab. "Well, if you feel woozy you can—oops!" He held Dish erect from behind as, legs shaking, she slumped in slow motion against the sink. Lamar did not take Merry from Dish. Merry was calm in Dish's arms as the therapist, leaning with elbows in the sink, was supported by Lamar. If the tiny girl refused his touch, he could use Dish as go-between.

Moments later, Dr. Matson found the trio still grouped at the sink. Chuck Matson moved with a hint of bounce that irked most of the faculty, especially those in middle years who did not, as Matson did, make a point of physical conditioning. His voice assumed its usual authority: "All right, Miriam. I'll take her. Um. Well, this little lady is lucky—doesn't look like any serious damage." Matson kept up the spiel, working on the silent Merry while risking glances at Dish. Warren Lamar began to clean the floor. "In fact, Miriam, I'd say her color is better than yours," Matson smiled faintly.

"Don't rub it in, Dr. Matson. I just empathize so much with children—my specials most of all."

Matson grunted, then quizzed the therapists on the accident. They freely gave details, Lamar volunteering blame for leaving the observation window.

"I don't expect perfection," Matson replied, finishing a suture clamp, "but this is the fourth injury this season to one of your autistics, Miriam."

"My special children," Dish implied the correction, "have special problems. They get hurt here less than in their own homes."

"Besides which, you have releases from Merry's parents," Lamar put in. "The university isn't liable."

Matson shrugged, finishing the bandage. "I was thinking in terms of blood, not dollars. I'm an administrator second—and general practitioner last, to judge from this bandage. Maybe I should be glad you two keep me in practice." Matson faced the angry pair with absolutely no readable expression, a legacy from years of riding herd on psychologists. "You research people are so defensive! If I didn't approve of your work, you two wouldn't get some of those research grants," he amended.

"We're getting there," Lamar replied evenly. "I'm a straight Skinnerian but Dish here keeps coming up with wags about programs for these kids."

"Wags?"

Dish snorted, a sign that her composure was returning, and stood erect. "W—A—G . . . wild-ass guess—Warren's term for any hypothesis that probes into the so-called black boxes of a child's mind. Take King Smith, now . . ."

"And condition him as a Harlem Globetrotter," Lamar cut in with forced humor. "Let's test our wags out, Dish, and then talk about 'em."

Dish saw behind Lamar's easy smile and made an eyebrow. *He's right*, she thought, *there's a right time to spring mind-bending new ideas. And seven thousand wrong times.* She drew a deep breath, felt the scrape above her kidney, and staggered. Matson's repairs were only half done.

Under Matson's sedative, Merry Mohr was tractable as a puppet. Dish's wounds were only superficial, with no clamps necessary from the hand tool which Matson could use almost like a stapler. Within the hour Dish and Lamar, with a student assistant, had the lab in shape again. They made explanations to Merry's mother at pickup time, then spent a final session reviewing the videotape records of King Smith, a profoundly

autistic black child whose behavior patterns were
disturbing in a very special way.

Freezing the video on a frame, Lamar studied
the elapsed-time rig. "Eighteen minutes and some
seconds again," he said. "You'll hate this Dish,
but we need to program some experimental frus-
trations on King—just backup data."

Dish pointed at her calculator display. "Haven't
you got an ethical bone in your body, Warren? We
have enough hard data now to publish results.
King Smith has an intermittent eighteen-minute
feedback loop in his head and that, probability
point nine-nine-five, is that. Why punish the poor
little guy on purpose?"

"Higher statistical confidence level."

"Any more assurance than we already have
would be statistical masturbation, and you know
it."

Lamar frowned at the video. It framed a scene
recorded in the special children's playroom that
day by automatic cameras slaved to follow the
transmitter on the back of King Smith's belt. The
gangly six-year-old played alone even among
other children. Bereft of speech, seemingly blind
and deaf at times, King might develop a sudden
interest in a toy another child was using. Often
King simply took it, the other child shrugging off
the invasion as one might accept an act of God.
This time it had been different: the offended boy
had punched King squarely if clumsily in the
mouth, then ducked away. Lamar's video frame
held a full-face shot of King, the handsome
broad-nosed little face as expressionless as an
administrator's even while the other boy's fist
snapped his head back.

"Right on the button," Lamar mused. "If that

isn't a pain stimulus I'm a Matson's uncle." And eighteen minutes later on that videotape—Dish's prediction was correct—came King Smith's sudden response to—something. Something very like a wallop in the mouth.

For many years, therapists had classified grossly inappropriate responses as elements of the syndrome called autism. While some children responded to certain regimens of behavioral engineering, others remained untouched and lost within themselves. It was taken for granted that autism might have several functional bases, any of which might yield that small horror, autism. A lone child, monotonously tapping two blocks together, might suddenly begin to duck and dodge, or be overwhelmed by tears, or rage. Clearly responses—but to *what*? To the objective world, that response was inappropriate. Usually it was impossible to query the silent, impassive, uncaring child who could not or would not commune with others. For the most part, the autistic child lived in a world exclusively, heartbreakingly, his own.

Then one day as Dish vainly tried to interest him in a simple tactile puzzle, King Smith had grabbed a wooden piece and swallowed it—or almost. He then sat inert, gradually turning brownish gray, finally slumping from anoxia as Dish extracted the block from his windpipe. Dish used mouth-to-mouth procedure, a dangerous process when applied to a child half doll, half wild animal. She anxiously watched the pale skin flush to healthier tones, and noted the time.

Shortly thereafter, Dish was in conference with parents of another child when Bill Fletcher, the student assistant, burst into her office. "It's King

Smith, Miz Deshong," he burst out. "He must'a swallowed something!"

It took a fast, chancy fluoroscopy to convince Dish that King had swallowed nothing. His performance had been convincing enough: thin fingers scrabbling in his mouth, eyes wide, terrified little lungs pumping as fevered bellows. Presently he quit this inappropriate behavior with startling abruptness, and Dish was too relieved to think beyond the moment—for the moment.

Later, Dish described her experience to Lamar. "Now that I think of it, his lungs were working beautifully," she said. "I was too freaked out to realize it but there couldn't've been any serious blockage in the trachea." Suddenly, in a luminous flood, the memory of King's earlier experiment with the toy blocks washed over her mind. "Anyway, I was trying a new tactile program with King—ah, what was I saying? And, ah, portions of this program . . ." She trailed off, thinking hard on a shining concept new to her.

". . . were prerecorded," Lamar finished laconically. "Dish, you have that glazed 'eureka' look again, it always . . ."

Dish raised both hands to her cheeks, mesmerized with the thought. "Well you sarcastic son of a bitch," she breathed, eyes elated. "And you thought you were so cleverly metaphorical—but if it's true, what do we do about it?"

"Whaddawedo about what?"

It took Dish ten minutes to convince Lamar she was serious, and another ten days to separate him from the notion that she was hallucinating. Gradually, using automated videotape tracking of King Smith in daily playroom routines, Dish built a case for a delayed mental feedback loop amenable to cybernetic theory.

When King Smith walked into a cushioned
wall, or fell hard, or was forcibly restrained from
some dangerous behavior, he might respond instantly. Or, especially if the jolt was severe, he
sometimes took the stimulus with absolute calm.
And sometimes, eighteen minutes after failing to
respond, King Smith would burst into frantic,
violent action which would have been appropriate eighteen minutes earlier. They spent weeks
amassing data, Dish impatient, Lamar increasingly cautious and slow.

Now, glaring at the display, Lamar slapped the
console switch off. "You're right, Dish. Some of
his sensory inputs are going into a reproducible
holding pattern. No point in foot-dragging, we
can present this stuff and get a special grant." He
whispered a popular tune off-key, the usual tipoff
that his formidable circuits were busy.

She was loath to interrupt him, but: "I hope you
aren't going to propose an aversive stimulus program. It isn't necessary."

Lamar broke off quickly, swung from his chair,
and snatched at a mighty yawn. "Right on, luv."
Dish despised every nuance of their old phrase
but ignored it. "We need a paradigm of that intermittent feedback loop, probably an n-stage
synaptic amplifier with low acetylcholine bal-
ance somewhere after state one. If we have a
model of it on paper, it may give Chris Maffei a
hint on how to modify it chemically. And if he can
do that on a predictable schedule . . ." He spread
his hands in a show of enthusiasm which Dish
found herself doubting.

"That's a pretty glib analysis," she probed, "unless you've been convinced all along. Think there
could be a better explanatory model?"

"I'll think about it on the way to K.C. There may be something in the literature, maybe old Cronk-hite's 'Strangers in Paradigm' monograph. You might digest some drug therapy stuff; ah, maybe start with Berger's work about thirty years ago, say, 1960." He paused at the door, donning his tattered driving gloves. "Or you *could* have a drink with me."

The previous year, Lamar would have taken that drink for granted, and so would Dish, who had begun an abortive affair with him soon after her arrival at their midwest campus. But if Dish admired the stolid behavioral engineer's side of Lamar, she longed for some sign of emotional warmth in him. She could never find it. The night she dreamed she was in bed with a machine, Dish awoke in cold sweat, dressed, and left Warren Lamar's Kansas City apartment without waking him. She never went back. It was characteristic of Lamar that he did not complain, never demanded an explanation. At the university, forty miles from the city, they still worked well together. For this Dish was silently grateful.

Yet, "I've got some books to flog," she lied, adding impishly, "And you've got a randy look about you."

"My title is *therapist,* not *the rapist.*"

"The only difference is in spacing," Dish said to his departing figure. Then she began to ponder a new hypothesis about Merry Mohr. She wasn't ready to hit Lamar with this one, God knows he was reluctant enough to accept the obvious in King Smith's case.

Merry, however, was another side of the coin. Dish herself scarcely dared to entertain what, she felt, was the most waggish of wags. With a great

sigh, Dish began to review videotapes of the play
periods featuring Merry. To avoid missing the last
monorail shuttle across the gully-wrinkled plains
to Kansas City, she'd have to run an accelerated
scan. This had an unpleasant corollary: a pounding headache. But she had to be sure.

Five minutes later, Dish's gray eyes were smoky
with anger. Her first impulse was to squander
money on the fast taxi lift from campus to K.C.,
find the oh-so-careful Lamar, and lash him for
being a thirteen-thumbed *schlemozzle*. But she
had made stupid mistakes herself; there had to be
a first time for Lamar. Dish secured the lab and
walked to the shuttle dock wishing she, like Lamar, had a sporty electrabout three-wheeler. Driving it might have erased the awareness that somehow, idiotically, Warren Lamar had made his own
erasure—the essential afternoon segment of Merry's videotape.

Dish had little time, the next day, to complain
about the erased tape. First came a group of student assistants and their briefings for subpro-
grams she ran for Lamar. Then a class in phonet-
ics, followed by words with her chief assistant
who wanted to take Merry Mohr, bandages and
all, to a test room on Lamar's orders.

"I'm sorry, Bill," she said firmly, "Merry needs
no stimuli, if we can help it, for the next few days.
Doctor's orders."

The youth moved on one foot, a parody of inde-
cision. "Well, you're the boss, Miz Deshong, but
Mr. Lamar is bosser, and if we miss a session with
Merry he's gonna take my head off at the waist."

Dish repressed her grin with a cough that fooled
no one. "And if we don't, Dr. Chuck Matson Him-

self will tack our collective hide on his office wall.
He's the doctor, and them thar's the orders, Bill."
She excused herself and rushed to the staff meeting with other factions of the Speech Department.
Therapists and thespians mingled in the same
department, which still administered programs
from frontal lisp to Freudian dialog. Dish occasionally sat in on debates and drama tryouts.
Lamar generally sent Dish to meetings, claiming
seniority. It was a dull meeting; Dish got her en-
tertainment on returning to the lab.

"Deshong, keep the hell out of my experimental
programs," was Lamar's greeting as she closed
the thick door. Something in his voice made Dish
look twice. She had never seen Lamar truly angry
or frightened, but there was something of each in
him now.

She flicked her babushka away, unconsciously
preening her hair for him. It was an expiation but
Dish did not know her sin. "You mean Bill
Fletcher and Merry? You know Matson's orders. I
supposed you'd forgotten to tell Bill. I don't know
what you're doing but . . ."

"But you countermanded me anyway," Lamar
gritted. "Next time, don't. I know what I'm doing." He swept perspiration from his temples
with both hands and continued, but with a sudden shift to softer tones. "Maybe we should take it
up with Matson. D'you think we can confide in an
M.D., administrator, health nut, politician, et cetera?"

Dish was about to say she was damned if she
knew when a silky baritone from the corner startled her, literally, speechless. "I wouldn't. Nor
anyone else yet, Warren." He lazed astraddle an
old chair, his forearms folded over its top. Dish's

first impression was of a stocky graying man with
outsized sinewy hands. Then he stood up. He was
taller than Lamar by several inches and, uncurl-
ing from the chair, he seemed to have fluid drive.
"I'm Neil Fox," he said, moving to her. His handshake was completely unaggressive.

"Miriam Deshong," she responded. "Take *what*
up with Matson?"

"First things first," the newcomer said, palms
out toward her, his smile gentle, beatific.

My God, Dish thought, *this is one attractive
cop—and why do I think he's a cop?*

Fox went on in his soothing, steady pace:
"First, my name is Fox only so long as this surveillance lasts. Next, I could show you my ID but you
cannot confirm it. You'll have to take Mr. Lamar's
word that it can be confirmed. Will you?"

Dish frowned toward Lamar whose expression,
over folded arms, was part leftover irritation, part
smugness at her confusion.

Dish gave Lamar an old, old look, a questioning
gaze of confidence and affection sculpted from
memory. She could see its effect on Lama. *Gotcha,*
she thought, *I can play dirty, too.* "Can I take your
word, Warren?"

"Absolutely," he managed to say, struggling to
decipher this strange woman's ways.

Dish turned a dazzling smile on Fox. "I take it
that you're police of some sort."

Fox's smile slowly broadened, saying volumes
in nonverbals Dish could not quite read. The lin-
guist in her scanned his accent—neither foreign,
nor mainstream, and not moneyed, but arrogant,
alert, busy—a metropolitan dialect. She gave up
trying to place him as Fox answered, "Of some
sort. Really, it's a routine—even picayune—

matter. The agency helps fund some scholarly research, and once in awhile we find more than one group working on identical problems. It may be happening here. Don't worry, we won't take your money away." A chuckle of confidence. "But even more interesting, you may have some data on sensory delay that could conceivably be of, ah, national interest."

He cocked his head, a faint request for response, and Dish saw the play of light on gray-black sideburns, recently trimmed. A *most* attractive cop. "I'm glad of course," Dish stammered, "but what can I—we—do? Or have I done it?"

"You almost done it this morning," Lamar aped her delivery, "and we'll be much obliged if you don't do it again. I'm running programs with some kids. Merry what's-her-name, Mohr, was one of 'em. For the next couple of weeks just cover for me, Dish. Don't let anything screw up any of my sessions with the kids. That's all."

He knows Merry's name as well as I do, Dish thought. *Is he playing coy with Mr. tall-dark-and-craggy?* "You're the chief therapist," she admitted. "I just hope the university likes the explanations you give when it's all over. I hope I do, too."

"In due time, Miriam," Fox soothed. "We don't like to complicate things more than we have to."

Lamar put in, a bit too quickly, "And you may be helping a whole lot of kids, not just a few."

Dish nodded in a forced show of confidence. "Speaking of complications, Warren, did you digest the stuff I laid out for you on Deaner?"

"Someone I don't know?" Fox asked. The notion did not seem to please him.

"A chemical," Lamar explained. "Diethyl-aminoethanol; which is a good reason to call it

Deaner. There's a pharmacologist M.D., name of
Maffei, who has better stuff. Best of all, Chris
Maffei lives within shuttle distance, in Omaha.
Talked with him earlier, and he's happy to work
with King Smith on our IOU, at least until your
people get my grant request by normal channels."

"I've heard of Maffei," Fox said wisely, approvingly.

"Will the Smiths let King go to Omaha?" asked
Dish.

Lamar savored the moment, then: "They came
for him this morning, Maffei's arranging it at his
end. Rest easy, Dish." His grin was one of genuine
pleasure.

It may have been gratitude that prompted Dish
to choose that moment. "I have some news, too.
King Smith isn't the only kid with a sensory tem-
poral displacement."

In the momentary silence that followed, Dish
felt a chill run from hairline to fingertips. It was
not all anticipation; Lamar and Fox waited with
identical catatonic expressions. "You're going to
think I'm freaked all the way out and back again,"
she said, then realized she was stalling. She
rushed on, "All right, here's what started me
thinking. A few days ago, Merry Mohr was in the
playground when she ran full-tilt into a wooden
pole. She lay there for almost a minute, but before
I could cross the playground, she was up." Dish
grimaced at the memory, then wailed, "And she
ran into the goddamn pole *again*! She didn't respond to either impact. I put her under observation, but I guess she wasn't any more gaga than
usual.

"So later, I'm studying a videotape of free play
when I see Merry sitting quietly, playing with a
piece of string. Suddenly she bursts into tears and

claps her hands to her left temple. And while I'm
watching this so-called inappropriate behavior
die down—this syndrome we take for granted
dammit, you know we do—she jerks her hands to
the right a little and uncorks another fit."

No change from Fox or Lamar. Both might have
been statues. Dish took a deep breath. "When I
checked the time-pulse on the video I couldn't
believe it. Merry's delay was thirty-seven minutes
long, but *it was in the wrong direction*. Warren
Merry Mohr felt the blows a half-hour before they
happened! And I think she's done that lots of
other times, but I haven't been able to spot 'em yet.
I will. I'm ninety percent certain Merry has a feedback loop; only it isn't feed*back*." She chirped a
laugh at the two men who seemed guided by the
same puppet master. They were both slightly
openmouthed now. "Warren, it's—it's a feed*forward* loop! I swear it is."

"Absurd." One corner of Fox's mouth twitched
up, the spell broken. "You're joking, Ms. Deshong."

"You're putting on an old on-putter," Lamar
chimed in. "I've modeled the Smith boy's loop as
primary and secondary synapse chains which
everybody may have, but King's secondary
doesn't always fire on schedule so the stimulus
input is stored as a sort of precognitive labile
memory until . . ." He trailed off. "Well, Maffei
and you will both get copies. And this, this feedforward loop won't fit that paradigm at *all*," he
said. He punctuated the complaint by chopping at
the air in frustration.

Dish laughed ruefully. One corner of her mind
marveled at Lamar's ability to grasp, in seconds,
new concepts. "Okay, I'm weird," she said. "Cal-

t just a hypothesis. But I think I can prove it in a
few more days. Today a hypothesis, but . . ."

"Tomorrow the world," Lamar grunted, then
flashed a glance at Neil Fox. "Just repartee," he
said weakly.

If Fox had been startled, he was quick to recover. "I think we'll be happier with a circuit
pardigm of feedback than with the, ah," he
paused and enunciated carefully, "bizarre claims
of time travel. It's not the sort of claim you make
without a long and leisurely study."

Dish knew she'd handled it badly. Lamar angry,
Fox contemptuous, both hinting that she played
her mental cards with half a deck. "Maybe you're
right," she said. "I can't really believe it myself.
Look, I—I have a lunch date." She retrieved her
babushka, retied it, and opened the lab door.

"Dish Deshong, my autistic adult," Lamar repeated an old affectionate insult. "It's the wildest
wag you ever had, but it has charm." He grinned.
"King Smith hooked up to a while ago, and Merry
Mohr with a hookup to tomorrow."

"More like half an hour," Dish replied softly.
"Nice to meet you, Mr. Fox. See you, Warren," she
promised.

But Dish could not keep that promise.

Dish knew her lie of the lunch date was trans-
parent and did not much care. She felt only relief
when young Bill Fletcher, moving at his normal
breakneck pace, brought news that she would be
taking over Lamar's afternoon lecture. The senior
pathologist, it seemed, would be off-campus with
his visitor. Dish covered for Lamar, took on her
own usual duties, and blessed the chime announcing the end of classes. Perhaps now she

could begin the tedious videotape reviews tha
might verify Merry Mohr's incredible deviance

The videotapes were blank.

Dish stood at the tape storage bank for lon
minutes, mute and numb. She eliminated ever
impossibility, and was faced with the stark ce
tainty that only Lamar, who alone with Dish ha
the code to the highspeed erasure mode, coul
have destroyed months of audio-visual record
ings. It could not have been an accident. Go
damn Lamar, coldly and logically forcing her t
obtain new data! Warren Lamar's lexicon did no
include the term *fair*, but he was always cautiou
and professional. Always until now. She felt ho
tears on her cheeks and let them come, stumblin
about the lab to secure the place, enclosing herse
in a cocoon of misery. It occurred to Dish that he
respect for Lamar was a cornerstone of her worl
and it was crumbling under his wanto
shortsightedness. If this was his way of dissuad
ing her from a peculiar wag, it was nothing sho
of childish.

She left the campus by shuttle, walked under
crisply clean evening sky to her apartment, an
went from Drambuie to books to stereo to sleep
None of it was very restful.

She overslept, of course. She accepted puff
eyes and a stomach that took to its trampoline
thoughts of breakfast, and Dish barely acknow
edged familiar faces on the shuttle to campus.

Halfway through the ride, Dish snapped fro
her dark reverie. Most of the passengers were un
versity people, intent on the overhead vide
where a reporter's voice-over gave brisk details
a pictured freeway smash.

". . . impact was so great that the victim could not be freed immediately. Debris from the electric twoseater forced rerouting of private vehicles from the air terminal interchange.

"No other vehicle was involved in the early morning crash. Officials noted that Lamar was licensed for manual control, and stressed the need for more stringent regulations."

Outwardly she was calm. Acquaintances were watching her. There were thousands of Lamars in the area, no doubt, but she knew with leaden certainty that she would never singe Warren's ears, now. He had paid dearly for his beloved manual control; first in taxes, and now—And she had seen the iridescent sun-yellow glint from the shattered electrabout: the color Lamar chose. Dish bit her lip, closed her eyes, and feigned sleep until she reached the campus.

The department chairman, Dr. Bishoply, was in the Speech Path lab when Dish walked in. He assumed from her appearance that Dish had been crying and misunderstood her motive. 'Miriam—Dish—I took the liberty of canceling your appointments this morning. I . . . oh, *hell*, what do I say," he moaned, turning half away. He was not a large man, nor always very strong under pressure. But unfailingly he did the very best he could.

Dish felt a surge of affection, even pity, and croaked out her thanks. It did not sound like her own voice and with instant objective clarity Dish saw herself miserably broken. And by what? A heartless, self-serving cheat snuffed out halfway through a new dissertation in dirty tricks. Finding her anodyne in anger, she masked it. "I'll be okay," she said, vowing to make it true.

Bishoply nodded. "And when you feel like it,
come talk with me. Galling as it is, we have to pick
up a lot of pieces." He left quickly. They had not
even obliquely mentioned the fact that her hated,
beloved Warren was dead.

Dish shook her head free of the thought and
began to collect Lamar's lab notebooks. She was
composed enough to watch the 9 AM newscast.
There was no doubt whatever that Warren Lamar
had marmaladed himself against an interchange
abutment ten miles from Kansas City just before
dawn. The official statement was faintly self-
righteous in citing a combination of alcohol and
marijuana. It was official—a dead man, a dead
issue. *Maybe it's official,* she thought, *but it isn't
all true.*

Dish was glad of hunger pangs that took her
attention from the newscast. Maybe she could
promote some scrambled eggs at the faculty club.
She forced a smile at the children as she strolled
past the playground. Merry Mohr, her plastic
bandage raveling to lend her a waifish look, followed Dish with her eyes but did not, of course
return the wave.

Dish was comforting herself with plans for
Merry and chasing a scrap of egg with her fork
when the adjacent chair was whisked away.
When it returned, Matson Himself occupied it.
Dish fought an urge to flee and continued to
persecute her egg.

Matson slouched back and regarded her for a
long moment. "One helluvan egg to justify all that
industry," he offered.

Silence.

"Pulse sixty-eight and rising," he said presently. "Under the circumstances, a miracle."

"Am I instrumented, or are you just omniscient?"

"Omniscient. Actually you watch the wrist and count the pulse. Easier than counting money." Seeing no response, he added, "Or was that unfair?"

"I'm sorry, I wasn't listening," Dish mumbled.

"My humor is never very successful. And I don't feel very funny, I feel—shocked. Lamar's loss is a shocker in surprising ways. I'm glad you weren't with him."

Dish glanced up sharply. "Why would I be?"

"You don't even know what I'm talking about," Matson said as if to himself. "By Christ, I believe it." He peered around at the other late breakfasters. "Do you play chess?"

Dish, amazed at this nonsequitur, signified no.

"Table tennis?"

Dish, with a quizzical look: "Used to be fair. Why?"

"Unless that cut bothers you I suggest—no, I prescribe a game to loosen up."

Her face said Matson was a fool. "Now?"

Matson played it for her. "Well, not here in the dining room no. In the lounge."

In the same irked, bantering tone she said, "Give me one good reason."

"Here's three: it develops hand-eye coordination, it keeps you trim, and," his voice dropped, "the table tennis room is soundproof."

Dish saw that Matson was deadly serious, his corneas like black ball bearings under the straight brows. She signed her chit, pushed away, and

strode out silently. In the hall she turned toward
the table tennis room, Matson following with his
aging athlete's gait.

"Ping for serve," Matson said, grabbing a pad
dle. "It isn't completely secure in here." He drove
an honest, efficient serve. "Been talking with . .
people in K.C . . . about Warren's accident," he
said, returning a wild forehand from Dish. "And
I'm worried . . . about some details. Was he into
drugs? Or gambling . . . though gambling didn'
. . . seem his bag."

"He didn't even have . . . the penny bag," Dish
chided. "Not even pot . . . but he drank a little
Warren didn't gamble . . . period." She
punctuated it with a slam and made it.

"But cannabis in his ashtray," Matson per
sisted, "and alcohol . . . in his blood . . . his
system."

Dish began a furious volley. "Planted. Had to
be. He'd tried pot . . . and hated it," she grunted
"None of this . . . fits Warren," she missed an
easy shot. "Damn you. Come on . . . out with it."

"Just between us . . . Lamar raided his account
. . . several times . . . in the last . . . two weeks
Always put in . . . lots more than he . . . too
out. Borrowed from the . . . credit union . . . a
first." Matson missed another of Dish's super
sonic forehands and retrieved the ball. For a mo
ment he watched her, motionless. "He started
with eight thousand and parlayed it to a hundre
thirty thousand, then asked his banker about
Swiss accounts. Late yesterday he took it all out."
He shook his head and served. "Miriam, that is bi
money. How?"

"Aren't there laws . . . against prying . . . int
private accounts?"

"Laws and laws . . . against misuse of funds . . . and bankers I . . . play handball with," Matson puffed. "Lamar had . . . a free hand with . . . research funds. You both did. It wasn't . . . a pretty picture." He watched her futile slam sail away. "Lamar may have been running for the jetport."

"And you think *I've* been into the grant money? Chuck Matson, I can't even afford a tri-D! My account will show that—only I won't permit it."

"I already know, your account was at the same bank since when you and Lamar—well, anyway," he finished lamely.

Dish gnawed her lip. "Who else knows about Warren and me?"

"Only everybody with a milligram of romance in his veins. Did you think it was a secret?"

"I thought it wasn't anybody's bleeding business! Can't you people stay busy in your own affairs?" The game forgotten now, both of them spoke with soft intensity.

"This *is* my business, and Lamar wasn't too busy to squeeze God knows how much, maybe over two hundred thousand dollars, out of someplace. But was it *here*?" He struck the table with his paddle edge and Dish saw the muscles cording in his neck.

"I don't know. But you sound like Warren isn't—wasn't the gambler, but the house."

"Exactly. He was onto an absolutely PVC pipe cinch, a nongamble gamble. He wasn't a gambler. Not like you are."

"Me? What did I ever bet on?"

Matson almost smiled. "Your forehand smash, and Warren Lamar. And with him I don't know if you lost, and I don't want you to tell me."

Dish laid her paddle down very carefully instead of throwing it at him. "All you want me to do is assassinate his character, posthumously."

As Dish headed for the door, Matson moved to intercept her. "Assassination? Men have done it for less, Dish! And Lamar is dead. Christ, now you're in charge of the funds yourself! Is there a big hole in the money? And how fast can you find out?"

Dish stopped, her eyes distant. "I hadn't thought of that; there are the kids to think of. You aren't worried for your precious administrative bod, of course."

It did not pass him. "If you believe that, you'd believe anything. But think, Dish: where or how did Lamar get a pipeline to the money tree in fifteen days or so? Not gambling, nobody guesses that well without knowing the unknowable."

"A hookup to tomorrow?" With her quote from Lamar, Dish felt the sunburst tingle of sudden knowledge. MERRY MOHR! She clasped her temples, a dozen possibilities fighting for focus. In seconds, one chain of reasoning hammered itself home. *If Merry is prescient, Lamar could've guessed.* Another piece of the puzzle dropped into place: *If Lamar could profit from it, he could ruthlessly keep it hidden.* She looked up at a worried Matson. "That's why he erased the tapes," she said aloud. "He guessed about Merry before I did."

"Talk sense, Dish."

"I can't. Just wait a minute." He saw the gleam of purpose return as she said, "How could Warren profit if he could see thirty-seven minutes into the future? Don't tell me it's impossible; answer my question!"

Matson gaped, then leaned against the game table. "State lottery? Nope, only once a month anyhow. Sports, maybe. Stocks? Hm, but they aren't all that volatile."

"Volatile?"

"Economist's term," he waved a hand vaguely, then jerked his head up. "Like commodities. I guess it's possible. But . . ."

"Shut up. Have you ever heard of a government cop named Neil Fox, or any cop, dropping into a research lab without going through normal administrative channels?"

Now Matson did smile. "Almost unheard-of. Since the seventies they're very, very proper. Who's this gent, Neil Fox?"

Dish threw open the door, nearly decapitating Matson. "Not our agent, and not a gent," she snarled. "And he's after one of my kids! Come on," she called, sprinting down the hall.

Matson was winded from running and furious with confusion when they arrived at the empty playground. From Dish's few words en route he realized they were searching for Merry Mohr and, seeing Dish dart into one room, he opted for another. In moments they knew that Merry was not with the other children.

Bill Fletcher followed Matson into the hall. "Doc, don't worry about Merry, I know where she is." Dish heaved a huge breath of relief, then heard young Fletcher say, "The big visiting fireman—uh, Mr. Fox?—asked me to let him observe her in the lab."

Fletcher stared in disbelief as Matson charged off toward the lab, Dish just behind. The youth followed.

The lab was empty.

"When did you last see them?"

Fletcher blanched. "Ten, fifteen minutes ago. Jeez, what'd I do wrong?"

"Nothing," Dish snapped, fighting for breath and courage. "Bill, get the provost on the line."

"Hold it," Matson grated. "Dish Deshong, you are directed *now* to tell me what's happened. I can help you or stop you. And you don't look all that stable."

Dish began her reply with a slap that rattled Matson's marbles. "That's for suggesting I'm hysterical when I'm goddamn mad." Her voice was rhythmic, steady, between hard breathing. "Merry Mohr has been kidnapped, as you can clearly see, by a man posing as a government agent. I'm sure he had Warren fooled; Warren didn't toady like that to mere mortals."

Matson rubbed his jaw, then with sudden alertness, said, "Son, did Mr. Fox have authorization of any kind to take the Mohr girl from the lab?"

Fletcher glanced around from the vidiphone. "No, sir."

"Then we move." Matson went to the phone. His exchange with the provost was briefly thorough: contact all campus security, stop anyone at shuttle or taxiport without campus ID, especially if he had a small blonde girl in tow, and search every outgoing private vehicle for the girl, relay any questionable ID to Matson at the Speech Pathology lab. Matson did not explain when the provost, an old friend, asked why he was speaking oddly.

"Speaking oddly," he grumped. "I'm lucky to be coherent after that haymaker, Dish. Now *you* be coherent. Why is this man after an autistic child?"

Dish took a deep breath. "I should make up a plausible lie. You won't believe it."

"You'll have to try me."

After sending Fletcher out, she told him.

"You're mighty right," Matson laughed. "I don't believe it—but maybe your Mr. Fox does. Great God, you don't suppose he *is* a government agent?"

"Whatever he is, he's gonna be a sick one when I see him. If you wonder why Fox is convinced Merry has this deviance, ask yourself how else Warren could get rich so fast on the stock market."

"Hm, you have me wavering," Matson half-smiled. "But how could he ask questions of a tiny girl who can't even talk?"

"I don't think he did, exactly." She raised her voice to Fletcher, who was instantly back in the room. "Bill, did Mr. Lamar have any unusual interactions with Merry lately?"

"How?" Bill fetched a broad shrug. "Merry wouldn't let him near her recently in her normal response patterns. Some of those weird prelim routines of his may've hurt her. He had me give her the mild stimulus routines the past few weeks."

Dish bored in. "Not normal stuff, Bill? What, then?"

"Nothing painful, just mild electrical stuff; you know, twitch responses on her arms and legs. She didn't like the straps one bit. This bastard Fox may have a double handful, 'scuse me, Miz Deshong."

"This bastard Fox may *be* a double handful if he can use Merry," Dish said with a hard look at Matson. "But Warren used a whole lab to feed stimuli to Merry. Knowing Warren and the prin-

ciple of parsimony, if he used it all, he needed it
all. Including an assistant."

Bill Fletcher was near weeping. "I used to take a
schedule every morning from Mr. Lamar," he
said, "and zap that poor little kid starting at nine-
thirty on the nose. Thirty-second intervals for
about ten minutes. You mean it wasn't to help
Merry?"

"It may yet," Dish soothed, "if I can convince
Dr. Matson that Merry is worth stealing. When
does the market open?"

"Ten in New York; that's nine, here," Matson
said.

Dish studied her sandals blindly for long seconds, then murmured an affirmative, "Uh-huh.
He was feeding stimuli to Merry thirty-seven
minutes *after* seeing her responses."

Matson squinted. "You've lost me."

"Okay, imagine Warren with a list of, uh,
twenty commodities at, ah, eight fifty-three,
watching Merry through an isolation window.
She glances at her arm—say, the left one. That's
his signal that Commodity A goes up significantly
during the first half-hour of trading. Thirty seconds later, from what Bill says, Merry might look
at her right arm. That's Warren's signal that
Commodity B goes down during that period. And
so on for twenty items, one every thirty seconds."

"But Lamar wouldn't know what stimuli to
program until later!"

Dish fed him a pitying look. "Of course not. I
know for a fact that Warren kept himself clois-
tered away next to an isolation window with a
vidiphone every morning recently from before
nine until nearly nine-thirty. He was keeping the

channel open to some broker. See, by nine-oh-three he'd have Merry's responses completed and would plunk down bundles on those commodities, and only those, for which Merry glanced at that left arm. And he could tell the broker to sell the whole batch of purchases at nine-thirty." She glanced quickly at Matson: "Or can you sell a commodity instantly?"

"You can these days," Matson admitted.

"Then it'd work," Dish insisted. "What's crucial is that Warren had to make his unalterable decision, *before he began to watch Merry*, that he would program the arm and leg stimuli depending on what the broker told him about the trading flurries by—oh, just about nine twenty-five. You understand, I don't say Warren did it exactly this way in every detail, but I know that he *could* have."

"Slow down. You say Warren told the broker to make very short-term buys at around nine-oh-five. What did he do then?"

"He stayed on the horn and ordered the broker to give him a simple yes-or-no checklist of those unalterably chosen twenty commodities by, maybe, nine twenty-five or so. Do any of 'em really jump?"

"Sometimes—and both ways. I think the market's honest, but it can fade you like a Cheshire cat."

"Well, those items that rose quickly and early got a quick 'left-arm' checkmark on the stimulus chart so Bill, at exactly nine-thirty, would start feeding arm-twitches to Merry in the predetermined order."

"So Lamar could get twenty answers in a minute or two from the broker, translate 'em into stimuli marks, hand the schedule to Bill a minute later, and—then what?"

"Then go count his loot," Dish shrugged. "He'd be done. You see, he'd already got the responses to those twitches thirty-seven minutes before they were made."

Matson, studying her, scratched an ear reflectively. "Let's say I'm Lamar, and I see left-arm glances for items A, D, and G. At that point I already know what items to buy. What if I just made my buys and didn't program any stim—oh," he finished.

"Oh indeed. It all hinges on the sure decision, before starting, that you *will* run the schedule when the time comes. Is Merry's delay exact to the second? I doubt it, or Warren could've run the stimuli quicker."

"Wouldn't the muscle twitches come early, too?"

"You're a doctor: think! Muscular responses are synaptically local; it's only her cognitive responses that lag. And she'd probably keep glancing at her parts as long as she felt funny business. When you're autistic, you don't get bored easily."

"Why did he have to ask the broker for the list? Why not just program those stimuli he knew, from Merry, were the right ones?"

Dish sighed. "Because in the communication system Merry is only a link. The broker is the source. Part of that unalterable bit is that you do what the broker says."

"Seems to me," Matson said, "that broker'd be sniffing the air hard and maybe talking about it after this happened a few times, ethics or no ethics."

"Could be. I have a satchel-mouth for a banker,"
Dish said darkly.

Matson injected, "I wonder if this could be
done on a two-step basis? Multistep? I mean, use
his nine twenty-five data based on what Merry
might know thirty-seven minutes after *that!* God,
it gets complex. Bill, did Lamar observe Merry
later in the day or run more stimuli on her?"

"No, only once a day," Fletcher replied. "I was
he only work-study he used for this. The stuff
with Merry was Greek to me but *this*, boy—this is
Linear B!"

"It's just as well. Chuck, Fox probably can't
make use of Merry while he's ducking campus
security and carrying a little bundle of barbed
wire. But why did Warren ever bring Fox into it?"

"Maybe Warren's sudden success brought Fox
into it. We don't know whom this man Fox works
for."

"I got a tougher question," Fletcher said. "What
if Fox gets off-campus with Merry?"

Matson and Dish exchanged lost looks. "He
might get rich," Matson said. "Or his government
might get a slight jump on the space-time con-
tinuum. And that, Dish, is what worries me. If Fox
is any government's cop, he gets Merry or nobody
does."

"How do you know that?"

"I don't; but I can guess what he'll try. Either he
gets her, *or*. He knows what other governments
could do. Horseshit; *will* do, if they believe in
his nightmare deviance!"

"Why should they? You don't."

"You ask too much. I'm on the fence, and that's
something."

"And here we sit *waiting*," Dish moaned.

"Can't we alert the state police?"

"Done. My neck's out a mile but I'll accep
kidnapping by this lunatic Fox. We're waiting fo
security to do its job, he can't leave the campus o
the ground or over it. What else is there?"

"Omigod, the sling tubes," Fletcher breathed

Matson slapped his forehead with the heel o
his hand. "Underground! Damn, I'd forgotten."

Dish watched Matson stab a vidiphone code
"But that's only cargo pods, isn't it? I though th
system was on the fritz."

She learned differently as Matson quizzed Ph
Royce of the university's physical plant staf
Conceived as a rapid-transit system, the slin
tubes were favored toys of the engineering schoo
The cylindrical pods accelerated magneticall
along the maze of tunnels and required parti
vacuum for efficient operation. Much of the tim
its safety interlocks denied a transit, thanks t
seasonal changes in the broken plains and the
effects on the too-shallow tunnels. And at best th
power requirements were high. Tunnels ran
several campus buildings requiring massiv
supplies and to parallel tunnels arrowing off
the Kansas City Quay area. This week, Royce a
mitted, it was working. And this week its pr
gramming staff were all at a Chicago seminar.

"Open all comm circuits to the pod terminals
Matson snapped into the vidiphone, "and try
spot a big man with a small girl. And dig out th
system prints, we'll be there in a minute." On th
way out he shouted for Fletcher to relay calls
the physical plants. He dashed for the parking l
Dish running after. She stole a glance at h
wristwatch. It was past noon. Merry Mohr mig
already be dead.

Matson, with a master access code to all university vehicles, dived into the first runabout he saw, Dish claiming the second seat. They slid to a halt minutes later outside the central control of the campus physical plant.

Phil Royce was waiting inside with blueprint tapes on his main console display. "If you intend to use the tubes now," Royce began, "forget it. System's down until one forty-five and there's no damn thing we can do about it."

Matson barked, "Why not?"

"Power requirements. This place pulls too many amps around noon, so there's a basic downtime programmed into the whole sling tube system until one-fifteen. Then it takes another thirty minutes to pull the necessary vac on the tunnels again. Don't tell me it's a helluva way to run a railroad. I know." Royce frowned.

"It's lovely," Dish beamed. "It means Fox can't have left here."

Matson was scanning the display, muttering to himself. Then, "How much slop in the timing?"

Royce shrugged. "None. Vac is usually up a few minutes early but the system is stupid. No sling power until one forty-five."

"If there were some way to monitor all the campus terminals," Matson began.

Royce said, "If it's only the on-campus terminals I can help. Like so," he added, turning to the display control.

Under Phil Royce's sure fingers the display wiped away the system diagrams. A mosaic began to appear, each a picture of a loading dock somewhere on campus. At a few locations, workers were exploring lunch bags. The gaping clamshells of sling tube pods could be seen in some of the pictures; several rectangles were blank. "Always got a few dead videos around here," Royce grumbled. "When're we gonna get remote focus rigs, Dr. Matson?"

Matson ignored the question, staring hard at the display. Dish had never studied a cargo pod closely. It seemed to have a fold-down seat near the front, but in the murk of the pod she could see little detail. If it were dark in the pods, Merry Mohr would raise total hell because she hated the dark like . . . then Dish flashed one of her sudden suppositions. "Mr. Royce, are there lights in the pods?"

"Supposed to be, but the engineering boys are a long way from using the system on a regular basis. Nope, no lights, spooky as hell riding one. Every little erg of power . . ."

"Good. Merry's records show that when she first began her autism she was two years old—and she already had a deathly fear of the dark! Fox may just have bedlam in close quarters."

"Lotta good that'll do," Matson spat. "He'll already be halfway to K.C." Then he saw Dish's face alight, her vigorous headshake contradicting him. He stared at her an instant, then grimaced, "Oh Dish, Dish, can we seriously believe that little girl will throw a fit a half-hour before then?" He glanced at Royce as if for help. Royce understood nothing of this exchange, and it showed.

"One of Merry's strongest aversive stimuli before her illness was the dark. If she hasn't been responding it's because we didn't know when to watch!" She closed her eyes briefly. "Ah, thirty-seven minutes back from one forty-five: one-oh-eight. If they're holed up near a terminal that's when Merry will tell the world about it."

"*If* Fox is near a terminal," Matson stressed. "Well, it's twelve forty-seven. Phil, think: how can you rig this display for maximum audio and video information to search the terminals?"

Royce frowned over his console, fingers roaming gently. After some false starts he sat back. "On the left, display of the master print again. To its right, small displays of every campus terminal. Forty-four of 'em, five videos down but all audios are up. Numbers on the print match the indices I punched into the videos. When you see something, find its location on the master print."

"Are all audios live simultaneously?"

"Right. Seven columns of pushbuttons here, seven terminals to a column except for the last column, with two. If you hear something special, start cutting columns out. When the noise goes out you've narrowed it to that group of seven terminals. Then cut in that column again and start cutting, one by one. It's pretty quick, really."

Matson passed a hand over his eyes. "Phil, I know you're working with patches on patches with old equipment, but it seems pretty risky to depend on it. You know we're hoping to find a six-year-old girl yelling bloody murder shortly after one PM. Dish, go to the runabout and point it toward the main campus. Master access code is oh-oh-six-oh-one. Keep the doors open. Saves seconds."

Dish obeyed. Matson was on the vidiphone againe as she exited. She didn't trust Matson; he was as likely to order her stuffed into a straitjacket as to check on Fox.

Dish parked the runabout on a lawn dowslope near the steps, nervously checking fuel-cell read-

outs and, every thirty seconds, her watch. At one
fifteen she could take inactivity no longer and
scrambled from the runabout. In the distance, two
campus security men stalked the hedgerow on the
campus perimeter. Both held the rarely seen tele-
scoping billies, proof that Kemper, the security
chief, was taking it all seriously.

As she entered Royce's office she saw the
school president, Karl Frye, framed by Matson's
vidiphone. Matson saw Dish but did not pause in
his discussion. "But there's reason to think the
pair is still on campus, Karl. Are you absolutely
sure we can't . . ."

"Positive," Frye said firmly. "It's not within my
power, Chuck, and perhaps not even very smart.
Picture gangs of student vigilantes converging on
the sling tube terminals, and someone mistaking
an aide for your suspect. Now ask yourself something: are you sure you aren't overreacting?"

Matson drew a long breath, then said, "Not
entirely." His flickered glance at Dish was
eloquent—*look what you made me do.* "All right,
Karl; thanks for the support, I'll get back to you."

Frye's laconic, "In an old vernacular, you better
believe it . . ." was flicked off as Matson stood.
For a moment he and Dish stared each other
down, then Dish quickly checked her watch. Only
ninety seconds since she left the runabout? Impossible.

"Sorry about the one-oh-eight deadline," Matson said quietly.

Phil Royce, at his console, shamed them with
his calm. "Just thought of something. I could
patch in a voiceprint match, if you have an audio
record of the little tyke or the guy. I didn't take an

MA in tech comm for nothing. That'll let us pin-point the terminal quicker, too."

Dish brightened, raked her memories, then nearly sobbed. "Not a thing on either of them. I could *kill* Warren Lamar!" She stopped then, the cold irony of the phrase careening through her mind.

She was near a breaking point and, she knew, Matson could see it. "It may work yet, Dish," he said, and touched her arm gently. "How's that scrape on your back; giving you fits?" It was a free excuse for tortured nerves and Dish managed a smile.

But, "You know that's not it," she husked. "Look, some of us are built for stress situations and some of us, well . . ."

"Don't lecture me on your function. I have eyes," Matson grinned.

Dish was only half-irked. "And a wife, and a weird sense of humor at a time like this," she sighed.

"Dr. Matson, Ms. Deshong, we're getting some-thing!" Phil Royce rode the audio to full gain, a welter of noise cascading from the speakers. As he flicked columns of buttons, they heard the step-by-step shift in the audio mix. Dish wondered whether she heard, or only wanted to hear, a faint nasal howl. Royce cursed and reopened all columns of input. "Nope. Thought I heard a kid yelling but—damnation, what am I thinking of." His long strong fingers played over the console as he spoke. "We can see most of the videos anyhow, we only need audios on those where there are pods ready and no staff working . . ."

Royce froze over the console. A thin wavering

cry ululated inhumanly, like a muezzin in hell—
from which terminal? "I've lost it, I screwed it
up," Royce crooned, his hands an ambidextrous
blur.

"Merry," Dish breathed. "That's Merry Mohr."

"Say again, say again," Royce begged softly,
concentrating on two columns. The quality of the
sound mix shifted again and they caught two
more salient outputs: a soft male curse, then a
muffling of the rage in Merry Mohr. A moment
later they had lost it.

Matson straightened, arms akimbo. "Okay,
what are the locations?"

Royce gestured at the print layout. "Ad build-
ing annex. Stadium. Fine arts center. Book de-
pository. Repair dock. Two others but there are
repair crews around 'em."

"Great, sites all over the effing campus," said
Matson.

"Wait!" The men turned to Dish who stood
wide-eyed, staring as if blind. "Of all those places
there's only one with that kind of echo."

"What echo?" From Royce.

"Where?" From Matson in the same instant.

"In the prop room of the fine arts auditorium,"
Dish shot back, already heading for the runabout.

"That's where the terminal is," Royce called to
the two retreating figures. "I'll pass the word." He
would have added that the video there was up,
and showed nothing, but no one was left to listen.
The time was one twenty.

Matson flung himself into the driver's seat
while Dish, in culottes, was only fractionally
slower. As the runabout ghosted over the green-
sward, Dish said, "Speech pathology gives you a

tuned ear, Chuck. There's a flattish metallic little
echo down below the big stage in the Fine Arts
Center. I was over there last week; they're working
up a production of *Medea*. Anyway, I could hear it
counterpointing Merry."

Matson, reaching for the dashboard commset,
said, "You seem awfully pleased."

"Merry's alive—and kicking, I hope."

Matson contacted Royce by his only available
channel, the radio. Though fully automated trip
programs were built into the runabout, the innovation was only three years old. The legal prohibition of front seat video had not yet been changed
in mid-America and, though private vehicles
flaunted the law, state vehicles did not.

"Video and audio are both working there,"
Royce reported, "but I'm not getting any action."

"Phil, I need you as a go-between. Call security
and ask for a chopper to the Fine Arts Center.
We're ten minutes from it with no weapons;
someone may be closer or better equipped." He
veered onto the twin ribbons of an access road,
beeping the two-tone urgency note at a bicyclist
just ahead. For a man who didn't really believe in
any of this, Dish reflected, Chuck Matson was
cutting a lot of corners.

To a suggestion by Royce, Matson was firm.
"Don't say anything on your audio to let Fox
suspect we've pegged him. Not unless you actually see him entering the pod. And don't punch
off, Phil, keep me posted."

They crawled at an exasperating forty miles an
hour, listening to Royce's office sounds. Presently
Royce coughed. It had apology in it. "Uh, Dr.
Matson, security's on the horn here. He'd like you
to contact him."

Matson stared hard at the road ahead. "Is it Vic Kemper?"

"You can say that again."

"Does he have anybody who can beat us to the center?"

"Neg," Royce replied, "but he's pretty insistent—even heated, you might say."

"He can't help yet, but we're doing his thing, right?"

"That, and the likelihood that you're walking in on an A-and-D."

"Say again?"

"Armed and dangerous. He got me with that'un too," Royce chuckled.

A marginal pause. "I'm not receiving too well, Phil. Fact is, I'm having a rough time with words."

"Not happy with the ones you hear?"

"*Plus ca change, plus c'est la meme merde.*"

"Say again?"

"See, you're not getting me either. Tell Kemper that. And urge him to get his martial ass in gear with all possible speed." With that, Matson punched off. He ignored further lights from the commset.

The clump of gleaming mushrooms that was the Fine Arts Center grew by proximity to become a complex of sprayed ferroconcrete buildings. The wall of a sling tube emerged from swooping green contours to penetrate the lower auditorium structure. They whirred into the parking area in the shadow of the complex. The lone vehicle they saw seemed huddle to itself in the vastness. Matson stopped nearby, glanced inside the small sedan while hurrying past it, then stopped short.

"What's wrong?" Dish was impatient as Matson dropped to his knees, peering under the sedan.

In answer, Matson flopped on his back and reached beneath the car's rear. In a moment he was up again, wiping fluid from his hand as a puddle appeared beneath the electric car. Matson rejoined Dish with, "Very cute. There's a rotary engine in that thing with whopping mufflers. What we used to call a Q-ship, a racer in overalls. Also very illegal. Also," a tight grin, "should seize up in minutes with all his coolant drained. I wonder if Lamar supplied him with it—and with his information on the sling tubes."

Dish nodded. Matson asked cautious questions—good. And in physical confrontation he'd give away too many years and forty pounds to the desperate Fox—not good. They were both panting as they reached the ramp to the prop room area, and Dish pulled Matson to a halt.

"Breathing time," she begged, "and thinking time too. We can't just barge in and say 'hands up.' "

"Hell we can't. Our function is to delay Fox 'til Kemper shows. You have a better idea?"

"Yes. Let me go ahead."

"Out of the question—and if you slap me again I'll flatten you."

Dish pressed on quickly, "Our chance of sneaking up on him in this place is roughly zilch. But he knows me. If I can flush him with you out of sight, then maybe you *can* flank him. He's a very big, ballsy guy, Chuck, and I could make him overconfident. Must I give you a goddamn syllabus?"

Matson's wry smile was admiring. "My marriage is legally open. I haven't seen Therese in weeks," he answered.

"Why tell me *now*?"

"It's now I think you are some kinda lady, Dish." He jerked a thumb at the door. "I'll give you twenty seconds lead. Use it before I lose my resolve."

Dish's watch, as she started down the hall, read one thirty-eight. Her first impulse was toward the loading dock with the fateful sling tube and its silent open pod. Then she recalled the narrow spiral staircase that began near the loading dock and emerged on the huge stage above for special effects. It would be unnatural to tiptoe. Dish strode through the cavernous prop room, noting that the lights were on. Simultaneously with the echo of her footsteps came a faint whooshing rustle, then silence. It could have been a stage curtain—or a soundproof door.

The main stage was directly above, but the center boasted a small practice theater complete with its own proscenium and flies. It adjoined the prop room. Dish swallowed her heart, walked to the door of the little theater, and slid it open.

She was met by full incandescent lighting. Squarely in the center of the miniscule stage sat Merry Mohr, toying silently with dacron cables tied to her wrists and ankles. The soft slender ropes were slack but ran through a metal ring and ended with half-hitches linking Merry to the throne which dominated the upstage portion of the stage. Dish felt liquid nitrogen in her veins, staring at the big man who lounged on the prop throne. Neil Fox smiled easily at Dish, obviously enjoying the moment.

Dish made herself a foolish stereotype. "Mr. Fox, my goodness! What on earth? And isn't that one of our special children?"

Fox uncoiled—he seemed to like doing that— and as he arose, gripped a support of one throne arm. The support snapped. Fox stepped between Dish and Merry. "The person I least expected. How symbolic it all is," he purred, relaxed and easy. "You people even call them 'special,' without knowing how special. In another quarter, children like this will be *sp'itsiyalniy*. The same word, really, but with somewhat different research orientation." Again that damnable warm smile.

"Is that a Russian word?" Was she talking loudly enough? Could she divert the feral Fox from the doorway? She looked her question at Fox and moved around him as if to see Merry better.

"I believe it is," he said. "Though not presently Soviet research." He glanced at his own watch. "Our charade is pleasant; Lamar named you well. But in a moment I must take my small charge and go, Dish Deshong." An earnestness crept into his tone. "We value this little person very much. If you do, you won't force me to hurt her. Or you."

"I valued Warren Lamar, too. And it seems to me you force very easily."

"I have only limited regret for Lamar. He was a selfish one—and a superb guesser." His eyes widened slightly as Dish stepped nearer.

"I'm right about the girl, then? She does have a feedforward loop." Dish held his gaze, forcing her eyes to ignore the flicker of movement at the doorway.

Neil Fox answered vaguely. "Perhaps unique at this time. You can't possibly appreciate the expense of taking her with me. If it's any comfort, I was ridiculously unprepared to act so soon. And," his voice suddenly chilling, "you are much too close." He waved her back, a single slashing chop suggestive of military arts.

With smoothness that seemed choreographed Fox stepped away, dipped to pull the knot of Merry's bonds from their mooring, and hauled Merry aloft, while watching Dish closely. Uncomplaining, the tiny girl hung across the massive shoulders, a trophy of the hunt. Perhaps it was the very lack of volition by Merry, or the sight of the silken silver-blonde hair tumbling to hide the little face. Dish cried out and leaped at Fox.

The impact was too sudden to hurt; the heel of his free hand jarred her chin precisely enough to stun, not enough to fracture. Dish, rising to hands and knees, saw through her own jumble of hair as Fox bounded to a squat table, where the play's props rested. A rhinestoned cape, a trick goblet for the sorceress Medea, other small objects swept to the floor as Fox deftly snatched the crucial item, Medea's dagger.

"Oh God, don't!" Dish's scream froze a tableau. Fox, his small bundle now held as if weightless against the formidable chest, held the dagger point gleaming an inch from Merry's viscera. Matson, teeth bared, held both hands before him as if imploring, only steps away from Fox who now saw Matson, and respected what he saw. In one of those imploring hands Matson held a trimming hatchet from the prop room, rusty with disuse. Very slowly, Matson lowered his hands, his eyes forged to the blade of Fox's weapon.

"You primitives," said Fox in soft contempt. He flicked an impossibly quick glance at his wristwatch, the knife blade glistening in the light at his motion, then pulled Merry close. The big man backed past the doorway, Merry held high on his chest, Matson following helplessly with Dish in tow.

"Three things," Matson croaked, proceeding more strongly, "we've blocked the sling tube up ahead, every exit is manned anyhow, and some very rough types are about due here." Finding no response he added, "You want murder one on top of kidnapping?"

Fox moved near the open pod. They could all see the emerald READY FOR USE legend shining in its surface. "My briefing says you lie," Fox said almost to himself.

"Try it and see."

"My notion exactly."

As Fox shifted his burden, Merry began to whimper and Dish made her decision. No time to explain or threaten: she reached the littered workbench in three steps and grasped a hefty injector for instant-set foam, lying between matched scenery molds. Now Merry was fully active as only a wild child can be. Dish kept the tiny fingernails closely trimmed but at least one caught Fox across an eye. The craggy head snapped back, trying to keep Matson and Dish in view while a spitting ball of pure energy shrieked and raked his face. At that instant, a monstrous voice resounded through the area.

"FREEZE RIGHT THERE!"

For Dish there was no mistaking the booming volume of the loudspeaker; she knew it was Phil Royce speaking from miles away. Fox whirled completely around, searching wildly, as Dish used the distraction to bound near him. Matson began a clubbing swing with the hatchet but Fox, sidestepping, avoided it. Then Dish triggered the foam cartridge around the big man's feet, then up to his knees. The stuff air-polymerized with phenomenal speed and enough exotherm to blister. Viscous brown slurry puffed on Fox's legs and his footing was suddenly uneven. Fox crashed to one knee.

"Blame yourselves," Fox howled, and plunged the dagger against the little girl's unprotected body, and again, and still again.

Matson, fearful that a wild blow might strike Merry, was waiting for a less hazardous moment. He shouted as the knife struck Merry and caught the little girl as Fox dropped his dacron cable. Not for an instant had Merry ceased her tantrum, nor did she stop when Matson scooped her up, his hatchet falling forgotten to the floor.

"Dish, foam the pod, the goddam *pod*," he called, sprinting to a jumble of stage furniture. Any one such blow could be fatal to an adult, let alone a child. Matson snap-judged that her chances were roughly nil. He placed Merry on a musty divan and wheeled to aid Dish, who might live or die depending on his next moves.

He saw Fox, tumbling into the pod, hurl the dagger straight into Dish's midriff. Dish staggered, whooped an insane laugh, and aimed the foam cartridge into the pod. The dagger skittered across the floor and Matson dived for it as Fox, who had found the dagger ineffectual against the growing mass on his body, struggled to take something from his coat. Matson saw that Fox might escape if he had a projectile weapon.

Fox's weapon was strange to Dish but she knew it must be that. Foam spattered over the hand that

ıeld it, the stream of slurry beginning to wane as
he cartridge emptied.

It was enough. Neil Fox, his face and upper
orso caught in the same swelling mass, made a
convulsive leap from the pod. A soft pop from
nside his cocoon swelled it further as Fox,
ɔerhaps accidentally, triggered the weapon.

One arm was free, the other caught up in the
ɔamed mess. Matson fell on the free arm with an
.rm bar hold, applying it as well as might be over
he puffy mass on Fox's torso.

From inside the cocoon came horror. Long
.huddering gasps, then the terrible sounds of a
ɔig animal strangling on the contents of its
tomach. Matson was literally hoisted from the
loor, the great hand tearing away his shirt front in
ts spasm. Matson rolled away cursing, incredu-
ous, and sprang back. Fox, lethal still, flailed
vith the free arm at his ghastly prison, raking a
rail of broken fingernails and torn foam from
.im.

In seconds the arm became rigid, outstretched,
ıngers splayed against the floor. Foam crackled
s Fox's back arched. A moment later he lay still.

The extended arm, the heels, and the back of the
ıead formed a shallow tripod holding the body
lear off the floor. Wafting his hand above the
ɔam, Matson sniffed at the air. He knew no sub-
tance so antipathetic to relaxation of the striped
ıuscles but there was something in the air be-
ides the smell of foam catalyst.

"Don't touch him," Dish began in terror, but
Matson was already trying to retrieve the life he
ıad so recently fought. He began by cutting at the
ɔam with the dagger. Then he saw the vicious-
ɔoking blade slide up into its hilt. He watched it

twice before he could take the datum in.

"Good God, Dish, this knife's a fake," he whis
pered, then looked quickly at the body of Merry
Mohr. The body was sitting up, crooning softly
playing with the pretty fibers of the cables tha
bound her. Merry lived in her own subjectiv
world, but she lived. "Ahhhhhh, crap," Matso
sobbed his laugh, and began trying to remove th
cocoon from Neil Fox.

Scenery foam, Matson found, was efficien
stuff. It exuded an oily film to slicken its surface:
Matson tossed chunks of foam into a corner as h
worked with the hatchet, holding his breath, the
scrambling away for a few fast breaths before re
suming.

He was much too late for Fox. As the foar
peeled from the agonized face Matson saw onl
whites in the open eyes, and retreated unprofes
sionally from the rest. The foam piece he still hel
was faithful to violence, a perfect death mask fc
the imponderably potent Fox. Matson dropped
in revulsion and pity.

Dish untied Merry, who seemed content to cor
tinue playing, and Dish saw bruises on the sler
der arms. "Chuck, could you take a look at Merry
She may be hurt."

From long expertise, Matson gingerly ir
spected the small body without disturbing i
play. He was astonished to find Merry so ur
marked; even the suture clamps he had applie
two days before were intact. He spoke rapidl
"Dish, we're stretching our luck."

"Not entirely. Fox was so cocksure he didn
even check that prop dagger. From watching tr
outs I knew it was harmless but I couldn't ve

well say so, he could've broken Merry in pieces with those terrible hands. I had to wait for the right moment. Still, we were lucky. He had time to get Warren somehow, but after that I think he was improvising all the way."

Matson snorted softly. "So far we're luckier than you seem to realize. Look." He leaned toward Merry head down, continuing in almost inaudible tones. "Phil Royce is recording, sure as hell. When Kemper's people arrive I hope you'll be incoherent. Mild shock, incomplete sentences, the works. We must have time, Dish." He turned to stare at the silent Fox. "Time," he repeated to himself.

"Will Merry be okay? Did that devil hurt her?"

Matson shook his head wearily. "Oh, the tad's just bruised a bit, any active kid can accumulate worse. He could've easily trussed her up tight and gagged her, you know. Or sedation—any number of things if he had been prepared. I don't think he meant her any harm . . ." Seeing Dish's angry silent O he stammered, ". . . except in extremis. I don't know. I'm really tired, Christ but I'm tired."

The stentorian whack of copter blades drew them outside, Dish extinguishing the lights from force of habit as they moved toward the hall. Matson carried the inert Merry and, as they emerged into the light, asked. "What's the time, Dish? Exactly."

"One fifty-six."

Matson grunted, "One damn coincidence too many," and went to meet a quietly angry Vic Kemper as Dish eased Merry into the runabout jumpseat. Royce, watching the fight from his monitor, had kept the security man in touch.

Matson took a frontal approach, stating the

barest facts. Fox an apparent suicide, the area in need of ventilation to counter an unknown toxic substance, and both Dish and Merry needing treatment for shock. "The little girl is completely aphasic," he added darkly.

Kemper glanced at Merry and grimaced. "Well I'd be obliged to hold you here until the state police arrive, except . . ." He shook his touseled head sheepishly.

"Go ahead, Vic."

"Except you really *are* the doctor. And you wrote my job description."

"And I haven't made doing it any easier today?"

"A sack fulla ten-fours on that, Doc. Can we get your statement later?"

Matson swung into the runabout. "At the dispensary," he agreed, and urged the little vehicle back across the campus. He was tempted to contact Royce and thank him, but decided to wait. He had more pressing problems to consider.

The dispensary was ideal for their needs. Matson gave orders for Merry's care before ushering Dish into a secluded consultation room. He spent long minutes thinking, conjuring a potion for them both, then eased himself into a couch next to Dish. "The cola's flat, but it's thirty percent ethyl," he grinned, and sipped. "Gaaah." Dish failed at a smile and waited for him to continue.

"All right, you called the shot," he said finally. "What convinced you—Fox?"

"Partly. And Merry setting up a howl we heard on Royce's monitor thirty-seven minutes *before* you doused the prop-room lights." He slumped further on the couch studying his glass. As if to himself, he continued, "And if I buy that, I have to admit the possibility that this Fox is mixed up in the future somehow."

Dish stared at him dumbly, her mouth slack, hanging open.

"Maybe he was some government's agent, somewhere, but I—well, hell, he called us primitives! The overconfidence of a bad anthropologist among campesinos. He spoke of taking Merry as if it would take incredible amounts of money or energy to move her—and you can vacation in New Delhi for a couple of thousand bucks."

"You think he was from another time?" Dish saw confirmation in his face and waved at the air. "But then he'd know everything—would be like God almighty! We couldn't've stopped him."

"But we did; which means, maybe, the future can be modified. Dish, I'm just hypothesizing—wagging. We have some serious decisions to make, honey. Like what we tell the police."

A pause, then a giggle. "Not that we bushwhacked a time traveler. I like my job."

"I like you in it." He reached out, palms up, and received her hands. The barest of squeezes, then mutual release. "So we avoid talking about Merry's very special deviance and play dumb. Let somebody else theorize where or when Fox came from." He chuckled slowly, relishing the idea. "Nobody's going to figure it as we do, no-o-o-body."

"Except the people who sent Fox," Dish said, and saw new seriousness in Matson's nod. She watched gooseflesh move across her forearm, then shrugged the shudder away.

"And whoever it is wants Merry there, or dead," Matson gloomed. "The big question is, what's our ethical choice? Maybe they need her. Do you realize you could shut down the DEWline if you had Merry Mohr for an early warning system?''

Dish stared at Matson, aghast. "You think we should've handed Merry over to that monster? 'Kiss off, Merry, you're in somebody's army now'." An unladylike snort. "Nobody who would sacrifice a helpless child should control her. And it isn't our ethical choice, it's *mine*. Even legally, if you want to get sticky about it."

He raised a hand in conciliation. "I'm not recommending, just broaching an option."

Her shoulders squared, Dish Deshong no longer seemed so small and vulnerable. "I don't see an option, I see a duty to a little kid. Merry Mohr is lost in her own synapses and I intend to find her."

"And when you do, what will we all have lost?"

"A thirty-seven minute crystal ball. How many children would *you* sacrifice for that?" The words came crackling out.

"It isn't the money, Dish. Never for money."

"Hell, no, for science! I can see you weighing it in that big-picture brain of yours. Do we try hard to find the little lost girl in that body, or do we drag our heels just a little, see if we can use her in the name of some catchphrase: science, money, national security, the good of man."

"Pretty important, some of 'em." Matson insisted softly. "I admit I'm pinched between principles."

"And ignoring the most important one."

Silence.

"*She's not a volunteer*," Dish cried. "I know; she can't be, but that only makes it clearer. I won't

let Merry be sold on the block of any principle that
keeps her as she is. Maybe she'll always stay like
this but I am committed, with Maffei's therapy or
whatever else it takes, and the next handsome
weirdo who looks at her crosseyed is gonna find
me—what'd Kemper say?—A and by-God D!"

Dish had never heard Matson guffaw, and was
startled when he did. "You have a way with gor-
dian knots," he said. "Not that it matters but I
agree. The thing we have to do now is kill Merry,
or cure her—to the media," he amended quickly.

"Ah! Publicize the idea that she's no longer
useful? You're a devious administrator, Chuck
Matson."

"I could promote a full-time guard for Merry
from other funding, but it'd excite a lot of comment."

"Not if she's snuck out to the Maffei clinic in
Omaha," Dish put in. "And you know what? A
few special children have been 'cured' by concus-
sion."

Matson cocked his brow. "Pretty rare, isn't it?"

"Right—and newsworthy. We release a fatuous
item about my brilliant deductions at Merry's
sudden remission. Warren Lamar going paranoid,
making wild claims about prescience when Merry
snapped out of it—Warren can be useful despite
himself," she said, essaying a sad smile.

"And one more thing," Matson said, "for the
record. We say Merry ran to you when you found
Fox."

"Yeahhh, which would make him say something to imply he'd been mistaken."

"Like, 'it's the wrong child,' or something."

Dish snapped her fingers. "She isn't a sp'itsiyalniy! That was his term, Chuck, we can claim we think he was Soviet. I think they might take that bait—whoever hired Fox."

"Or whenever," Matson added.

The official records noted that fingerprints, photographs, and retinal patterns all failed to identify the man, Neil Fox, whose weapon was finally identified as of contemporary French origin. Phil Royce's videotape recorded the fight at the sling tube and did not complicate the story offered by Deshong and Matson. Nothing anachronistic, nothing very special among unsolved cases. And nothing nearly so newsworthy as the human interest story that broke from wire services in Kansas City. Announcing the miraculous cure of little Merry Mohr, it preceded the truth from Omaha by eight months. But, as Dr. C.D. Matson remarked one evening to Chief Therapist Deshong: Merry's announcements had usually been a bit premature.